£9.45

Nov.

Jessica and Me

First Edition

April 5th 2014

Copyright

Ronald Shadbolt

ISBN 978-1-291-87863-9

Published by

LULU.COM

Jessica and Me

Contents

Introduction 7

Chapter One 7

Chapter Two 14

Chapter Three 32

Chapter Four 35

Chapter Five 40

Chapter Six 45

Chapter Seven 51

Chapter Eight 57

Chapter Nine 60

Chapter Ten. 63

Chapter Eleven 69

Chapter Twelve 73

Chapter Thirteen 76

Chapter Fourteen 78

Chapter Fifteen 80

Chapter Sixteen 87

Chapter Seventeen 93

Chapter Eighteen 101

Chapter Nineteen 105

Chapter Twenty 106

Chapter Twenty-one 112

Jessica and Me

Chapter Twenty-two 116

Chapter Twenty-Three 118

Chapter Twenty-Four 122

Chapter Twenty-Five 131

Chapter Twenty-Six 133

Chapter Twenty-Seven 138

Chapter Twenty-Eight 141

Chapter Twenty-Nine 145

Chapter Thirty 147

Chapter Thirty-One 149

Chapter Thirty-Two 153

Chapter Thirty-Three 155

Chapter Thirty-Four 158

Chapter Thirty-Five 161

Chapter Thirty-Six 165

Chapter Thirty-Seven 167

Chapter Thirty-Eight 174

Chapter Thirty-Nine 179

Chapter Forty 181

Chapter Forty-One 183

Chapter Forty-Two 186

Chapter Forty-Three 195

Chapter Forty-Four 200

Jessica and Me

Chapter Forty-Five 202

Chapter Forty-Six 207

Chapter Forty-Seven 209

Chapter Forty-Eight 212

Chapter Forty-Nine 214

Chapter Fifty 217

Chapter Fifty-One 219

Chapter Fifty-Two 222

Chapter Fifty-Three 228

Jessica and Me

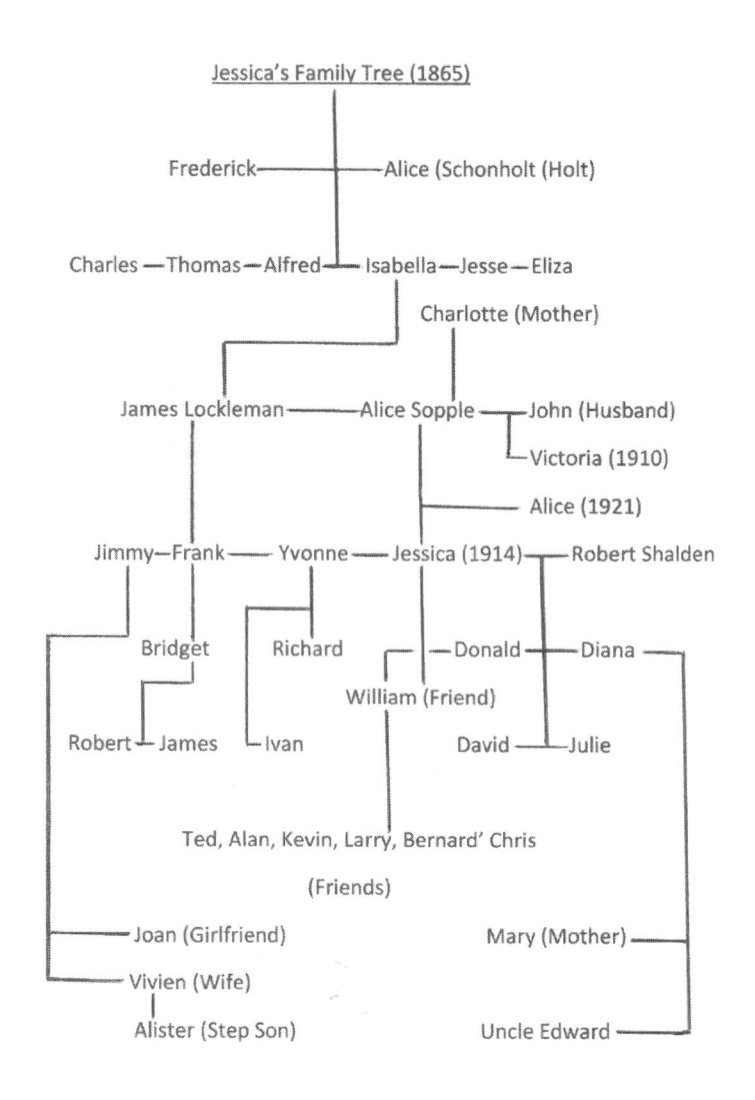

Jessica's Family Tree (1865)

Frederick ——— Alice (Schonholt (Holt)

Charles — Thomas — Alfred — Isabella — Jesse — Eliza

Charlotte (Mother)

James Lockleman ——— Alice Sopple ——— John (Husband)
　　　　　　　　　　　　　　　　　　└ Victoria (1910)

　　　　　　　　　　　　　　　　　　Alice (1921)

Jimmy — Frank ——— Yvonne ——— Jessica (1914) ——— Robert Shalden

　　Bridget　　Richard　　　— Donald ——— Diana
　　　　　　　　　　William (Friend)

Robert — James　└ Ivan　　　　　David ——— Julie

Ted, Alan, Kevin, Larry, Bernard' Chris

(Friends)

——— Joan (Girlfriend)　　　　　Mary (Mother) ———
——— Vivien (Wife)
　　Alister (Step Son)　　　　　Uncle Edward ———

Jessica and Me

Introduction

Jessica was an unwanted baby. For some reason that will be revealed in the book she was given to a family who lived in Fulham. Compared to other families in the street they were reasonably well off to the extent that the Step Mother called Isabella was a money lender and she had been widowed just before Jessica was born.
Jessica's son Don began researching her life and found that the Step Mothers parents were very rich when they lived in Germany prior to settling in England in the 1860`s.

Chapter One

Isabella at the age of 20 was in love but the path to true love was not easy. The man she had fallen for came from a working class background. In the 1890`s getting involved with people out of your class created problems. Isabella`s family were very rich living in the Regents Park area. The boyfriend James lived in Fulham which wasn`t anywhere near as affluent and his job as a decorator didn`t help either as it was looked on as a service industry being just above being a servant.

Jessica and Me

Isobella

It was while James was working in Isabella's house that he came across this beautiful girl. He knew he had to get to talk to her but how could he when he was covered in paint and hadn't shaved for days. Isabella took no notice of the dishevelled man as she passed him in the hall. He spluttered out something but she carried on down the hall

Jessica and Me

and when he upset the paint pot, she kept walking. James knew he had to attract her attention so he climbed the ladder and promptly fell off shouting out for her to help. At last James got her attention as she ran back down the hall to see if she could help him. This was just what he had wanted but he was still too nervous to talk. Isabella managed to help him into the kitchen to clean him up. She said 'Take off your overalls and vest so I can wash away the paint.' James began to relax in the girls company. He was able to use his charm and wit to chat to her as an equal and make her laugh as he joked about the accident. Isabella was intrigued and surprised by the way he talked and noticed his muscles rippling on his body. The way James talked showed that he was fairly intelligent which impressed her because her Father had similar intellect. This broke the ice which helped James to introduce himself as he asked 'Where do you live.' she said 'I live here' James said 'I haven't seen you before' she said 'I have just returned from finishing school, I can't talk anymore I must go and unpack we must talk again sometime.' As she began to walk away James grab hold of her and kissed her, she pulled away but he kissed again this time it was more passionate and Isabella kissed him back. After they parted Isabella said 'I must go I am having dinner with my parents but I can see you later'. He said 'I will try and see you tonight.' But the dinner went on to long and it was too late for them to see each other. James thought he must get to know Isabella and every time he saw her with the family he would try to get her attention but although she was intrigued with this upstart she kept her distance. This frustrated James but he could not stop thinking about her and tried harder to get to know this rich girl. When James did manage to talk to Isabella he said 'why can't we see each other'. It was then that her mother intervened and scolded her daughter for getting involved with the workman. Isabella said 'It was just a casual conversation and meant nothing.' The mother did not believe her and moved James to another part of the house away from her daughters room. This did not deter the decorator because he used the lunch breaks to get in touch with this beautiful girl who he was beginning to fall in love with.

Jessica and Me

Isabella's mother was becoming very concerned about her oldest daughter fraternising with the workman. Alice eventually let Frederick know about Isabella talking to the workman. This enraged her father and he said 'The best thing to do would be to send her to stay with her Aunt in the country.' Frederick hoped that this would help his daughter forget about the workman before it became too serious. When Isabella found out about her parents idea to send her away she ran to her room locking the door and lay on the bed sobbing her heart out. She shouted back at her father saying 'I don't want to go to my Aunty.' Frederick shouted back through the door 'You are going and that is my decision and you are to start packing right away.' Alice sent the maid up to the room to help her daughter pack. At first Isabella would not let the maid in to her room but the maid said 'If you don't let me in I will be sacked.' With that the door opened. The maid found Isabella on the bed still crying she said 'Please don't cry because it will be for the best, hear is James address you will be able to write to him and arrange to see each other at weekends.' Suddenly it came clear to Isabella that it would be alright because she would talk to her Aunt, who was a modern woman, to help her arrange to see her boyfriend. When the morning came Isabella had been awake all through the night tossing and turning in her bed crying to herself. Her mother sent the maid in to finalise the packing. The two women arranged a plan to make it possible for James to keep in contact.

Finally Isabella completed her packing and with tears in her eyes she said good bye to her parents. James looked on from one of the rooms looking out onto the street below, although he was sad to see her go the thought of being able to keep in contact helped him deal with the departure of Isabella.

After a long journey Isabella arrived at her Aunt's house on a large country estate. Aunty Flo came out to greet her niece with a kiss on both cheeks and said 'Do not worry everything will work out just fine, I am sure we will get on well together.' Isabella said 'Can you keep a secret?' Her Aunt said 'Of course I can what is troubling you?' Isabella told her about her relationship with James and how she wanted to see him weekends. Flo said 'If that makes you happy then

Jessica and Me

of course you can see James but your mother will be very angry if she finds out.' Isabella was pleased with her Aunts attitude and said 'That is why I want you to keep it secret.' As soon as she unpacked Isabella wrote a letter to James telling him what train to catch and where she would meet him. James hadn't been outside London but that weekend he boarded the train to make his way to see Isabella. When he got off the train Isabella was waiting on the platform and when she saw him she ran up to him and flung herself into his arms, they kissed each other and they got on the waiting coach and horse to go the rest of way to the house. Flo said 'James you can stay in one of the guest rooms and I am putting you on your honour not to see Isabella during the night.' James said 'Thank you for putting up with me, it will be difficult to keep that promise but I will try my best to keep away from your niece.' The couple spent a happy weekend together but the days quickly turned into Sunday night when James had to get back to London.

Isabella continued to see James at weekends throughout the summer but when the winter came it became difficult for James to make the journey and Frederick was giving him more work to do around the house. Isabella kept writing to her boyfriend but he wasn't very good at letter writing. With the visits and letters drying up Isabella became unhappy living in the middle of nowhere and longed for the life she had in London. Isabella eventually apologised to her mother and father. She wrote a long letter pleading with them to let her come home and promised not to see James. Frederick said 'Providing you keep away from the decorator then you can come home.' Isabella jump with joy and quickly packed her things to catch the train to London. She didn't mean to keep her promise and when she arrived back home the first thing she did was to get in touch with James to arrange a secret meeting. After seeing each other secretly for several weeks Isabella decided to confront her parents. When she said to her parents that she was seeing James again and was in love with him her father began to lose his temper again but this time

Jessica and Me

Isabella was ready to make him understand saying that whatever he said it would not make her stop seeing him because she was serious about her relationship with the decorator and said 'I am over 18 and if necessary I will run away to Scotland to marry.' Frederick calmed down realising he couldn't win and after lengthy discussions finally agreed to let his daughter see James but with the proviso that it would be in the presence of a chaperone. In the 1800's chaperones were used to enable parents to keep an eye on their unmarried children when they were going out on social occasions. Usually it was an older woman probably one of the family. Isabella and her boyfriend would try to hide from the old lady but she was up to their tricks and the couple would only be on their own for a short while. Eventually James got up the nerve to ask Isabella to marry him. She said 'You will have to get my father's blessing.' James was a bit apprehensive as he knocked on the door, the maid answered and he nervously said 'Could I have a word with Mr. Schonholt.' He was shown into the study where he paced up and down waiting for the father to come in. After what seemed an eternity Frederick strode in and sat behind his desk and said 'what can I do for you, I can guess what you want, come on man out with it.' James was so nervous he had trouble getting the words out and when he did he was stuttering, something he normally never did. Eventually he gained enough composure and managed to ask the father his permission to marry his daughter. The father had been tipped off by Isabella about the proposal and was ready when James blurted out his request of marriage. Frederick didn't let on that he knew about the couple wanting to get married and kept talking about other things keeping him on tender hooks and the longer it went on the more nervous the boyfriend became until he shouted out 'For goodness sake can I marry your daughter or not.' Frederick burst out laughing and said 'Of course you can marry her but you have got to get a better job because at the moment the

Jessica and Me

money you are earning will not support my daughter.' Isabella was pleased that her father gave his blessing and agreed that James should earn more money. She asked her father if he could get in touch with his friends in the club to see if they could get her boyfriend on the rung of a decent career. Frederick said 'I know someone who is in the insurance business; I will ask him if there are any vacancies.' Frederick managed to get in touch with the friend in the club and while they were playing snooker he mentioned that his future son in-law was looking for a job, the friend said 'there may be something; I will let you know when I get back in the office.' After few days the friend got back in touch with Frederick saying he would like to interview James for a job as an insurance salesman. When James heard about the chance of getting a job he became very nervous saying to Frederick 'I know nothing about insurance.' The father said 'Don't worry about your lack of experience you will be trained on the job.' The interview went well to the point where the manager said 'I want you to get started as soon as possible because the person who will be training you will be retiring soon and you will take his place when you finish your training.' Isabella was so pleased that she took James out that evening to celebrate and as she paid the bill she said 'In future you can pay because you will be able to afford it when we go out.'

Jessica and Me

Chapter Two

With the marriage of his oldest daughter becoming a reality Frederick began to think of the day when he was getting married. At the time he was living with his parents in Germany during the 1860's. His family were Jews called Schonholt and they were in the business of manufacturing musical instruments. It was very successful making them very rich and a power within the Jewish community. Frederick had a charmed life courting a girl called Alice. They were very much in love and planned to get married one day. She also came from a rich and powerful family. Although on the face of it everything seemed to be going well, there were undertones of unrest amongst the locals which had very poor people in and around the Jewish gated community and every time they went in a possession to pray at the Synagogue gangs of people would shout abuse and sometimes throw rotten vegetables at them. To start with these demonstrations were only a small section of the town but the envy amongst the poor was growing and Frederick could see that things were going to get worse making life very uncomfortable especially when the Jews felt that their life was being threatened. Frederick and his girlfriend were riding in their horse and carriage to go on a picnic when they were suddenly confronted by a gang of youths shouting at them to get out of the carriage. Frederick said to the driver `don't stop; get us out of here as quickly as you can. ` The driver used the whip to make the horse break into a gallop and as they sped passed the youths he used the whip to stop them getting onto the carriage. When they reached the house, Frederick said to Alice 'Let get married and get out of this country.' She said 'It's an unusual proposal but I will marry you but where shall we go?' Frederick said 'I have friends in England, we can go there.' When their parents heard about the plan they were very angry that the youths had forced the couple to think of leaving the families but with all the racial tension going on all around them they could see that they didn't have much choice and agreed that it would be for the best and said 'If we were younger we would do the same

Jessica and Me

thing.' As soon as they could Frederick and Alice applied for a marriage licence and went to the synagogue to be married by the Rabbi to go through the full Jewish ceremony with all the family, friends and neighbours in attendance. When the group came out to go to the reception the youths were waiting outside shouting abuse and it took the police some time to disperse the crowd to let the Jews make their way to the party.

Frederick's father decided to shut the factory and retire to the country. They gave most of the proceeds to Charles. This enabled him to use the money to start up a business in England.

Frederick managed to draw all his money and shares from the bank. A close friend bought the house and the factory. The couple hid their valuables such as Jewellery and ornaments in their baggage. They changed into working men clothes to disguise their Jewish background to avoid being noticed as they made their way through customs. There were a few scary moments when they saw people ahead of them being searched but Frederick was a tall man and made a good job of hiding his Jewish nationality. A friend had modified his passport to show that he and his wife were of German origin. The authorities waved them through without searching their luggage and they sighed with relief as they sat down in their first class carriage. The couple still had to avoid border checks along the journey.

By the time Frederick and Alice arrived in England they were exhausted. The journey was long and they had to change trains as they sped through Europe and then board a ferry to cross the channel. The sea conditions were rough making Alice seasick. When Frederick reached London his wife was feeling better and they were glad to see a friendly face walking towards them. He was an old friend that they met while he was on holiday in Germany. His name was William and came from a Jewish family. He said 'I have found a flat that you can rent while you look for a house to buy.' Frederick thanked William and said 'How far is the flat.' His friend said 'It is very near to where I live.' At last the couple felt things were going their way and they could begin to plan their future in a new country.

Jessica and Me

Frederick opened a bank account and bought shares in well-known companies to start earning interest on his money. He began looking for a factory around the Hampstead area to continue his father's business of manufacturing musical instruments. Alice found a large house in the expensive area of Regents Park. It took nearly all their money to buy the property but Alice said 'It is worth the outlay because we both plan on having a large family.' When Frederick saw the house he agreed with his wife that it would be just the place for them.

After a long and difficult search Frederick found a factory large enough to carry out the operations required to manufacture and assemble the instruments. William helped him to find people that had the skills required to produce the various instruments that Frederick planned to sell to the orchestras of the day.

Alice found that she was pregnant and as soon as they moved into the mansion a decorator was employed to create a nursery for the baby. Frederick was delighted that his wife was expecting a baby and gave Alice all the money she needed for the baby when it arrived. After a busy nine months Alice gave birth to a healthy baby boy and when Frederick saw him he said 'His name will be Charles after his Grandfather.' Alice employed a nanny to look after Charles who grew to be a healthy boy getting into all sorts of mischief. This was the beginning of the couple's life in England away from the troubles of Germany. In the following years Alice gave birth to another five children. In 1874 the children were Charles 12, Thomas 10, Isabella 4, Jesse 2, Eliza 1 and Alfred just born. Alice said to her husband 'As much as I love you I can't cope with any more children.' Frederick agreed because he realised his wife's health wasn't very good.

As soon as the boys reached five years of age they were sent to boarding school and although it was expensive Frederick was now a very rich man. The girls were taught at home by a governess.

Charles and Thomas were at boarding school, they were very clever children. All the children at that age were encouraged to participate in an army course that the teachers took very seriously getting the

Jessica and Me

children to wear a full army uniform. The children took part in parade marching, kit inspection and exercises in the field just as if they were in the real army. There were ranks starting with a private, corporal, sergeant and captain that the children would have to work through. Charles and Thomas managed to become captains of their regiment. Thomas enjoyed the army course, but Charles wasn't that concerned and really wanted to concentrate studying maths, science and English, but he also liked cross country running.

The discipline at the school was very strict and the older boys would help to keep the younger children in control. The bothers outlook was different with Charles being serious and business like and Thomas having a future in the army. They got on well together and protected each other from the school bullies. They took part in boxing matches and managed to win prizes being champions at their weights. It was an all-boys school but this did not stop those seeing girls outside the school when they went into the local town. It was never serious as they were warned by the school master that if they got any of the girls into trouble then they would be punished and expelled from the school. Some of the boys couldn't resist the temptation of being involved with the girls and were duly punished for their misdemeanours. Charles and Thomas enjoyed their days at the school and were sad to leave when they reached sixteen years of age. As a welcome home from the boarding school Frederick said `I will take you on a skiing holiday in the Swiss Alps. ` The boys had not been skiing before and their father organised lessons for them. Frederick was an accomplished skier as he had enjoyed the sport as a child in Germany.

The brothers soon picked up the art of skiing down the slopes and enjoyed the thrill of racing each other between trees. Best of all they were able to meet girls in the hotel where they would enjoy the nightlife.

Frederick met old friends that he hadn't seen for a long time and he left the boys to themselves Charles arranged to meet the girls on the slopes the next day. When they went as far as they could go by the cable car and began walking up the mountain the weather started to

Jessica and Me

close in making it very windy, Charles said 'We should turn back.' but at that moment there was an enormous rumbling noise and as they looked up they saw the snow erupt starting an avalanche .Lucky for them there were clumps of tree and bushes to seek shelter as the snow and boulders engulf them. Fortunately the trees protected them from the full force of the snow and they were able to dig themselves out. One of the girls was hurt and had to be carried down the mountain. The trek back was treacherous as the weather continued with heavy snow and strong winds gusting creating snow drifts The group could hardly see where they were going and kept falling and straying from the descent. Frederick was in the hotel getting worried about the weather conditions realising all was not well. He said 'a search party is needed to head up the mountain to find my sons.' The blizzard conditions made it very difficult to keep going but Frederick was determined to carry on because he had to find the group and to go back would be a disaster. The sons used torches to shine a light through the gloom and hope someone would see them. After going for some time Frederick managed to see the lights shouting 'stay where you are and keep shining the torches to direct me to you.' The search party soon found them to rescue the group and take them back to safety.

   Charles and Thomas were shaken up with the experience of the avalanche but were unhurt. The girls had sprains to their ankles and were upset by it all but lucky to be alive and thanked Frederick for his quick response in rescuing them. The next day saw the boys out on the snow again but not straying too far away from the hotel where their Father could keep a watchful eye on the skiing. Apart from the problems of the avalanche the holiday went very well seeing Frederick making contacts with people that could help him with his business. There was one woman who took a shine to him and when the boys were not around. The woman said 'Could I treat you to a drink. Frederick agreed and they chatted for a long time finding out that they had a lot in common. This was unusual in these times for a

Jessica and Me

woman to be on her own and being very forward in her dealings with men but she was very rich and didn't have any respect for protocol. This made Frederick have feelings he thought he never had although this was only going to be a brief holiday affair and would end when he returned to England. However, Frederick thought to himself that he would enjoy the moment and the woman thought the same way. After the holiday Charles and Thomas treated life a bit more seriously having realised that it was precious and not to be taken lightly .It would see Charles studying more to enable him to enter business with as many qualifications as possible. Thomas decided to make a career in the Army. The girl that Charles had met on the holiday wrote to him asking him if they could meet each other with a chaperon of course. This was how young people met each other in those days and Charles was pleased to agree with the arrangement. The girls name was Clare and was very beautiful and intelligent and when Charles met her he knew she would be the girl for him. Their romance blossomed he said `Could I see you without the chaperons. ` The pair loved riding and dancing plus going to musicals to see Gilbert and Sullivan were very popular at that time. Thomas also had a girlfriend, but it wasn`t to last as his army career would be first in his relationship and she thought she would not see too much of him. Thomas managed to enlist into the cavalry division of the army. This was all he wanted as he loved being with horses. His horse was a thoroughbred Egyptian and was very well trained. Thomas made friends with the horse and they bonded well together. Every day they would be out riding and go through the paces that might be used in the fighting situation. The horses name was Ben and was very knowing for his age of five years. Thomas was billeted not too far away from his girlfriend and said `Could I see you over the weekends.` She agreed but knew their relationship wasn`t that serious and it would stay that way from the start.

Jessica and Me

One day when Thomas was out riding on the road the carriages got too close to his horse and it reared up and sent Thomas crashing onto the road and injuring his back in the process. Somebody called an ambulance he was rushed to hospital to see if he had broken anything. Fortunately there were no bones broken but he had to stay in hospital to be treated for shock and rest his back. Thomas's girlfriend along with his brother Charles visited him bringing grapes and card to keep him occupied, some of the other family came to see him during his stay. Gradually his back got better and he joked with the doctors and nurses. He got on well with one of the nurses and said `Could I see you when I get home. ` The nurse gave him her address and said `I would be pleased if you could manage to see me when I am off duty. 'When Thomas didn't tell his girlfriend as he knew she wouldn't understand. When he got home he began dating the nurse going out to theatre and dancing. His old girlfriend became suspicious and decided to follow him and she discovered the awful truth that Thomas was seeing somebody else. She confronted him with her suspicions and he said 'I don't want to see you anymore.` She wasn't surprised but was still upset and she found out where the nurse was living and knocked on her door to discuss the matter more fully but sadly things got out of hand and they ended up fighting. Thomas arrived and he had to break it up, he managed to get the two girls apart and his old girlfriend ran back into the house leaving him to console the nurse who was very upset and couldn't understand why she was attacked by a girl she didn't know and also to find out that Thomas had another girl in his life and she was devastated, she didn't speak to Thomas for some time after the fight. Thomas was desperate to make it up with his new found love and seek the advice from his brother. Charles advised his brother to persevere with her, he said `Keep sending her flowers and little gifts and keep talking to her.' This would make her aware that it was all over with his old girlfriend and telling her he loved her and promising to be honest with her at all times. The nurse's name was Annie and she tried to keep away from Thomas but she missed him and his constant attention

Jessica and Me

won her round and they got together becoming serious and confessing their love for each other.

The Schonholts were a very close family with them all living in the mansion where Frederick and Alice could keep an eye on their children making sure they kept up with their education. The only one that was away from home was Thomas as he was in the Army but he would spend all his leave at the family home except when he saw his girlfriend. Sunday was the day for the whole family to be together at Church and have their mother's roast dinners. This gave Frederick a chance to talk to his sons regarding the affairs of the business. He encouraged the brothers saying 'both of you should take an interest in the amount of money that is being made.' He let them know how their shares in the company were progressing. Charles was very interested in how the business was progressing and he wanted to make his career in running the business one day. He could see this being very soon as he had finished his schooling and was looking for something to do. Frederick sensed that his son was interested in starting work and as Charles recovered from his holiday he made it clear that his intention was to work for his father and was given a junior position in the firm.

Isabella's family lived in the upper class area of Regents Park. Isabella was the oldest daughter. The father Frederick and his wife Alice were deeply in love and lived in an idyllic life in the mid to late 1800`s·

When Isabella was born it was a fairly peaceful time for Great Britain and from 1876 there was some important inventions such as the telephone by Alexander Graham Bell and patent for the phonograph by Thomas Edison also in 1879 the electric light bulb was invented by Thomas Edison, all this helped to make things easier for the Schonholts family to run the business.

Before the invention of the light bulb the candle was the main source of light in the Victorian households and the factories. The horse and carriage was the main source of transport in London. There were so many horses on the road that the pollution from the manure was a big problem. The smoke from the houses and the factories was creating

Jessica and Me

very dense fog during part of the day and night. This created a lot of illness among the young and old people and Isabella was lucky to stay fairly healthy during this period. Fortunately she was one of the elite to be sent to a boarding school on the edge of London where the country air wasn't as polluted.

Isabella loved reading books and studying music along with ballet dancing. The other children tended to like her and protected her from the bullies. She was especially popular due to the fact that she was able to help her classmates with their homework charging 6d a time for hand-outs of written sheets for copying. Isabella progressed through school achieving various certificates in her subject and her ballet lessons were coming along as well. Her Mother and Father were very proud and showered her with many gifts such as jewellery and books to help with her studies.

Isabella had met several young men whilst she was at finishing school, but she didn't get too involved with them as she thought they lacked the character her father possessed. All they wanted was a one nightstand but she was saving herself for someone she might marry who was similar to her father who she adored. When Isabella reached the age of 16 she left the boarding school to go to a finishing school for young ladies in Switzerland. Here again she excelled in all the subjects although some of the bullies managed to make life uncomfortable. She was pleased to leave by the time she was 18 and return home to the mansion in Regents Park.

As a young man James was mixing with people that were drinking heavily in the pubs he frequented. Now that Isabella was officially his girlfriend she didn't agree with his social life. Her parents didn't approve of James but because they had agreed that they could marry there wasn't much they could do but they still thought that he was after her money which was in a trust fund maturing when she became 21. This was only a few years away and James realised that he had to move slowly in the relationship with Isabella and withdrew from the scene for about eighteen months.

The oldest son Charles was destined to take over the company after he had worked his way up through the firm. The other sons were

Jessica and Me

more interested in playing instruments. The daughters were mixing with the upper set in the neighbourhood with the exception of Isabella who was interested in creating a career for herself although she wasn't too sure of the type of work to take up after leaving finishing school. Meanwhile, her parents were trying to find a suitable suitor to court their eldest daughter. Every time a young man was deemed to be the one that the parents approved of, Isabella would see him for a while but very quickly loose interest. The rest of the family were in relationships that would lead to marriage. Isabella's parents were worried about her attitude towards men being such that she could become a spinster for the rest of her life.

The business was doing well in the late 1880's creating a secure future to enable them to carry on their luxurious lifestyle. Britain in the late 1800's was a very rich and prosperous country although the gap between the rich and the poor was quite dramatic. Charles Dickens books were very famous at this time about the subject and they were selling very well especially in America.

Isabella decided to take up art and enrolled in the local art classes to help become an accomplished artist. The teacher would supply numerous models of men and women to pose in the semi or naked form. Isabella revelled in this kind of art and was fast becoming an expert. The teacher soon recognised this saying `you could reach the highest standard to enable you to exhibit in the local gallery.'

Isabella asked her mother to arrange an engagement party in one of the large hotels near to where they lived. She also commissioned the invitation cards to be sent to the family and friends including the Lockleman family. The two families had not met before so she decided to invite them round for a high tea one Saturday afternoon.

The Locklemans were working/ middle class and spent most of their lives drinking and smoking. They lived for the moment and were not worried about saving money. This put them in a different league to the Schonholts. Isabella was fearful of the meeting and told James `Try and keep control of your family.` This wasn't an easy thing to do and they started arguing over where the party should be held. James said `The party could be held in a large pub that I have frequented. `

Jessica and Me

This was very popular with people that knew Frederick. This seemed to be the compromise both families were looking for and they were pleased with James suggestion.

Isabella and her mother lost no time in starting arranging the party. She was in her element being very good at coordinating the contractors that would supply the orchestra and decoration plus the food. Also they would be no delay in supplying the servants to create a professional touch to the party. The mother made sure that it would be the talk of the neighbourhood and no expense was spared.

The one thing that could not be controlled were the prospective in-laws as they were heavy drinkers and could easily upset the other guests who had never mixed with this kind of people. When James and his two brothers got together they became an unruly lot and when they had too much to drink they became argumentative and anyone that disagreed with them got a good tongue lashing with a lot of foul language being used. James hadn't reached the stage of be as drunk as his bothers and soon realised things were getting out of hand and tried to calm things down by taking his brothers outside and he said `Behave yourselves or you will be banned from going back into the party.' One of the brothers collapsed due to being in contact with the air and the other one decided to go to another pub on his own.

The Lockleman's outburst didn't affect the party which went very well. The orchestra played Viennese waltzes, Isabella enjoyed this dance but James wasn't a good dancer so she danced with her cousins and other men all evening. James wasn't happy but he didn't say anything because he didn't want to spoil her enjoying herself.

There were areas set aside for card games and James liked playing although he didn't have enough money but this didn't stop him and he began winning so he put more money in and lost it all. He interrupted Isabella's dancing and said `Could I borrow more money to carry on gambling.` She reluctantly gave him some but she wasn't happy and wondered if this was going to become a habit with him keeping on borrowing from her. James lost again but had the sense to pull out and eat at the buffet because it was the first meal since

Jessica and Me

breakfast. The lack of food could have been why James brothers were suffering by the amount of alcohol they had consumed, drinking on an empty stomach wasn't good for them.

The party carried onto the early hours of the morning with everybody enjoying themselves and the skirmish with the Lockleman's largely forgotten with the exception of Isabella's brother Charles and father. The pair were incensed with rage over the Lockleman's behaviour and told Isabella `Consider your future with James if things don't improve we will try to stop the marriage taking place.` This was bad news for Isabella and she rebelled against her father and brother to the extent that it threatened her relationship with the family. It was only James intervention with the family that cooled things down because by now James was completely sober and was now acting as a different man from the drunken one from the night before. He somehow managed to talk his way out of trouble, this was the start of many encounters that James would have with the Schonholts prior to the marriage that seemed a long way off.

Isabella tried to put her problems behind her by going on a shopping spree in Oxford Street not far from where she lived. She took her sisters Ivy and Jessie with her.

The two sisters tried to get Isabella to forget her problems and even tried to match her with a man called Henry. He was a tall handsome young man but he didn't have a character of her James, but he was attractive and help her cheer up and for a moments she began to relax and enjoy herself in his company while they were shopping and anyway she told herself that her sisters were acting as chaperons. Henry didn't seem to take life seriously with his happy go lucky character which for a while appealed to Isabella. She saw Henry again and went on a few dates with him. For the moment James seemed to be out of the picture. Her new boyfriend enjoyed all the sports that James wasn't good at plus he liked riding which was one of Isabella's passions. It appeared that Isabella was seeing less of James and more of Henry. James sensed this and started trying to see his fiancée again but he was up against Henry's carefree attitude.

Jessica and Me

James had to gain his fiancées trust before it was too late. He started showering her with flowers and gifts but it was an uphill struggle.

Meanwhile Isabella's brother Charles announced his engagement to his long-time girlfriend who came from a similar class of family therefore his parents gave him there blessing. He said 'I want the wedding to be within the year and I want it to be a lavish affair. 'Once again his mother stepped in to say she would organise everything but the future brides family said 'We would like a say in the wedding plans.' A meeting was held between the two families and unlike Isabella's party everything was agreed in an amicable way with the mother doing most of the organisation but letting the mother of the bride do her share as well. Isabella said she would be getting married in two years much to James surprise and delight although she said this depended on how her boyfriend behaved himself. The Schonholts were still wary of James behaviour and said they would also keep an eye on their prospective son-in-law. This put a lot of pressure on James but he resolved to improve his ways because he would not throw away his chance of letting Isabella's fortune fall through his fingers although as he would find out to his cost the plans he had thought up prior to his marriage would not work out in a satisfactory outcome.

Charles was also looking forward to following in his father's footsteps by becoming the managing director of the business as he was thinking of taking early retirement. He had been running the company since his early twenties due to his father's death in his forties leaving Frederick with little experience to run the business. Fortunately the young Frederick had been well educated in financial matters at university where he obtained a BA degree to allow him to become a factory manager and this gave the experience to understand the production side of the business to equip him with all the knowledge to have complete control of running the company. His other brothers took up managing positions to take charge of the drawing and buying offices. One of the sisters ran the sales office making it a truly family run business.

Jessica and Me

James Lockleman was still grinding away at his job as an insurance clerk. This was to change because his hard work made him stand out as promotion potential and his manager made him up to an insurance salesman. This enabled James to get out of the office to sell policies to people in their houses to protect their homes against fire and theft plus any damage to household ornaments etc. James revelled in this kind of work where he could meet people especially the wives when the husbands were out working.

Isabella managed to get a job as an artist in a small office painting pictures for magazines. Isabella didn't need to work because her father was still giving her an allowance that she could use to live on but she wanted to be independent of her family as much as possible.

Charles' wedding was, as expected, a lavish affair, money being no object as the Schonholts pulled out all the stops out paying for the whole wedding. James was invited but without his family which annoyed him. He went along with it because he realised his family would probably upset everyone. He set about enjoying himself at the reception mixing with the guest with his eye on making contacts to further his career prospects. When the happy bride came out to say goodbye to begin their honeymoon the bride threw the bouquet up in the air and who caught the flowers but Isabella that indicated that she would be next in line to get married.

By 1894 Alice was busy arranging her daughter's wedding. She had managed to persuade James to go along with a lavish affair that her son had, although his family were not happy as they would be in the minority of Alice's rich friends and would be put in shade as all the women would be dressed in glittering dresses that the Locklemans couldn't afford.

On the wedding day as predicted Alice's rich friends turned up in their finery and ignored James family in the church and the ceremony went without a hitch and everyone made for the reception where the Locklemans went straight to the bar to start drinking as much as they could and after a while they became their usual loud and obnoxious selves falling about and bumping into the guests. By this time Isabella had to pull her new husband to one side she said 'Tell your family to

Jessica and Me

either quieten down or leave the party. ` James managed to get the message across but they were not in the mood to listen to him and eventually made their exit from the party. The reception carried on at a pace with everybody enjoying themselves. Isabella's sisters changed out of their bride maids dresses into the latest fashion with very tight waists and frilly top and fall length skirt. They looked beautiful with hair up and make up which their Mother let them wear for the first time as they were still young girls and they had just come out of finishing school. All the young men were clambering after them and their book of dances were full. Jesse and Eliza were more adventurous than their older sister because the Mother had not been as strict on them as she had been with Isabella. Also they were more musical being able to play the piano and the violin. They decided to join the orchestra and play more Viennese waltzes and other dances that were in fashion at that time.

Charles and his younger brothers Thomas and Alfred were playing cards and gambling for money with James. As usual James started off well but started to lose heavily. Once again he had to borrow off Isabella who wasn't best pleased with his gambling which was becoming a habit. Isabella was getting angry with her husband when suddenly he said `Get changed to go on our honeymoon.` She agreed and forgave him and they kissed and made up as they changed into their going away clothes. Everybody came out to see the couple off and wish them bon voyage on their journey which was a closely guarded secret even Isabella didn't know where they were going until they boarded the orient express train to travel across Europe to Budapest.

Isabella was overjoyed with James for organising such a trip and they made love in there cabin as they sped on through the night missing breakfast and would have missed dinner if they hadn't started feeling hungry. The train stopped in Paris and the young lovers managed to see some of sights before boarding the train to carry on with the journey across to Switzerland. This was where Isabella went to finishing school and she showed James where she stayed with the view overlooking the Alps where she used to ski on

Jessica and Me

the slopes. The train sped on towards Budapest and the newlyweds revelled in the atmosphere of the train especially the dining car with the choice of exotic food on offer and the waiter service was excellent. James flirted with the waitresses much to the annoyance of Isabella but apart from that the honeymoon was very much to the fore with the couple making love at every opportunity. The train rumbled on its journey with its rich passengers including other honeymooners on board which made it easy for the couples to exchange their experiences with each other during the time spent in the dining car. There were a lot of rich people that James could meet and make contact with them by giving them his business card with a view to selling insurance when he got back to England.

When the train pulled into Budapest station the passengers were able to get off and stretch their legs. There were art galleries and museums to visit but James was interested in the music halls and the couple went to the shows. They liked Gilbert & Sullivan and were surprised that a show by them was on one of the theatres although the language was Hungarian they still enjoyed it because they recognized the music and Isabella liked the costumes.

Gilbert & Sullivan were very popular back in England and it appeared they were making their mark in Europe as well. They were very much part of the Victorian music halls and Isabella and James had grown up with the music ringing in their ears since they were babies.

The honeymooners boarded the train to carry on the journey to Constantinople originally known as Istanbul in Victorian times and this was far beyond what they had ever been to before. They were very excited at the prospect of seeing strange people dressed in clothes suitable for the hot climate of Eastern Europe with traditions they had never seen or encountered before. The religion, politics, and architecture made this a new adventure for them and it was very hot which didn't suit there Victorian clothes. The couple had to shed a lot of there under ware and just wear the minimum amount of clothing. Isabella used a sun umbrella and to the locals she looked and acted as a very rich lady that was normal for her but for the Turkish people

Jessica and Me

it was very unusual as they stared in ore. The merchants soon gathered round the couple trying to sell all sorts of items such as rugs, ornamental statures, clothes and food. Isabella declined to buy any of the items that were being pushed at her except for a silk scarf.

The couple stayed on in Constantinople and travelled by horse and carriage out into the country side. James had his eye on the villas and wondered if they were for sale. The couple came across a market in one of villages and were impressed by the amount of fresh food and rugs etc. that were being sold. The heat in the middle of the day was very hot and Isabella said `I want to go up the mountain.' Although it was a long way ahead they decided to go, the higher they went the cooler it became although when they came across a lake with a water fall it was still hot and they changed into bathing suits a plunged into the water. They swam to the waterfall and stood under it where they made love kissing each other until they fell in each other's arms to rest under the water spray. Life was great at this time and Isabella couldn`t have had a better honeymoon. After a few days the pair boarded the train to return to London. James managed to get involved with a gambling set in one of the cabins and left Isabella to get on with her sowing. As usual James didn`t do well and had to borrow money from his wife to pay his debt and she was now becoming worried about James increasing habit of getting involved with gambling but she kept quiet thinking she would confront her husband when they returned to London.

When Isabella reached London she made straight for her new home in a Victorian style terraced three stories building in Highgate where she began designing the interior to enable the decorators to start work for the couple to live comfortably and have enough room to plan a family for the near future. Isabella became so busy dealing with the house and talking to her family and friends about how she enjoyed the honeymoon that she forgot about confronting her husband regarding his increasing gambling problem. Meanwhile James carried on acquiring new business for the insurance company travelling around the Highgate area and becoming very popular with the

Jessica and Me

housewives being invited in their homes for tea and cakes in the afternoon when their husbands were away at work.

Isabella was unaware of James exploits and after two years of seemingly blissful married life the couple were blessed with a healthy baby boy and they named him James after his father but he was to be known as Jimmy throughout his childhood. He became very mischievous as he got older and Isabella dressed him in the latest fashion and was the best of everything as rich kids were treated in those days. Soon there was another addition to the family of a baby boy and his name was Frank. He was more of happy go lucky kid where Jimmy was more intense with an eye on the girls in the nursery. The two boys were sent to boarding school as their Mother and at the same place.

Just as Isabella was getting used to bringing up two children after two years she fell pregnant again and this time it was a baby daughter and they named her Yvonne. Isabella called a halt to having any more children as she was finding it difficult to bring up three children although they employed a nanny to help her but truth was that she was being worn out by her husband's attention and didn't want to go through child birth again.

Meanwhile James hard work as an insurance salesman was paying off and he was promoted to a supervisor. This was to become his undoing as he became older with extra money he was able to indulge himself in drinking and gambling. His new position didn't stop him doing the rounds in fact it increased because he now had to keep an eye on all the insurance salesmen on his watch plus visiting the households with the juniors to show them the technique of selling policies to the families.

Jessica and Me

Chapter Three

It was 1902 and life was changing for the rich families like the Locklemans and the Schonholts. As far as the Schonholts were concerned the music industry was now up against competition from the film studios. More people were seeking entertainment going to see film shows at the newly built cinemas and this was having an effect on the music halls which in turn reduced the sale of musical instruments although the sale of pianos were still ok because the cinemas were using them to provide backup music for the film shows.

Queen Victoria had died in 1901 and her son Edward VII was King of the Empire and Great Britain. A new era had begun with people more flamboyant and being adventurous with their dress shedding the strict regime of dress code that the Victorians followed. Chamber music being played in the rich men's clubs and houses was being replaced by more melodic music that was to be called jazz. A film star called Charlie Chaplin was becoming famous with his slapstick humour.

The advent of the car was replacing horse drawn transport albeit slowly at this time because only the rich could afford this expensive mode of transport.

The next twenty years would see an increase in the above mentioned changes plus a war that would become the worse disaster that the British had experienced for a long time. The Locklemans would see big changes in their life style as well. The Schonholts were going through changes as well. Charles was looking at the business and thinking of creating a company in America. His younger brothers were in the army and the sisters were married to wealthy business men. Frederick and Alice were retired and living in Switzerland near the Alps. Charles decided to go to America to see if he could start in New York. He discovered that there weren't that many factories making musical instruments and went to the banks to obtain a lone to buy a factory. He also wanted to buy a large house in Manhattan where his family could join him when the business was up and running. The bank agreed to finance the venture and Charles moved

Jessica and Me

to a rented apartment. This enabled him to buy the machinery and fit it into the factory. The next job would be to employ and train people to start manufacturing the instruments. He had managed to employ salesmen to create contacts that would buy pianos and violins etc. It took a bit of time to get the business off the ground; once it did everyone was delighted with the product. Charles and his family were able move into the mansion he had been dreaming of living since he came to America to rent an apartment this enabled him to buy the machinery and fit

Charles eventually shut the factory in England and concentrated building up the business in America where his wife said 'I am happy to settle; we can find a good school to enable the children to be brought up as American citizens.'

Isabella could no longer rely on hand outs from her family to help bolster up James gambling debts and money from her trust fund was beginning to dry up too. Although this didn't stop them from enjoying a good life style for the moment and anyway James salary and commission was managing to support the family in a style that they had got used to. Yvonne was having private piano lessons and Jim was making good progress at school but Frank was struggling with his lessons because of his happy go way of dealing with life enjoying himself going fishing and playing football. Jim was a serious boy wanting to follow in his father's footsteps although this was not a good thing as the coming years would show and Jim would find it more of a struggle to make a good life for himself.

Isabella carried on with her art work although it wasn't bringing in much money it kept her busy and stopped her thinking about her husband's problems and at the moment didn't have much of an effect on their life style. James bought a motorbike to help him with his work when he visited his clients and the women in his life liked the idea of this modern man cutting a dash in his outfit and he would give them a ride on the back with their hair blowing in the wind. He would take them to the pub for a drink to get them in the mood to buy policies that they couldn't really afford. Isabella didn't know of James exploits at that time.

Jessica and Me

In the early 1900's the motorbike was very basic with fixed suspension and no speed ohmmeter. Telescopic suspension and ohmmeters would come later. Wearing a crash helmet was virtually unheard of because if the riders did wear anything it was a leather skull cap and goggles plus heavy weight gloves and trench coat with riding boots that would have normally been worn when horse riding.

Isabella wouldn't go near the vehicle preferring to ride in a horse and carriage if she was travelling more than a mile or two. A few years on found them buying a car which was gradually becoming more popular although it was generally reserved for the upper class. Cars were not that fast and would break down often. It wasn't until a partnership between Rolls & Royce that would see a really reliable engine but this came at a cost so only the wealthy could afford to own them. The first cars on an assembly line were in 1885.

Jessica and Me

Chapter Four

By 1910 King Edward was in his seventies. Heavy drinking and smoking took its toll and after a short illness he died leaving his son to reign. When King George V came to the throne the relationship between Great Britain and Germany was deteriorating as the Kaiser Wilhelm II was making more demands on claiming territory from the French and Belgium nations. The French were building their defences to try to stop the German army invading but this proved disastrous in the coming years. The troubles were affecting the Schonholts due to their family ties in Germany and they decided to change their name to Holt which would be more acceptable in England and America.

James was spending more than he was earning due to his drinking and gambling, his heavy smoking which was affecting his health was getting worse but he carried on with living the high life. The couple were now dipping into Isabella's trust fund.

The Schonholts family had gone their separate ways with Isabella's parents living in an old people's home, her brother Charles making a life for himself in America and his brothers were still in the army. The sisters were married with children living in France and Germany. Germany wasn't the best place to live during this time and the sister decided to leave before the First World War started. Isabella's children Jim & Frank were in their teens and managed to find work as a greengrocer's assistant and a laundry boy local to where they lived. Yvonne was at school in the senior grade and couldn't wait to leave. The boy's earnings went into the family pot as times were beginning to get tough. Jim started going to night school to study electrical engineering which was a popular trade. Frank in his happy go manner carried on working in the laundry and Yvonne had private lessons playing the piano. Her lessons would have to stop soon when the money was needed to help with the running costs the family were

Jessica and Me

incurring especially with James carrying on with his drinking and gambling.

In 1911 the Lockelmans were just about ok with their finances and enjoyed entertaining their friends. Isabella would get Yvonne to play the piano for the guests in the Highgate home. Jim would play the piano but he was heavy handed and played in the vamp style that was popular in those days. Isabella and James would go to the music halls and the theatre but the teenagers wanted to go to the movie theatres that were becoming popular with the younger generation.

By now the film industry established in 1903 was becoming big business and the leading actors were earning big money but films didn't cost that much because the actors that had bit parts and the extras weren't paid that well. There was a class system in the film industry with actors tied to long contracts and this would go on for a long time before it was changed to enable the actors to have a better say on how they were treated and also to enable them to earn more money.

Films in the early 1900's were in black and white and silent except for the live piano playing in the pit in front of the screen. These films were known as silent movies therefore actors and actresses didn't have to have a good speaking voice but they had to be able to move well and be good looking and in fine suits and dresses. Along with the comedy there were cowboy and Indian films that showed the action in the wild west of America and one of the actors that was doing very well was Wild Bill Hitchcock. A lot of the films would be very violent and full of action with the cowboys always winning against the Indians which the audience lapped up.

By 1912 Frederick Holt (Schonholts) was in his 70's which was a good age in those times and if you had a serious illness the doctors couldn't do much for you and Frederick who had been in poor health in over two years became weaker and the doctor said he couldn't do any more for him and soon after he passed away peacefully in his sleep in the old peoples home. This left Alice heartbroken and she nearly gave up but she was a strong woman and with the help of Isabella she was able to carry on living for a few more years. Isabella

Jessica and Me

looked after her as best she could but with her husband getting into debt with his gambling and constant drinking it wasn't easy. Jim was a good son and gave as much money to his Mother as he could afford and Yvonne gave up her piano lessons and took up cooking for the family to ease the burden on Mothers shoulders.

The family moved out of their large house in Highgate and moved to a smaller property between St. Pancreas and Camden. With the money from the sale they were able to buy the new home and carry on living in the style they were accustom to. They were still in the above standard bracket but this wasn't going to last too long as the coming years would show.

James was enjoying himself in his job visiting houses showing the junior salesmen the art of selling policies to families especially to the women who would invite him in for a drink or a cup of tea and flirt with the young salesmen. It was on one visit that James met a young house wife called Alice Sopple. Her family were living in a three story terraced house in Fulham near Bishops Park. She was a good looking women and lonely because her husband John was always away working as a chauffeur driving his boss all over the country. Alice liked James calling on her and he said 'Let's go to the local pub for a drink.' They would talk a lot during the short time they were together. The pair would begin to see more of each other finding different places to meet and be alone together. After about a year James managed to buy a lease on a flat just off the Fulham Palace Road and the couple would spend time in the love nest having romantic dinners and sleeping together. They were very much in love.

Alice had a daughter called Victoria who was born in 1910 and when James and Alice were in the flat the grandmother would look after Victoria. Alice's mother Charlotte knew about the affair but didn't approve of James but she kept quiet about their acquaintance as she didn't want to cause trouble between her son-in-law and daughter plus the fact Alice seemed much happier since she met James. Alice went with her boyfriend to the casinos to gamble and she seemed to bring him luck and he begun winning at the table although the money wouldn't last because he spent it on her giving her expensive

Jessica and Me

jewellery and high fashioned clothes. Alice was over the moon with so much money being spent on her because as a child she had a hard upbringing. She was one of ten children all of them being adopted due to her father dying in his mid-forties and the her Mother remarried to enable the children to have a father figure head, she didn`t really love him and he knew this but he liked playing and bringing them up in a family atmosphere. He wasn`t a wealthy man and Alice and her family often went without food and clothes until he managed to obtain money from charities that operated in these times. The family lived in a poor part of Fulham and when Alice reached eighteen she married John who was the first man to come along and became her lover. This enabled her to get away from the family and John was being paid very well by his employer who would give him cast off clothing for Alice and they managed to afford the rent for a three story terraced house in the better part of Fulham. The couple were happy to start with but with John away so often this was when Alice started seeing other men and when James came along flashing his money about and taking her to places she had never been to before she couldn`t resist his charm and thought he was very wealthy which he wasn`t but he managed to fool her for a long time before she found out the truth and by then it was too late because Alice had fallen in love with James and things would become very difficult and a great change would come and affect her and Isabella's family in a big way.

Isabella and her teenage children were oblivious to her husband's affair because the last few years the couple hadn`t seen much of each other and she had got used to James being busy working and being out in evening drinking and gambling with his so called friends and his wife didn`t mix with them. This was just as well because the friends were really Alice.

Jim was in the middle of his studies to become a qualified electrician and at the time working in the grocery store. Frank was still working in the laundry and wasn`t interested in studying for any qualification instead he concentrated on having a good time going out dancing and seeing films in the cinema. It was when he was out one night at the local dance hall chatting up the girls that he saw a very beautiful girl

Jessica and Me

on the other side of the dance floor chatting with her friends. He tried to catch her attention but she took no notice of him preferring to be with her girlfriend. It was obvious that Frank had taken a shine to her and having little success in attracting her attention from the other side of the dance floor he made his way over to her and after making his way through the crowd he eventually found himself standing in front of her where he sheepishly said `Could I have a dance. ` To his surprised she said `Ok let's dance. ` From that moment Frank knew she was the girl for him.

   The new girl in Franks life was called Bridget and she reminded him of his mother when she was her age as she was just as beautiful. Her family was part French and she was a very good dancer and could keep up with his drinking. He could drink a lot and unlike his brother who became nasty when he got drunk, the younger brother would act silly and laugh until he collapsed in a chair or on the floor and fall asleep. Bridget would often have to get friends to help her carry her boyfriend home and leave him on the floor in his mother's kitchen much to the annoyance of Isabella's daughter Yvonne who was different from her brothers not liking to go out but staying at home cooking for the family. She was pretty girl with long flowing red hair down her back but she was very serious and disliked her brothers drinking so much but she would find somebody later on that would change her life although after a while she would revert back to being a stay at home dutiful wife.

Jessica and Me

Chapter Five

By 1913 James was losing so much money at the gambling tables that the couple had to sell their large house in Camden and move to a small terraced property in Fulham. At the time this area was classed as a hamlet by the river Thames with daisy fields leading to the edge of the water which gave it a country feel on the edge of London. Although it wasn't all country because just a few minutes away there was a coal fired power station which would be enlarged in 1936. Isabella's house was opposite fields within walking distance of the River Thames. The fields were to be built on in the near future to make way for an oil terminal owned by the Shell Mex Company. The fields were not fenced off which made access to the river easy and the family used to spend Sunday afternoon sun bathing and having picnics which made life easier to deal with since there move from Camden.

Their home in Camden was within a few minutes of the City of London which the family used to visit but now they had to adapt to a more rural way of life but they could still travel to London albeit being a longer journey which wasn't too hard to bear. The family settled into their small terraced house and quickly made friends with the neighbours. The houses had been built during the late 1800's and were completed by 1910 and covered a large area. The population had grown considerably during that time. The industrialisation of the area was to create problems for the inhabitants with increase of pollution from the power station but they were more worried about the threat of war gathering on the horizon at this time with the news paper's full of stories from Europe about the troop movements in Germany. This was going to affect everyone in the coming year as Jim would find out as he reached his late teens.

Their move to Fulham still enabled them to have money from the sale of the house in Camden. Therefore, compared to families living in their street they were considered to be rich and people would come to Isabella to help them with their money problems so she became a money lender and a figure head amongst the community. At

Jessica and Me

Christmas time the family created an open house where everyone that they knew would come and pay their respects and thank them for the support they had been given throughout the year.

Jim and Frank were still working in the grocers and the laundry. Yvonne carried on cooking for the family but was also teaching the local children piano lessons in her spare time. All this was the lull before the storm for the family.

James health wasn't getting any better, he wasn't helping himself because he carried on working hard and seeing Alice when he could. His gambling and drinking increased plus he was smoking a lot as well. Although he was only in his mid-forties his life style made him look much older. Isabella wasn't very happy moving to Fulham being away from her friends and family in Highgate but this would pale into insignificants with the problems she would have to face in the coming years.

Soon after the family moved into the house the neighbour's called round to welcome them with bottles of beer and food to help them settle in and make themselves known to Isabella and was glad that it appeared she was going to have good neighbours to rely on if things got tough. The family stopped unpacking and had a house warming party there and then. The people next door were called Blundle and had three children and were a jolly lot. The Head of the family had been an amateur boxer when he was a young man and liked singing in the pubs. His oldest son took after his father and also liked boxing but he was also an all-round athlete getting involved in running on the sports track and his name was Richard. His younger brother Simon was also into sport and preferred to play football. The daughter Harriett was the youngest child and liked to watch her older brothers boxing and playing football.

Yvonne was a similar age to Richard being in their early teens and became good friends but that was as far as it went at that time but they would get more involved later on when they were in their twenties.

Jessica and Me

In those days kids would play in the street because there weren't many cars or Lorries on the road and the nearest park was too far away.

Jim bought a second hand motorbike & sidecar which became his pride and joy as he drove it at high speed through the local country side although motorbikes in those days were more than likely to be only able to go at 50 mph which was classed as fast at that time. Jim wanted a skilled job and when he saw an advert in the local paper for electrical trainees to work at the Power Station he jumped at the chance and applied for the job and went for an interview. When the manager found out that Jim was already studying electrical engineering he immediately said. `You have got the job. ` This enabled him to get involved with the practical alongside the theory that he was being taught at college.

People were travelling about more and Jim loved to ride his motorbike travelling out to Marlow near Henley where he could relax by the River Thames or stroll through the village and have a drink in the pub. This was where he met a girl called Joan working behind the bar who was very beautiful and friendly. He took an instant liking to her and said. `Could I buy you a drink.` She said `That would be nice.` After a few drinks they both got to know each other and Jim said `Could I meet you again.` She agreed despite being very popular with the local lads, she was attracted by his charm and sophisticated manner that the locals didn't have. Joan was intelligent and had a sense of humour, she was out of town and away from the other girls Jim knew in London. This allowed him to pick and choose between his girlfriends to keep himself from getting too involved with them.

Frank and Bridget were still going steady with each other but they were not planning on marriage as they felt they were too young.

Life in Fulham towards the end of 1913 was better than the Locklemans thought it would be. This was because they had managed to control their expenses and Jim was putting more money into the family coffers although James wasn't helping with his dependants on alcohol and addiction to gambling but Isabella was able to cope due to the cheap rent and Yvonne was making a lot of

Jessica and Me

bread and cakes also Frank was growing a lot of vegetables on his newly acquired allotment.

There was a widower living next door to Isabella, he was called Harry Tovel. He was tall and good looking in a rough sort of way, similar in age to Isabella. He introduced himself and said `If you need any help I will be there to lend a hand.` He sensed that Isabella was lonely with her husband always away on so called business. Harry had been a widower for some years after his wife had died giving birth to a still born baby. This had knocked him hard but he was trying to build a new life when he met his new neighbour.

It was Christmas time in 1913 and it was to be the last one before all hell would be let loose on Great Britain for years to come. James did his usual thing on Christmas day by splitting his time up between his families and seeing Alice in the afternoon. Jim and Frank spent most of day in the pub much to the annoyance of Yvonne who was stuck in the kitchen cooking the turkey dinner and she worried that it would get cold before the family sat down to dinner.

The Blundles and Harry Tovel visited Isabella in the afternoon and had a party till the early hours of the morning everything went well with the exception of the father and son getting the worse for the drink and ended up arguing with each other and when it was all over everyone wandered what it was all about because they were so drunk that they couldn`t remember what started it off in the first place. Apart from the argument everyone enjoyed themselves and went home singing in the street before going inside their houses.

The morning after saw everyone in their houses still asleep except for Isabella and Yvonne who were clearing up from the night before and Jim and Frank were chatting about the party upstairs in their bedroom. The pair always liked to laugh and joke after the party and they would still be drinking until Isabella turfed them out of the bedroom to carry on clearing up the rest of the house. As usual Yvonne was angry and upset by her brother's antics and went to the kitchen to start preparing the dinner to take her mind off the rows of the night before.

Ronald Shadbolt

Jessica and Me

Everyone ate and drank a lot in those days and also lived for the moment because the news from abroad was getting worse between the Germans and the Serbs and it would only take a spark to set everyone at each other's throats. Britain and Germany were building battleships to defend themselves at sea and the French were building the defences on land. Things were becoming very tense.

The families in the street celebrated the New Year with gusto as they did every year. Isabella and family ignored the bad news and carried on with their lives. James began seeing more of Alice. Jim progressed in his job as an electrical engineer at the Power Station and his brother seemed stuck in a rut with his job at the laundry although he didn't mind as he wasn't very ambitious and all he wanted to do was to have a good time with his girlfriend Bridget. Yvonne stayed at home doing what she enjoyed most which was cooking and looking after the house.

James was going away to seminars for at least two or three days at a time and he would take Alice with him. He would book her into the hotel as his wife to enable them to share a bedroom. Alice didn't see her daughter that often as she was looked after by her grandmother when they were away. Victoria didn't mind the arrangement as she got on better with her grandmother who spoilt her buying toys and clothes and taking her out shopping in Oxford street. Victoria was enjoying herself so much that she would cry when Alice came to collect her to take her home. The grandmother didn't mind looking after her grandchild but she was worried about the parents and could see things going from bad to worse with the marriage and wondered what would Alice do.

Jessica and Me

Chapter Six

Going into the year of 1914 Britain was increasing their production of battle ships and trying to keep up a dialogue with the Kaiser Wilhelm but he was an awkward customer and seemed determined to carry on building up his armoury and the aggressive proper gander that was coming out of Germany wasn't helping the Diplomats with their negotiations to try to avert the onset of war.
   The Locklemans were trying to get their finances in order but it wasn't easy because of James spending habit. As soon as any money was saved he would raid the money box and go off with Alice to have a good time at the casino. Isabella would confide in her next door neighbour Harry and he would sympathise and try to give Isabella all the moral support he could give her. Harry would try to speak to James but it was like water off a ducks back because he didn't seem to care how his wife felt.
   Jim was seeing more of Joan in her home town of Marlow which was a small village surrounded by farm land and had the river Thames running through it. Jim liked going into the local pubs and chatting to the local farmers. Frank would go with his brother and liked fishing. When the pair got together they were a force to be reckoned with and they would make the locals laugh at their antics when they were in the pub.
   The land around Marlow was relatively cheap compared to modern times and Jim had his eye on plots just outside the village but he held off making any offers because at that time it would have stretched his resources but he would keep the idea to himself and look at the situation at a future date.
   James was infatuated with Alice and their love making became more intense and sure enough by the end of March Alice became pregnant and the same time her lover became very ill. The illness was a shock to everyone as he was only 46 and seemed to be coping with his

Jessica and Me

drinking and smoking but looking at in the cold light of day it was obvious that this kind of life style couldn't be maintained and it effected his liver and his chest, this was destroying his immune system. Before James became too ill he summoned Isabella to his bedside and confessed all his indiscretions. Isabella was shocked to hear her husband's revelations and was even more distressed at his request that she should contact Alice and offer to help with the pregnancy that was due in December. James begged his wife to contact his girlfriend to talk about the best way to deal with the situation he found himself in. His mistress already had a child and she couldn't afford to keep another one and anyway the Husband didn't want to know about the baby especially when it wasn't his child.

James wife found it very difficult to come to terms with the news but realised she had no choice but to go along with her husband's wishes because she realised he was dying and she promised him saying `I will do all I can to find a way to take care of the baby.`

On top of Isabella's problems came the news that the break out of war was announced by the Prime Minister Lloyd George because in June the Archduke Franz Ferdinand was assassinated as he was driving through the street.

Kaiser Wilhelm encouraged the Austrians to adopt an uncompromising line against the Serbs and then he attacked Belgium, this triggered a war with Russia, France and Britain which would be known as World War I. By this time James was taken into hospital and within a couple of weeks he passed away. Isabella and Alice were by his bedside along with his teenager children who had just heard the news about their father's mistress and were devastated with their father's death and also seeing Alice pregnant.

Isabella gave Alice some money to enable her to cope with the pregnancy and said `Please get in touch with me when the baby is due so that I can be present and help you through the ordeal of the birth. `

As the end of the year drew ever closer the war in France was getting worse and Britain tried to get as many young men to join up

Jessica and Me

and go to the front line to fight for their country. It became a very patriotic thing to do and thousands of men went to the trenches.

Jim and Frank would have to consider their position with regard to joining the Army for their part in the war effort. Jim was first to be sent to the front line and Frank tried to join but it was found that he wasn't fit enough and he had to stay at home.

Alice gave birth to a baby girl on Christmas day in 1914 much to her annoyance as it spoilt her Christmas and she had been depressed worrying how she would cope with another child. Isabella visited her husband's mistress; the two women discussed the best way forward to deal with the new born baby. Isabella asked Alice `Have you named the child.` By her expression she realised that Alice had not given much thought regarding a name for the baby Daughter and didn't seem to care. Alice reluctantly agreed to think of a name and the two women went through various names before coming up with Jessica as a suitable name. After some deliberation a decision was reached when Isabella finally agreed to take Jessica and bring her up as one the family. Alice was very pleased with the outcome and said she would visit whenever she could to keep in touch with Jessica.

Alice and her husband hadn't been talking to each other since she fell pregnant and the relationship became worse after Jessica was born. Johns attitude didn't change when the Locklemans agreed to take the baby and bring her up as one of the family. The couple were living in separate bedrooms and Alice decided enough was enough and began looking for somewhere else to live. She hoped her lovers son would let her live in the love nest that she had spent with James but Jim had already let the rooms to lodgers and wasn't keen on associating himself with his father's lover.

Alice had to find another flat and managed with the help from Isabella to move into a property near Hammersmith. It was smaller than where she lived with her husband but it was better than nothing and Alice and her daughter set up home together. They were glad to be rid of John's abusive ways.

Alice had to find work now that she was the bread winner and she needed to start earning money as soon as she could to be able to pay

Jessica and Me

the bills and the rent. Her Mother offered to look after Victoria while her daughter was working. Isabella said 'There is a job going in the local laundry factory that cleaned industrial clothes', curtains, rugs from the local mansions. Work in the laundry was hard but Alice knew she had to keep going to bring the money in to help to pay for her daughter's education. Being a good looking woman she attracted the men working around her. The charge hand called Henry was especially taken with Alice and due to his position he was able keep the other men at bay while he pestered her for a date. Henry was tall and good looking in his early thirties with three children having to look after them alone because he had recently been widowed due to the death of his wife who had suffered with ill health for some time. He began showing Alice how to operate the complicated machinery and had a laugh when she got things wrong as it was difficult to operate the huge machine. Henry took his time getting to know the women who he nick named Ali and after she had settled in feeling comfortable with the work, Henry began asking if Ali could go for a drink in the lunch breaks. Seeing that the offer was in a local pub and during the day Ali agreed although she kept laughing at him when he tried to be serious about his intentions towards her. Ali asked one of the girls about Henry and she told her all about his past including that he was a widow. This surprised Ali and she began to try and keep Henry at arm's reach from her but by now he had fallen in love with her and he asked her why she was being so distant. Alice said 'It's because I am married so there is no future in carrying on going out with you.' Henry said 'I know you are married but I also know that you haven't been living with your husband for some time so that shouldn't stop you from going out with me.' Eventually Alice gave in and agreed to a dinner and dance in a local hotel. That evening was the turning point in their relationship because Henry had secretly book a room for the night and when he thought Alice had consumed enough drink and was completely relaxed and were in a very passionate dance, he whispered in her ear that they could go to room and continue to make love and to his surprise Alice agreed. Henry quickly whisked her up the stairs and as she was giggling lifted her up

Jessica and Me

into his arms unlocking the door and they fell onto the bed and continued to make love. That night was the best time Alice had experienced since she had been with her lover James. She soon realised that she had to forget about James and make a new life for herself and Victoria with Henry. After a few months she agreed to live with her new boyfriend but she warned him that they would have to be careful about her husband because he could be a nasty character. Henry said `I am not worried about your husband because I can look after myself.` It wasn`t long after that Alice got in touch with John and asked for a devoice but he refused and said `You can live in sin with this upstart as far as I am concerned because I don`t want to see you anymore.` Alice wasn`t surprised at her husband's attitude and while her daughter was crying she gathered up all her belongings to put them in a van that Henry had rented and set off for new life in his house that he shared with his grown up children. Despite Johns refusal to agree to a devoice Alice and Henry continued to live together and it wasn`t until John dyeing in 1949 that they were able to plan to get married in 1950. By this time they were in their sixties.

By 1921 the couple were still very much in love to the extent that Alice fell pregnant and when she told her lover he was over the moon with joy and asked when she was due to this she said `The baby would be born in seven months' time'. Henry said `I would like a daughter because my other children are boys. ` Sure enough when the baby was born it was a daughter and they named her Alice after her mother.

Victoria wasn`t that happy living with her stepfather and now there was another child in the family she was even more miserable but she continue to live with her mother until she was 18 years old when she met and married a local boy and moved to the other side of London in the county of Essex.

With all that had happened over Christmas Isabella had briefly forgotten about the war but suddenly it all came flooding back when she realised her son was in training to make him ready to go to the front line in France. This war was becoming the most disastrous war of all time with thousands being killed and wounded. The hospitals

Jessica and Me

could hardly cope with treating the men with horrendous wounds that included amputations becoming a common occurrence and also soldiers were coming back from the trenches suffering with shell shock although this wasn't recognised in those days and some men were so effected that they didn't want to go back but if this happened then they were classed as deserters. If they were caught then they were court marshalled. When they were found guilty they were treated as cowards and shot for desertion. Also a lot of injuries would be for blindness from gas attacks when they were in the trenches.

Jim pushed the fear of war to back of his mind saying to himself that it was his duty to go off to France and fight for King and country but he would soon change his mind once he got to the front line. Frank stayed at home working in the munitions factory making guns. He found this difficult because he hadn't trained in engineering and was not used to handling machinery but he would have a laugh and joke with the work mates and he became popular with the girls due to his good looks and he was one of the few young men around that they could get to know because most of others were away in the war.

Jessica was a bit of a handful for her stepmother and Yvonne had to lend a hand to help Isabella who was feeling the strain due to being in her forties , she realised her age was making it difficult to bring up a baby and began to rely on her teenage daughter to make it easier to cope.

With Jim in the army and Frank on a low wage money was becoming tight and a new baby in the house didn't make it any easier to keep the budget in balance. Yvonne managed to get a job in the local laundry and now she had to split her time between looking after Jessica and the job. Isabella helped as much as she could but Jessica was missing being fed from milk from the breast because Isabella couldn't do it and there was a food shortage due to the war raging in France. Yvonne being young and energetic was in her element doing a job, cooking and looking after a baby at the same time.

Jessica and Me

Chapter Seven

During 1915 the war in France and Belgium had been raging more than six months which was far beyond what people were led to believe because they thought it would have been over by Christmas. The politicians and the Generals were now realising it would be a long haul because the Germans had done a good job arranging their defences. They were able to fight from a very strong position in the trenches that were protected by heavy artillery and were able to bombard the French and British causing heavy losses as they advanced towards them. The allies were fighting an old fashioned war relying on using huge amounts of men to charge the enemy but every time they climbed out of the trenches the Germans would moan them down with machine guns and cannons. One day the losses were 60,000 men wounded or killed, it was carnage on a grand scale and the Generals didn't seem to be leaning from the horrific experience and if there were any gains it was only a matter of yards or if they managed to get to the enemies trenches they would be bombarded so much that they would have to retreat. Moral was at an all-time low in the ranks and officers were finding it difficult to rally the troops.

Jim hadn't gone to front line yet and every time leave came he would go home and try to support the family with the little money he had. He would also see his girlfriend Joan in Marlow but as the time got closer to being sent abroad the more he became depressed with the bad news being broadcast every day although the government were using all proper gander to keep moral amongst the population as high as possible.

Since her husband's death Isabella's life had changed dramatically. Gone were the days of leisure like riding in Green Park and shopping in Oxford Street for dresses that could be worn to go to parties and the theatres. Isabella missed her brothers and sisters and her parents had been dead for some time. She felt very lonely and it was only her neighbours that kept her going. The widow next door would pop in

Jessica and Me

and try to lift her spirits and she began to be attracted to him waking up feelings that she hadn`t felt for a long time.

Jim was eventually sent to France by sea in a troop carrier across the English Channel on a windy rainy day on a very rough sea making everybody sick. It didn`t seem to affect Jim who had a tough constitution. When they reached land the journey had only just begun and before they could get over the rough sea journey they were ordered to board a steam train that would take them to the fighting zone. When they eventually arrive worn out from the journey after a short rest they made their way to the battle area. The tented area was a muddy smoke filled chaotic scene with everyone rushing about looking after the injured and getting the new troops together with sergeants bellowing out orders to get them ready to go to the front line. It was a horrendous scene with the injured being taken to the field Hospital by the Red Cross ambulances as quick as possible. There was also the walking wounded struggling along the road and the nearer Jims platoon got to the front line there were shells exploding all around them coming from the heavy artillery being fired by the German lines.

Everywhere was in a chaotic state with Officers running between units blowing their whistles and directing the Red Cross to the wounded and those that were able to fight were being pounded by the big guns fired from the Germans. They were pinning the soldier down to the extent that if they put their heads above the trench then they would be shot at by the snipers. This war was much worse than Jim had been led to believe and he was scared out of his wits. Jim was a born survivor and managed to get to the trench without being injured unlike some of his comrades who were being picked off by the snipers. For next few years this would be Jim's life trying to keep alive and sane where some of his colleagues were going out of their minds with shell shock. The fact that this type of illness wasn`t being recognised made it more difficult to treat and all that was being advised was for the men to be sent home for rest and recuperation and when they were deemed to be fit enough the men would be sent back to the front line to carry on fighting. Some men were able to

Jessica and Me

carry on but others were not lucky as their reflexes had been slowed due to their mental state and couldn't react quickly enough when faced with being shot at and were killed. Many men lost their lives this way and the lack of proper treatment would mean it would go on like that for the rest of the war. Jim realised he couldn't survive in this environment and planned to get away somehow but it wasn't going to be easy because the military police were everywhere. To make his escape successful he would have to take his time and wait for the right moment.

Apart from the Western Front in France which covered 475 miles of trenches and fortifications there were other fronts such as the Eastern, Balkan, Middle Eastern and Italian Fronts. The vastness of Eastern Plains which had limited railroad network made it difficult to supply the war machine and fighting on the Western Front was in stalemate with each side cancelling out each other's manoeuvring. There was also hostilities at sea and in the air although it wasn't towards the end of the war that aeroplanes started shooting at each other, prior to that the air forces were being used as reconnaissance taking pictures of each other's positions.

The Japanese entered the war in August 1914 and the Italians came in to fight in April 1915.The Americans left it until April 1917 before they took part in the hostilities and this helped to break the Germans stranglehold on the war. The allies were beginning to stop the food and ammunitions supply to the German nation and in August 1918 the war came to an end.

When the Americans finally came into the war Jim saw his chance to get away and when he was on leave he went to see Joan and he told her that he didn't want to return to France. She said 'I will hide you in the cottage in Marlow. ' Living by herself she had managed to store a substantial amount of food and drink and she said 'If we are careful we could last for at least a year.' The pair of them hoped the war would end and with chaos Jim wouldn't be missed by the army. The military police did come looking for him but Joan managed to see them coming and found a good hiding place to stop the MP's finding her boyfriend. Isabella knew her eldest son was alive but Joan hadn't

Jessica and Me

told her where she was hiding Jim and with the family kept in the dark about where her son was hiding she couldn't let it slip out to anyone where he could be found. This arrangement was hard to live with but Isabella knew that if she said anything to anyone her son would be branded a deserter and probably shot.

   Isabella was seeing more of her neighbour Harry and her daughter noticed this and wasn't happy with her mother flirting with him and rows would break out every time the mother saw Harry. He tried to make friends with Yvonne but she would have none of it and she would go next door to the other neighbours for a bit of peace and quiet and talk to them about her problems. Richard had a soft spot for Yvonne and said 'Could I take you to the cinema.' It was her favourite film and after the show he said 'Could you be my girlfriend.' She said 'I would be glad to be your girl.' This was what she had wanted because she had always liked him from the very start. They went to the sports centre where Richard showed her the boxing ring he used and although Yvonne showed some interest to please him she wasn't really into sport but she wouldn't let him know because she was scared that he wouldn't continue with their relationship. Their friendship would become more serious and lead Yvonne to leave home but she held back from doing this for a while to make sure Jessica was able to look after herself. Jessica's real mother and her sister would visit now and again to see if she was ok but they were hoping that Isabella would give them some money and although she did it was only a small amount because she wasn't as rich as she used to be.

   While Jim was in hiding he couldn't erase the experience he had during his time in France because of the friends he made in the army and the way they were killed as they got out of the trenches which was called 'going over the top' was shear carnage and he felt guilty for surviving when so many had lost their lives needlessly. It was also while he was there that he met a young girl in her late teens, he was on a few days leave and he travelled to a village a few miles from the front line. He was surprised how quiet it was compared to the trenches a few miles away. The shops and the bars were open and

Jessica and Me

he went into the café/bar for a drink. He managed to make himself understood because the girl behind the bar spoke a little English and he knew a bit of French. For a while he forgot about the war as he laughed and joked with the girl whose name was Yvette and he later learned that she belonged to the resistance. She invited him to go upstairs to her bed where they made passionate love. During his time at the front Jim went back to the village as often as he could and Yvette introduced him to the men in the resistance and he said `I want to get away.` They said `We can't help because like you we have a duty to fight and you should also think about doing the right thing.` He thanked them for their advice and said `I will think of another way because I don't want to blow your cover.` Jim continued to see Yvette which made the experience of the war more bearable and he felt as long as he could keep his head down and avoid the snipers he could survive the terrible ordeal he was going through. He told Yvette `I have a girlfriend back in England. ` She said `I don't mind because the way things are it was best just to live for the day and forget about tomorrow.` For a young girl she had a wise head on her shoulders and Jim respected her views and was relieved that she hadn't thrown him out.

Back home the war was effecting morale as it seemed that it would never end and added to that despite the lack of news people were getting to know about the amount of men losing their lives and the horrendous injuries that a lot of survivors were being brought home to be treated in the hospitals and because of the lack of wards some of the mansions were being converted into Hospitals to treat the wounded.

Isabella was worried about Jim and she took solace in Harry's comforting arms as they became lovers but because of the way society viewed their affair they kept it as quiet and secret as possible.

By the time the Americans came into the war the future looked a little brighter as the Germans were being pushed back into their own country.

Jessica and Me

It took another year before the Germans capitulated due to them running out of men and materials. Kaiser Wilhelm II was forced to abdicate and he went into exile in the Netherlands.

Jessica and Me

Chapter Eight

As peace was restored to enable men to come back from France to be demobbed plus the reduction in Military Police allowed Jim to come out of hiding and return to normal life. He managed to get work at the Power Station.
Isabella found her husbands will through a solicitor and the family had a meeting with him. They were informed that there wasn't much money but Jim had been left the lease on a house just off the Fulham Palace road, this was where his father entertained his clients and mistresses especially Alice. Frank and Yvonne got a small allowance and their half-sister Jessica only had the security of staying with her stepmother. Jim decided to let the house out to lodgers and along with his wages it made life easier to live and not to worry about how to survive in the coming years. Jim stayed with Joan at weekends and lived with his mother during the week days. Frank returned to work in the laundry and Yvonne remained in the house doing what she had always done. Life was a bit drab for her but her boyfriend saw more of her taking her out to see films at the local cinema to help her through her periods of depression that would sweep over now and again.
Jessica was a bit of a tomboy playing with the kids in the street chasing the Lorries and hanging onto the tailgate as it sped down the road. Even at the age of five she was a very fast runner and Richard noticed this and made a note that he would take her to the race track to let her take part in racing other girls.
When Jessica's real mother and sister came to see her she would play with the sister but being four years older she would soon get bored with her. The mother was a rough and ready character but when she was at Isabella's home she would try to put on airs and graces as though she was a lady with a fortune and when Jessica sat on her lap and played with her buttons or bows the mother would chastise her and act in a snooty kind of way. Everybody knew what she was like and laugh behind her back at her antics. Jessica didn't realise it was her real mother calling to see her until she was a teenager and this would be a huge shock to her. Meanwhile Jessica

Jessica and Me

had a good life as a child because her adopted family treated her as one them and this would continue for most of her life. The main thing that began effecting Jessica in her young life was the amount of drinking that went on amongst the brothers especially when Jim had too much to drink and this was where he took after his father when he would pick an argument with anybody near him and this could end up in a fight and being a little guy he would invariably get the worst of it. He would take a long time to learn his lesson and although he still argued during the drinking sessions he would tend to hold himself back from going too far and avoid a fight. Like most children in those days Jessica had to make the best of her childhood and try to keep out of the way when the drinking sessions were going on. Yvonne used to help her cope by staying in the kitchen and cook cakes to keep their minds off the ruckus that was going on in the front room. The way the family carried on had a lasting effect on Jessica as a child and becoming an adult. She would swing from being a moody character to a really fun loving person.

Joan was good for Jim because she was the only one that could steer him away from trouble when he was drunk. Although the brothers could put the same amount of alcohol away Frank tended to act in the completely different way by becoming soppy and dance with everyone and laugh and joke with people which made him very popular with his mates.

After the war society became more relaxed and it seemed that the nation decided to have a good time enjoying the moment. In the 1920`s the music called Jazz was sweeping across America and it also became popular in Britain and everyone would go to clubs where there would be live music being played by mainly black musicians who had the Jazz rhythm in their soul and it was a defence mechanism against the way the white Americans were treating them in those days. There appeared to be a double standard because on one hand it was ok for them to play in the band but not to socialise with customers. Although slavery had been abolished, black & whites couldn`t go to same schools or travel on the same bus and if they did the bus was split in two with the blacks and white kept separate. A lot

Jessica and Me

of black musicians crossed the Atlantic to work in Europe with France being the best place to play Jazz. To a point Britain accepted them, but they were only allowed to play with the whites in the clubs but they lived amongst themselves in the poorer part of town.

Jessica and Me

Chapter Nine

In the early part of the 20's Jim was beginning to earn a lot of money in the Power Station and from the lodgers in his house in Fulham.

Frank had fallen head over heels in love with Bridget and wanted to marry her. He saved up enough money to book a fancy restaurant and during the evening he proposed to her. When he showed her the ring she was overjoyed because she had been expecting him to ask her that evening, she immediately said `Yes I would love to be your wife.` Frank was over the moon with excitement and they danced the night away.

Isabella was glad her second son had got engaged and looked forward to the wedding day. She liked Bridget and hoped they would be happy together. Her son didn't have much money so it was no surprise that finding somewhere live had to be renting a flat. They found a place in Clapham and he also managed to get a better paid job with the local council as a messenger. Bridget had never worked as her parents were reasonably well off and they gave her enough money to spend on an expensive wedding present which they used to buy furniture and a double bed to give them a good start in their married life together. They saved some of the cash preferring to keep it for a rainy day which was just as well because this would help them overcome the down turn that would follow the crazy 1920's.

After the wedding everyone made for the reception. The party lasted for days, nobody wanted to leave as they were having such a good time with endless supply of food and drink with the cost born by the bride's parents. Jim and his neighbours Richard and Harry were completely drunk and by the end they could hardly stand up. The women had to carry them to their beds struggling to calm them down so that everybody could sleep it off. By the next day they all had hangovers and suffered for days afterwards but they all looked

Jessica and Me

forward to the next party as this was how it was in those days with one party going on after another and with no regard for tomorrow. People were letting off steam and being thankful that they had survived the terrible war that had taken so many loved ones that they just wanted to forget the past and enjoy the present.

People in the years after the war were busy enjoying themselves living for the day and not worrying about tomorrow. This was all very well but this period wouldn't last.

Jim didn't want to get married because he was happy with the arrangement he had with Joan allowing him to be part of her life at weekends and pursuing his life in the week days where he would go to the pub in the evenings and socialise with his mates and have a good drink. This didn't appear to impair his judgement at work which was just as well because anybody else would have fallen down on their job. Yvonne and Richard were opposite to each other but this seemed to be the attraction and they were happy in each other's company. She liked staying at home whereas He liked enjoying himself on the athletic meetings at weekends and being in the boxing ring punching somebody silly. He also liked going to pub having a drink and singing to the locals. He was very popular being an extrovert whereas Yvonne was an introvert and as long as the couple allowed each other to do their own thing then it seemed their relationship worked.

Yvonne was increasingly becoming unhappy with her home life and when she reached 18 she decide to find a small apartment to get away from the arguing that would happen between her mother and Jim. It always started when Jim came home from the pub drunk and argumentative and when his mother told him off they would go at each other till the early hours of the morning. This happened on a regular basis and was getting on everybody's nerves. It would make Jessica cry a lot and misbehave to seek attention and Yvonne would go off on her own for long walks to get away from the constant shouting at each other.

Yvonne found an apartment and told her mother that she was moving out. Isabella tried talking her out of leaving but she would

Jessica and Me

have none of it and her mother understood her reasons and gave her blessing and they parted on good terms respecting each other's views. Jessica was still a young girl and relied on Yvonne to help her with her education and if her stepsister left home then this would be a big blow to her confidence.

Jessica would go and stay with her half-sister as much as possible which made her life more bearable and Richard helped coach her with running on the race track although her mother wasn't that happy saying `It is unladylike to take part in such a sport. ` Despite this Jessica carried on competing and became very good but she respected her mother's views and after a while she stopped racing even when everybody said she could have gone all the way to being a top athlete.

Bridget broke the news to her husband that she was pregnant and he jumped for joy saying `I hope it is a boy. ` Isabella was pleased about a new addition to the family and Yvonne started making clothes for the baby. Everybody pulled together to help the couple deal with the pregnancy by giving toys and clothes to make things easier for the arrival of the baby. When the baby arrived they named him Robert and he was a healthy boy crying his head off. Frank was very proud of his son and planned to have another baby.

Jessica and Me

Chapter Ten

Jessica was 10 years old and liked being an Aunt but she was devastated to hear that Isabella wasn't her real mother but it was the one that came to call now and again plus the young women was her real sister. Being a strong willed girl she quickly got over it but the worst would come in her teenage years when she went to see her mother who didn't want to know her. This would stay with her for the rest of her life. She never knew whether she had been adopted or just handed over and she would describe herself as being a door step baby because nobody spoke about it in those days. Isabella never said anything because it would bring up old wounds from the past and she had tried to forget about her husband's indiscretions.

Jessica knew that she had to make the best of things and enjoy the life she had and relied on friends to stop her thinking of how her real mother had treated her. One friend was called Joanna and the pair of them joined the girl guides movement. She liked the uniform and joined in the games and went camping in the country to study nature, but she wasn't keen on writing up about it and she and Joanna started fooling about and were accused of not taking things seriously enough and the Guide Mistress warned them that if they kept misbehaving then they would be expelled. This didn't deter the pair and they were duly thrown out of the guides. Isabella wasn't pleased with her daughter and banned her from attending the track events at the stadium. Richard wasn't pleased with Isabella's refusal to let her daughter carry on training but he couldn't do anything about it. The punishment didn't worry Jessica because being a teenager she was able to go with her friend Joanna to have fun going to the theatres to have a good laugh watching comedians doing so called stand-up comedy.

The theatres were very popular but the film shows at the cinema were beginning to attract an audience that would also become popular. There was also the advent of the radio although in its infancy was beginning to attract an audience that could stay at home to listen to the news and all the shows that could only be seen at the theatre.

Jessica and Me

The theatres managed to carry on with the introduction of musicals that came from Americas theatres on Broadway in New York. There were songs from a new breed of writer such as Irving Berlin, Cole Porter, George & Ira Gershwin, Jerome Kern and many more. There were dance halls with live bands playing the latest dance craze that everyone liked to dance to. The new dances were given names such as the Charleston, Tango and the Shimmy all played to the rhythm of Ragtime which was all the rage in the 1920's. The fashion houses changed their clothes from being restrictive tight corsets and large puffed up sleeved and long skirts down to the ankle that characterised the Victorian era to being free and loose with skirts above the knee and see through blouses.

A new kind of dancing was free to sway, hug and grind to the ragtime music. The young people lapped this up but the older generation didn't approve. Although in the early 1900's both the Waltz and the Tango were considered scandalous dances because they involved physical contact between partners during the dance. Once the dance crazies took Paris by storm and were demonstrated in America everybody embraced the dance and this became the norm. Dancing was a very good way to exercise and have fun at the same time.

Young people introduced their own fashion styles and so the 'Flapper' and 'Sheik' came into existence. Girls with short bobbed hair styles, close fitting hats and short skirts were referred to as 'flappers' and men dressed in raccoon coats and bell bottomed trousers were called 'sheiks'.

The popularity of the Charleston created other new dances like the blues dancing developed in the speakeasy clubs. The good times went on into the late 20's until the stock market crashed in 1929 called the black Monday in September. Towards the end of the 20's a dance called the Lindy hop swept America, it was named after Charles Lindbergh famous for his solo flight in his light aircraft. It was the beginning of the athletic type of dance where the men would swing and jump his partner around to the big band music that was being played by the black Negro bands and eventually white bands

Jessica and Me

as well. This type of bands would dominate the music scene until the early 50's and everyone liked dancing because it covered a wide spectrum of the dance from jazz to strictly ballroom. Dance schools were all the rage and there was a guy called Fred Astaire and his sister Estelle who performed the dances in the theatres. Fred would go onto expand his career in Films in the 1930's with his fantastic tap dancing with various partners especially a girl called Ginger Rogers and the pair captured the mood of the public and they would always be remembered as Fred & Ginger for many years.

When the stock market crashed Americas mood changed significantly and would be known as the great depression going on into the late 30's. It spread like wild fire to Britain and Europe. It took Governments by surprise and to start with it created mass unemployment that would last for years. People were out of work for three years or more. It took the new President of America to turn it around by creating work on the roads and the railways to stop people from starving.

In 1922 Yvonne and Richard became engaged. The couple were very happy although both families were surprised that they had become an item because Yvonne was a quite stay at home girl '; Richard like going out and enjoying himself socialising with his mates but it appeared that opposites attract each other and Richard needed someone to keep things steady when he was at home.

In 1924 the couple got married and both families were pleased for them and it was an excuse to have a party. As usual when Richard had a few drinks he would break out into a song and dance with everyone leaving his new wife to sit in a corner out of the way.

A year later Yvonne was pregnant and she had problems when she gave birth to a Son and she said 'I don't want any more children.' Richard was disappointed because he really wanted a daughter but it was not to be. The couple named their son Ivan and his mother doted after him spoiling him from the start much to Richards annoyance and to make matters worse Ivan wasn't that interested in sport and this kept Father and Son apart. Ivan was a very intelligent baby and his mother could see that he would do well at school.

Jessica and Me

The party atmosphere was still going strong in the mid 20's and Isabella had a new lease of life enjoying herself with the attention that Harry was giving her. She liked going to the theatres taking Jessica and Harry to see the live acts of the day. Harry was different to her late husband and they made a nice family and it was good to get away from Jim and Frank, their arguments often going on into the early hours of the morning.

Jessica's real mother was not seeing her much of her as she was growing up. Isabella wondered if Alice had someone else in her life that was distracting her from seeing Jessica. The family would soon find out when Jessica went to see her when she was sixteen.

Isabella's children were in their twenties and thirties when Jessica was reaching her early teens and she had to find friends outside the family circle. Boys came and went because although she was an outgoing girl she could also be moody and some boys couldn't deal with it.

Isabella invited Harry to live with her much to the annoyance of Jim as he didn't get on with him but he couldn't talk his mother out of it and he decided to stay with Joan. There were now only Isabella, her boyfriend and Jessica living in the house. This didn't make Jessica very happy because Harry was attracted to her and was always making sexual advances towards her and in those days abuse was kept quiet and in fact sex was never mentioned and love making between adults was carried out behind closed doors and usually on a Sunday afternoon when the children were at Sunday school.

Sunday consisted of the family going to church early in the morning and then to the pub before the Sunday roast prior to sending the children to Sunday school while they settled down in the bedroom to make love. Teatime would be another large meal made from bread and fish usually cockles, whelks and winkles bought from the street fishmonger early in the morning. All the neighbours knew each other popping in and out of their houses and this was how Isabella and Richards mother Agnes shared the local gossip taking up most of the morning. The radio was very popular in those days and people would

Jessica and Me

follow the news and plays including comedy and actors became household names.

When Jessica was in her early teens Jim and Frank took her to see the real mother. When she knocked on the door she was full of trepidation wondering how her mother would react and when she greeted her mother with a cheery `Hello I am your daughter.' The mother froze and said `I know who you are` appearing very nervous and just as she spoke a man's voice shouted out from the living room `Who is that at the door`. With that the mother replied `Oh it's nobody` and she quickly closed the door leaving Jessica upset and bewildered at her mother's attitude. This would affect her for the rest of her life and she never saw her mother again. It seemed that one of reasons Alice acted in such as offhand way was because the boyfriend didn`t know about Jessica and if he found out then she would be in trouble and possibly beaten up. It also seemed the reason why her sister didn`t keep in touch because the mother had poisoned her mind against Jessica saying `She is not a nice person to know`. It appeared that Alice had a new life which included a third daughter called Alice who was nine years old and her mother hadn`t told her about the existence of Jessica and she feared that it would upset her new family if they discovered her secret.

By now Frank had two sons Robert and James this was just what he wanted because when they were older he could take them fishing and to football matches at Chelsea where he was a member of the club.

Yvonne and her family moved to a house in the next street to Isabella and her husband got a job maintaining lorry's for Shell Mex near where they lived.

Jim was working in the Power Station and still seeing Joan. It was rumoured that the Station would be enlarged to have four chimneys the same as Battersea. This was good for the employment but it would prove to be a heavy polluter making the area a filthy place to live and would cause a lot of chest disease leading to many deaths although this wasn`t discovered until many years later and would lead to the Power Station being shut down and eventually demolished but

Jessica and Me

by that time it was too late for a lot of the inhabitants who hadn't managed to move away.

In those days most people lived near to where they worked allowing them to walk or cycle to the factory. Cars were too expensive for the working man and not that many garages around to maintain them or fix when they broke down which was often because they were inefficient.

Jessica and Me

Chapter Eleven

By the time 1929 came along the so called good life of the 20's came to a sudden halt In America people working in banks were committing suicide by jumping off sky scrapper buildings. Unemployment in America reached 25% and the farmers land on the prairies became dust bowls which forced them to leave the land but this didn't help them because there was no work in the towns. People stayed at home rather than go out on the town. They listened to the radio and read books by Agatha Christie, Raymond Chandler and Dashiell Hammett. The younger generation chose the cheaper seats in the cinema and the dance halls were cheap as well. In America Herbert Hoover was President up to 1932 but he lost the election to Franklin D Roosevelt who set about turning the economy round by getting people to work on the roads and the railways. It was called the `New Deal`. Herbert was unpopular because he refused to provide government aid to help the unemployed.

Europe was gripped by dictators such as Hitler in Germany, Mussolini in Italy and Franco in Spain. People were desperate turning to anyone that they thought would deliver them out of the recession but trouble lay ahead that would make them wish that the Dictators had never been given power to mesh up their lives.

It wasn't all gloom and doom because as mentioned before the dancing film stars Fred Astaire and Ginger Rogers lifted peoples spirits when they went to the cinema to see them tap dance their way through the films which were pure escapism. Most of the films were light entertainment with the exception of Charlie Chaplin's film about the working man oppressed by the employer called ``Modern Times`` this was unusual for Chaplin because he usually made films that were incredibly funny with their knock about humour.

Film stars in those days were on a seven year contract and most of them were happy with the arrangement but some felt that the studios had too much power over the type of films they could be in and they rebelled against the system. Eventually the actors formed the United Artists group which would allow them more freedom to pick and

Jessica and Me

choose the type of films they could be in and also they could share in the profits that the film made at the box office.

Jessica was growing up fast being a very strong character and the boys found her very attractive and despite the upset she had with her real mother she enjoyed going out with her friend Joanna to the theatre. One of them was called the Palladium where all the top stars used to put on a show. She also began going out with boys but it was never serious until she met a young man who lived in the next street and his name was Robert Shalden. He used to go to the shop where Jessica worked and when the other girls noticed that she was attracted to the boy they encouraged her to go out with him. He had bright ginger wavy hair and was two years older than her. Jessica liked the look of him but she realised it would take a while to get to know him because he was very shy being the complete opposite to Jessica's fun loving ways but this didn't stop her going after him and he eventually asked her to go out to the cinema on a date.

Robert was a carpenter in the building trade and like most people he couldn't find work because all the trades were suffering from the effect of the great depression. All together he was out of work for three years which was very hard to deal with and this would affect him in a big way for the rest of his life. He was one of seven children made up of four sons and three daughters. His father died in his forties which left the mother to bring up her family by herself, she was a strong women which was just as well because she wouldn't have managed otherwise. Robert was a weak child missing his father's guiding hand and his mother didn't understand her sons attitude and was very strict in bringing up the children. The other children managed to cope with their mothers out bursts but it had a bad effect on Robert and he would retreat into his shell and would bottle up his feelings and it would affect his nervous system making him a sickly child.

When Robert reached his teens he managed to overcome his nervousness and he became a more stubborn stronger person who helped him deal with being out of work for so long although this was only on the surface, underneath he was still in a nervous state. He

Jessica and Me

began smoking at school to calm his nerves but this brought on bronchitis. He would have to go to the Doctor regularly and he was advised to give up the habit of smoking because his father died from the same symptoms but he was addicted to the nicotine and couldn't give it up.

Despite their differences Jessica liked being with Robert. Being the stronger character, she was able to do what she liked except when he thought he was in the right and he would become very obstinate but usually Jessica would ignore him and carry on with whatever she wanted to do. Their courtship was a long one because they couldn't afford to get married due to the depression and they agreed to wait until things improved and Robert needed to get a job.

Jessica was becoming very unhappy at home because of Harrys unwanted attentions towards her and the last straw came when he tried to enter her bedroom while she was asleep. The sound of the door knob rattling woke her and before he could do any more she screamed out and rushed to put a chair against the door to stop him getting in. Isabella ran from her room and pulled Harry across the hall shouting at him to go away and wait for while she tried to calm her daughter down saying `Everything would be ok`. She would talk to him and find out why he was acting that way. Harry said. `All I wanted to do was talk to her nothing else. ` Isabella believed him much to Jessica's astonishment and disgust and she vowed to leave home as soon as she could.

The next day Jessica asked Yvonne `Could I move in with you because I am frightened of Harry and I don't know what he would do to me if I stayed. ` Yvonne was only too happy to let her stay because it allowed her to get back at her mother and show the type of man Harry was and that he could be dangerous.

Isabella was shocked at her daughter's decision to leave home and pleaded with her to change her mind and stay where she belonged. She said `I believe the story about Harry and I promise he will not do such a thing again`. Jessica didn't believe he would stop pestering her and said `I will leave at once. `

Jessica and Me

When Yvonne helped with the packing her mother came into the room but they ignored her and carried on filling the suitcase and when Harry appeared Yvonne gave him such a look that he hurried into the back yard and hid in the outside toilet. Isabella still pleaded with them to change their mind but it fell on death ears. They took the case outside where Richard helped them put everything on the back of a wagon and pushed round to their house in next the street. Jessica lived there until she got married.

Jessica and Me

Chapter Twelve

Despite the depression Jim was able to carry on working at the power station and he was increasingly staying with Joan in Marlow. One day he saw an advert in the local paper showing land for sale near to where his girlfriend lived. People were being encouraged to buy land to build houses although it didn't happen straight away because people couldn't afford this luxury. Most of them settled for buying a readymade shed and Jim did the same. This enabled the family to spend the weekend there to break the routine of living in Fulham. Jim said 'It would be a good investment'. He asked his mother to go into partnership with him to buy three plots at sixteen pounds per plot. His mother agreed and went to the bank to ask for a loan. Once all the paper work was completed the family went to see the area which was basically a field and set about clearing the long grass with a scythe to enable a shed and a tent to be erected. This was easier said than done but everyone buckled down and worked through the day to clear the area. The plot was only lived on at weekends and it became overgrown and it was very hard work to keep the weeds down.

Frank and his sons would go to the plot and take their fishing rods to the Thames nearby and they caught some fish just big enough to cook on a portable stove which made a good meal before making their way through the foot path to the pub. Frank had to leave his sons outside but he would let them have a week alcohol drink while he had a pint of mild & bitter. The pub closed in the afternoon so they would make their way back to the plot to sleep because they had been up since dawn.

Jessica and Robert would spend the weekend at Marlow along with Isabella because by this time they had settled their differences. Although Harry wouldn't go with them and nor did Yvonne either. She couldn't forget the past and refused any pleas from her mother to be friends and this was how it would be for a long time.

Jessica would stay in the shed with her mother while Jim and Robert spent the night in the tent. One night there was a terrific storm and the tent nearly blew away and the next morning Jim found Robert

Jessica and Me

asleep with his head resting on the iron bar that was part of the support for the tent. Jim said to Jessica `I can't believe how your boyfriend managed to sleep especially with his head on the bar`; It appeared that Robert could sleep anywhere and at any time of the day.

Although Yvonne got on with Jessica's boyfriend she didn't encourage the relationship because as she told her stepsister `You could do better for yourself by finding someone who had a better future and would be able to give you the security you craved`. Jessica said `Their couldn't be anyone else for me because I love Robert and I intend to marry him one day when I feel the time is right.`

Robert managed to find work making orange boxes but he had to live away from home in Tunbridge Wells. Although the money came in handy Jessica wasn't pleased with the arrangement as it meant that she didn't see him as often as she liked but she took her mind off her problems by getting a job in a fish & chip shop which kept her busy and it also meant that the money could be saved for the day when they could get married.

Life was still a drudge because it seemed the depression would never end. People were trying to make the best of their meagre existence. The radio programmes helped by producing a series of comedy shows that became very popular and there were plays to be listened to as well.

In those days TV had only just been invented and only a privileged few could afford to buy one to watch the restricted viewing on TV sets that were bulky and had a tiny screen.

The theatres, dance halls and cinemas were still the place to go for enjoyment and try to forget the problems that the depression was creating. It was amazing that people were still able to frequent pubs and afford to buy alcohol to help them forget their worries but this wasn't helping because many ended up becoming alcoholics and dying young. The National Health system hadn't been created and Private Health was expensive and only the rich could afford the Doctors fees. If you became seriously ill the chances of survival were

Jessica and Me

slim and the average life span was about fifty years if you were lucky to have a good constitution.

Jim was one of the few with a healthy body which was just as well because he could consume a great amount of alcohol and smoke a lot. He was a small thin man but strong as a thick steel wire rope.

Frank had a similar build to his brother and could consume the same amount of alcohol but he wasn't so strong.

Yvonne's son suffered from migraine attacks and he would have to retire to a darkened room and lie down until it went away but apart from that he was fairly healthy but he wasn't into sport except for dancing and rowing.

Jessica and Me

Chapter Thirteen

During the 1930's at the height of the great depression the Royal family had a crisis of its own when King George V died and in the tradition the Prince of Wales would become King but this particular Prince was having an affair with an American woman called Wallace Simpson. The complication that made it worse for the couple was that Wallace was a divorcee. The government got to hear about the Princes liaison with Mrs Simpson and tried to persuade him to give her up especially because he was to become King of England and the Empire.
  When the Princes mother Queen Mary found out about the affair she was devastated and along with her daughter-in-law Princess Elizabeth tried to talk to her son, known as David amongst the family, to give up seeing the divorcee. David was an obstinate man and wasn't worried about becoming King but he thought that if he was to take on the title then his mistress should be his Queen.
  When the government heard about his intentions they brought pressure to bear on the Prince to make him choose between giving her up and become King or if he married Wallace then he would have to give up the title.
  The Prince was very popular amongst the people but with the Royal family and the government against him it was becoming very difficult for the couple.
  With the death of his father David took the title of King Edward VIII but before the coronation took place everything took a turn for the worst when the Prime Minster Baldwin had a meeting with him and said `The relationship should come to an end and I am backed up by a letter signed by the Commonwealth countries`. This showed that they couldn't support the King marrying a divorcee.
  Wallace said that she didn't want to be Queen but David said `If this was how it is going to be then I will abdicate. ` Within hours he

Jessica and Me

announced on the radio that he would step down as King and the couple went to Paris where they eventually got married and the Duke and Duchess of York were crowned instead to become King George VI and Queen Elizabeth.

The depression was still affecting the daily life of the population with industry still in the doldrums including house building. The plot that Jim owned was still a field with a shed and tent standing; most of the other plots were in the same state. People were only using the fields as a weekend retreat to get away from the daily grind that existed during the weekdays. Some of the owners used goats to keep the grass down but Jim wasn't that lucky so he had to rely on the family to cut the grass while they were on one of their visits. Jim was advised to build a bungalow but he couldn't afford it and was hanging on to the land hoping things would get better to allow him to have a nice home to live in within walking distance of his girlfriend.

Joan was beginning to wonder if her boyfriend would ever ask her to marry her but Jim wasn't the marrying kind at this time of his life and kept avoiding the issue saying 'I am happy with the things the way they are.' Joan wasn't happy with his attitude and gave him an ultimatum saying 'Its marriage or nothing.' Jim was a very persuasive person and promised to marry as soon as the depression came to an end and he kissed her and they ended up making love in front of the fire in the living room.

Joan took her lovers word and accepted that it would be better to wait until things got better. He realised he would have to be careful with his girlfriend by keeping her happy and avoiding the question of marriage would prove to be a fine line to tread because she was no fool and sooner or later she would realise she was being strung along and when this happened all hell would break loose.

Jessica and Me

Chapter Fourteen

Meanwhile by 1938 Jessica and Robert decided they could wait no longer and they said to their parents 'We want to get married.' This wasn't greeted with much enthusiasm from both sides of the family and the couple realised they would have to arrange the wedding on their own.

Yvonne offered to make a wedding suit for her stepsister and they went to a second hand clothes shop to buy cloth, shoes and a hat. When the suit was completed Jessica put it on along with the shoes and hat. With a flower in her button hole and a bouquet she looked a picture and everyone admired her outfit. The couple met at the registry office in Fulham. Only a handful of people turned up at the service but the couple didn't mind as long as they were able to marry on a very hot August day.

Yvonne baked a cake and cooked sausages and various other tip-bits to be served at a reception in her house. The only people that turned up were one of Robert's sisters, Yvonne's mother-in-law and Ivan plus Jessica's best friend Joanna and Richard. The party was a success with every one enjoying Yvonne's cooking and when it was all over the happy couple went back to a flat above the fish & chip shop. Jessica's boss said they could rent the flat as long as they liked if they paid a small rent.

Robert could only stay at weekends as he was still working in Kent. Making orange boxes wasn't that demanding but it brought in money that could be added to Jessica's earnings that was just enough to live on. The couple weren't happy being apart but had to make the best of it so when Joanna asked her to go to the theatre's in London Jessica was glad to accept. When the two girls went out together they would have a good laugh at the expense of the actors on the stage. This upset some of the audience and they would complain to the manager who would ask them to stop making a noise with their incessant

Jessica and Me

giggling and if they carried on they would be thrown out of the building which made them laugh all the more.

During the late 30's the rumblings of war was gathering pace and there were exchanges in Parliament especially by a Politian called Winston Churchill. He was very concerned about Hitler stirring up trouble amongst the people with his nationalistic views calling for Germany to be for the Germans and he was creating hatred of other races especially towards the Jews who were running the banks and commercial enterprises throughout the country.

Hitler was busy building up his armed forces including bomber and fighter planes. Churchill's concern was that Britain was lagging behind in the arms race and he seemed to be the only one in Parliament showing any concern.

Yvonne found that the people in the flat below were moving and knowing that her step sister wanted a better place to live she let Jessica know. The couple were glad to move because the fish shop was smelly and noisy by customers outside eating the food from old newspaper. The ground floor flat was just what they were looking for although it was nearer to the Power Station but it didn't bother them at that time because the rumours of war was far more of a worry and would change their lives in a big way.

Jessica managed to get a job in a canteen in the Fulham Broadway area where the pay was better and she was able to dress in decent clothes that didn't smell of fish all the time. Robert was still working in Kent but the couple were happier living in a flat below Yvonne. Isabella said 'I would like to live with you.' Yvonne wasn't that keen on her mother coming to live with her but if it meant getting away from Harry then it would be ok but she insisted that her mother tell her boyfriend to stay away.

Jessica and Me

Chapter Fifteen

Just as the economy was picking up and people could see the beginning of the end of the recession the threat of war was becoming a reality. The Prime Minister Neville Chamberlain tried to avert the start of war by going to Germany to have talks with Hitler to draw up an agreement that would help keep the peace between the two Nations and when he got back to England and stood outside No 10 and showed the press a piece of paper saying `It is an agreement with Hitler to avoid going to war with each other.` Everyone sighed with relief at the news but this euphoria wasn`t going to last for long because Hitler couldn`t be trusted and everything took a turn for the worst ,Germany invaded Poland. Chamberlain announced that we were at war with Germany.

Panic set in when the sirens were set off and no one knew exactly what action to take and people were running to shelters that had been quickly erected. No sooner had the alarm been raised everywhere fell quiet and it turned out to be a false alarm and the next few days saw people going out as normal on their way in fact the next few months were quite as well. It was to be known as the phoney war but this was just the beginning and it appeared the reason for the silence was that the Germans were busy invading Europe and Britain`s turn would come when Hitler reached the coast and he could see the white cliffs of Dover.

Meanwhile everyone was going about their business plus building shelters and barricades because people were convinced that the Germans would be able to cross the Channel and then over run the country to defeat them.

The Government were in a panic and most of the Cabinet were in an agreement that some sort of deal should be arranged with Hitler to create a peace settlement. There was one man who wouldn`t except the deal at any price and that was Winston Churchill and he would change his colleagues attitude with his strong rhetoric saying that `Britain would if necessary fight the enemy on the beaches and in the

Jessica and Me

streets and never surrender. ` This clarion call was so popular with people that Neville Chamberlain was forced to resign and Churchill was given the job to lead the country in its fight to stop Hitler's army reaching Britain. When he held his first cabinet meeting most of the ministers were still convinced that a peace settlement could be brokered with Hitler and Churchill was up against Lord Halifax. He held firm to his belief that Hitler couldn't be trusted and managed to bring the rest of the Ministers round to his point of view and with that Halifax walked out and later resigned.

Meanwhile Jessica settled in the new home and Robert eventually got a job working for a local builder and he thought his travelling would be over but his first job was seven miles away although he could be home every night. Jessica managed to keep working in the canteen which gave the couple an improved security but now that war had been declared their area would become the target of bombers trying to damage the Power Station.

Yvonne was given a puppy by a friend who couldn't afford to keep it. It was black and she named it Prince and as it grew up it became very protective of its new owners and one day two delivery men came to drop off some furniture. Prince was in the hall and as they walked towards the dog he let them pass, when they tried to leave he stood in their way snarling and showing his teeth. The men were up against a very aggressive dog, making them so scared that they hid in one of the rooms and stayed there until Yvonne came home. She grabbed hold of the dog to enable the men to escape and run to their lorry swearing never to go near the house again. Prince also hated cats and he was always chasing them but they always escaped but one night he was in the back yard and he trapped a cat and as it ran away he managed to snap at its tail. The neighbours heard an almighty scream and the next morning Yvonne found part of the cat's tail. Prince approached his mistress in cowered manor and he seemed to know that she would be angry and sure enough he got a wallop and was told to go inside and stay there to hide from her anger. Prince was a good guard dog but if he managed to get out and roam the

Jessica and Me

streets he was a menace to other dogs and cats and the neighbours were always complaining about his antics.

Jim and Joan decided to split up because the war kept him busy at his work and his drinking made him more argumentative. Jim's earnings rose from his shift work and rent from his house, he was able to buy a large property in Barnes on the fringe of London and split the rooms into more lodgings and he used the rest of the area to live in. The house was on a long lease and in a nice position with a brook running along the bottom of the garden and within easy walking distance of the common, shops and pubs.

By now Jim was ready to settle down and one of the lodgers was an Irish woman called Vivien and he was attracted to her with her long auburn hair and a twinkle in her eye plus she would stand no nonsense with the way Jim behaved and he respected that. With all the trouble going on Jim wanted to put some routes down and wanted a son to carry on the family name and he asked Vivien to marry him. She thought about it for a while and after some deliberation she said `Yes I will. ` The couple got married in the local registry office. None of the family knew about it and surprised when the couple turned up at Jessica and Yvonne's doorstep telling them the news of their wedding a few weeks ago. Isabella cried when she heard the news because she thought her son would never get married. She was also suspicious of Vivien because of her Irish background and wondered if her new daughter-in-law was anything to do with the Irish army known as the IRA. In fact she had been on the fringes of the terrorist organisation but that was in Ireland and when she moved to England she gave up her membership but she used to speak out against the English treatment of the Irish but this was when the pair had too much to drink becoming over excited with the alcohol and the atmosphere in the pub. Jim loved it when his wife let off steam and they would end up in bed trying for a baby but nothing happened and he began to wonder if it ever would although he wasn't worried because he didn't want a child while the war was at its height.

Like many young men Robert decided he wanted to join the armed services and applied to go in the RAF to work on aircraft because he

Jessica and Me

wanted to do his bit but when he went for his medical the Doctors result wasn't good. He was informed that because of his week chest he wasn't fit enough to be accepted by the service.

Richard tried to join up as well but he was told that his job maintaining petrol tankers was already contributing towards the war effort. So the pair volunteered to fire watch when the bombing commenced.

By early summer of 1940 the army in France was outnumbered by the Germans who also had superior guns and tanks. Their army managed to push back the British to Dunkirk where the only area left to regroup was the sandy beaches. The only protection was the deep sand dunes and the only reason that was stopping the enemy from pushing the British into the sea was the strong rear-guard action and the barricades. The Luftwaffe were flying above bombing and shooting at the soldiers that weren't able to take shelter in the dunes.

The Navy came to rescue by using all the ships they could muster including small privately owned river craft that volunteered to cross the channel to pick up as many soldiers as possible. This wasn't easy because the boats couldn't get to the shore close enough due to the planes dive bombing them. There were about 400,000 soldiers that were ready to be evacuated. Only 7500 were pick up on the first day but by the end of May 338,000 were rescued.

After Dunkirk the German Luftwaffe attempted to win air superiority over Southern Britain flying over the English channel to destroy the RAF and also the aircraft industry and this was to be known as 'The Battle of Britain', Winston Churchill said of the pilots 'That never so much owed by so many to so few. ' Meaning that against all odds the British Pilots did so much damage to the Luftwaffe that after a few weeks they had to retreat back to France.

On seventh of September, the blitz of London began caused by a German pilot accidentally bombing central London. The British sent a retaliatory bombing strike to Berlin the next night. Hitler was so incensed that he ordered a merciless bombing on London. Churchill praised the composure of the Londoners as they strived to survive.

Jessica and Me

Jessica and Yvonne's family used the air raid shelter in the back yard for protection from the bombing while their husbands were on fire watch.

Jim carried on working in the Power Station which was regularly targeted by the bombing raids. One night he was ill with flu and he missed going on his shift and that was the night that the Station was hit creating massive damage and loss of life. Jim found out the next day and when he turned up for work his mates were surprised to see him because they thought he had been killed in the bombing. Jim thanked them for their concern but said he was fine and felt lucky to avoid the bombs that night.

The bombing was becoming more intense as the raids were being carried on by night and day and in the middle of the chaos Jessica found out that she was pregnant and expecting the baby to be born in the early spring of 1941. This news couldn't of came at a worst time but the family rallied round to support her and she thanked them all but said 'I want to carry on working to help Robert bring enough money when my baby arrived.'

Isabella and Yvonne busied themselves making clothes and knitting cardigans plus saving their ration stamps to be able to store enough food that would be needed for the new born child. Food and clothes were hard to come by because everything was being rationed due to the merchant ships being sunk by submarines called `U` boats as they tried to cross the Atlantic from America. The Royal Navy were finding it difficult to locate the submarines and therefore couldn't tell where they would strike next. This would be a major concern for the Secret Service as they worked day & night to break the enemies code that controlled where the `U` boats operated from.

Franks oldest son Robert joined the RAF and trained to become a pilot. He was hoping to be able to fly the most successful plane called the Spitfire that was causing havoc amongst the enemies' bombers and fighters.

The family was pleased when they heard that Robert had qualified and they all met in the pub to wish him well. During the get together Robert took his brother to one side and as they were drinking he

Jessica and Me

suddenly said 'I want you to look after our mother and father'. As he spoke there was fear in his eyes. Although James knew what his brother was trying to say he tried to put a brave face on it and hide the tears telling him 'Don't worry everything will be ok you will be back in time for my birthday. ' James couldn't hide his fear that his brother might not come back and when he told himself not to worry there was always that nagging feeling that wouldn't go away and he wished his brother hadn't spoken to him in that way

Robert was sent to an RAF base somewhere in the country. He was ordered to prepare himself to join the squadron for his first flight in combat. As he put on his flying jacket a sudden fear gripped him as he made his way to the plane and the foreboding grew as he started the engine to taxi along the runway to begin the flight. When he took off with other pilots everything became chaotic because he was not the only one that was a rooky and they were jockeying to find their position to fly in formation. The only training they had been given was about an hour in the air with the squadron leader on a one to one basis to enable them to understand the controls and fly in a level position. Nobody had trained them to fly in formation. Planes were criss-crossing each other at very close range and the squadron leader was barking out orders trying to get the rookies in formation. Just as Robert was beginning to understand what was required of him he heard a very loud noise from an engine and out of nowhere a plane loomed up in front of him and both planes collided with each other causing an almighty explosion. Instantaneously the two plane burst into flames as they dropped out of the sky at a terrific speed. Robert didn't have a chance of getting out of the cockpit as the smoke filled his lungs making him pass out as they hit a field causing another explosion. The Farmers saw the planes plummeting down and called the fire brigade but by the time they reached the field the flames from the wreckage kept them from any kind of rescue and when the flames died down the charred remains were beyond recognition. Apparently the other pilot was an American who had just arrived in England and volunteered and was accepted by the RAF

Jessica and Me

and after training was given the all clear to fly and like most of the pilots had little experience of flying especially in combat.

When the Officer walked up the path Frank knew it was bad news but he wasn't prepared to hear of Roberts death and he collapsed with grief and couldn't believe what he was hearing. When the rest of the family heard the news they were appalled at the horror of it all.

When the funeral took place Roberts mother fell on the coffin in tears and James and his father had to pull her away and huddled together to each other comfort in their hour of need. It would take a long time before Frank's family could come to terms with disaster that had torn their son away from them.

Jessica and Me

Chapter Sixteen

By 1940 the canteen where Jessica worked had to close down due to the increase in food shortages and the rationing meant that people were having gone without and makes the best of the little food they could get with their stamps and nobody was going to the canteen.

Being out of work wasn't an option that Jessica could afford and a neighbour said 'I know where there is a vacancy in a wood working factory in Chelsea.' She went for an interview with the foreman called William and although Jessica wasn't experienced in the work he gave her the job. The owner of the factory was his uncle and it was a family concern. Jessica had to be trained to operate the machinery and she soon acquired the skill and got into the routine and enjoyed working with other girls. Most of the employees were women due to the men being away at war. The only men around were too old or not fit enough to serve. William being that much older had already served in the army during World War I.

Jessica was a good worker and William arranged for her to assist him on the wood cutting machine and they had a good time laughing and joking while they worked. He liked her and built up enough courage to ask 'Could I take you for a drink in our dinner hour. ' She thanked him but declined the offer saying 'I am married and I have to get home to prepare the evening meal for my husband.' By this time William had fallen in love with Jessica and kept asking her out on dates. One day she approached the foreman to tell him 'Please stop pestering me and if you persist then I will have to give up working for you. ' All she wanted was to be friends. William realised she was serious and respected her views and agreed to be just friends. He kept his promise but from that day he never went with a girl and he would remain besotted with Jessica for the rest of his life.

Jessica carried on working through pregnancy and taking shelter from the bombing which was horrendous at times being so near the Power Stations in Fulham and Battersea but the they kept going despite the Germans attempt to blow the buildings apart and it was fortunate that our fighter planes were able to attack the bombers and

Jessica and Me

put them off their target but some of the bombs were hitting some of the surrounding houses.

When Jessica was omitted to hospital in March 1941 to give birth in Parsons Green the area was being bombed. Just when the baby was due the attacks were getting so bad that the Doctors decided to evacuate everyone to the underground shelters and after a long period a healthy baby boy eventually arrived in the make shift ward. Robert missed the birth of his son due to being on duty fire watching but when he got to the ward and saw his baby son he was overjoyed but tearful at the same time because he didn't know what had happened with all the bombing going on near the hospital. Jessica had gone through a bad time and she said to her husband. `I don't wants to go through that again. ` When Jessica came out of hospital everyone gathered round to see the baby and Isabella saw him she said `You look like a little rabbit. ` The couple decided to call him Donald.

The bombs were still falling on Fulham and one night Yvonne and Jessica with the baby went into the communal shelter and the noise of the bombing was making him cry and people's nerves were on edge and someone complained about the crying which upset Jessica. When Donald wouldn't stop crying she decided to leave the shelter with Yvonne and head for home. As they got near the house a bomb nearby exploded and part of the house was hit causing so much damage that it was too dangerous to enter. The pair's only option was to head back to the shelter where they met their husbands and when they heard the news they were in shock and wondered where they could find a place to live. Jim saw the bomb blast from the Power Station and immediately ran to the house to see if anyone had been hurt. When he arrived he came across his sisters and their husbands standing outside in bewilderment at the damage. Seeing the problem Jim said `I know a place in Barnes where you can all live. ` Both families agreed and managed to get their possessions out of the house and load a van that Jim rented for the day and they all climbed in the cab and made for Barnes.

Jessica and Me

When they arrived outside a butchers shop they asked Jim `Where is the house. ` and he said `You are standing in front of it.` They couldn't see what he was going on about until Jim pointed to the flat above the shop and then the penny dropped and they couldn't believe that this was where they were going to live. At first sight they weren't impressed but when they got inside they were amazed at the size of the rooms and Yvonne fell in love with the kitchen. They all agreed that this was the place for them although Robert wasn't that happy sharing the flat but he accepted the situation thinking that it would be temporary and as soon as the war was over he would move elsewhere.

The flat was central to the shops and pubs and near the common with a pond and the river Thames. Jessica agreed that the location was great but she was worried about travelling to Chelsea to work. With the families living in Barnes Jim asked Isabella to live with him, she hesitated at the thought of living with her Daughter-in-law because she didn't get on with her that well but she couldn't stand living on her own with all the bombing going on in Fulham and Harry had gone to live in the country with his long lost cousin. Isabella agreed to stay with her son and try to get on with Vivien.

Jim liked Barnes because there were plenty of pubs within walking distance and he regularly began at the Sun Inn by having a pint of beer before going to the Coach and Horse to have another pint and then visit the Bull Inn and the Waterman's near the Thames and if he had time he would go to the White Hart in Mortlake.

William heard of Jessica's problem getting to work and said `I can meet you in Hammersmith and take you the rest of the way by car.` She agreed but asked William `Could you pick up my husband and Brother-in-law as well.` He said `I will be able to take all three if you, could catch a bus into Hammersmith.` This arrangement would carry on through the war years and they were thankful that William could be such a good friend to them but this was how everybody got by during the war.

The sisters were happy living in Barnes because it was about eight miles from the centre of London which made all the difference as far

Jessica and Me

as the bombers were concerned and it was fairly quiet and allowed people to go about their business as normal as possible in those times.

Living above the butchers was very convenient and the sisters became very good friends with him and he would give them any extra meat although it wasn't much because of the tight rationing that had to be followed by the shops and if the butcher had been caught breaking the rules then he would face a heavy fine and even end up in prison.

Robert created a vegetable patch at the bottom of the yard which was long and narrow but opened out to a larger area. He also brought some chickens to supply them with eggs that were in short supply in the shops. One day there was a huge ruckus and Yvonne looked out of the window to find Donald amongst the chickens chasing them about in the pen and showing no fear as the cockerel stood its ground clucking and screeching to stop the child getting to the chickens and Yvonne just arrived to stop and pull the young boy away before he got hurt. The vegetable and eggs helped feed the families plus the extra bits of meat the butcher was able to scratch together to help get over the harsh rationing.

The bombing in London continued to disrupt the lives of the workers and kept Robert and Richard busy fire watching every night.

By now Yvonne's son was seventeen and working in the local engineering factory training as a Toolmaker. His apprenticeship enabled him to be deferred from the army and this was just as well because Ivan wasn't that eager to go to war. The work was deemed to be helping the war effort and being a clever young man made his work mates call him eccentric because some of the things he got up to were bizarre to say the least. He loved fiddling about with old motor bikes and listening to music on a record player he made himself. Towards the end of the war Frank's son joined up and was sent to Greece where he stayed until the end of the war. After the war was over he hardly went abroad saying that he had enough of being in Greece to last a life time.

Jessica and Me

The Blitz continued until May 1941 and then Hitler turned his attention to Russia.

Jessica carried on working at the factory in Chelsea and her husband was busy clearing the bombed out houses to enable rebuilding after the war was over although at that time nobody knew when that would be.

With the help of William using his car to ferry them back and forth to work the two families were able to cope with the devastation around them. Richard carried on maintaining the Shell-Mex tankers to enable oil and petrol to be delivered to the garages and the factories. He was very good at listening to the sound of the engines that he could more or less say if anything was wrong with them and this saved a lot of time when it came to repairing the lorries. Ivan was working hard qualifying to become a tool maker and he also worked on old cars and motorbikes whenever he could but the hours were long at the factory and by the time he got home all he wanted to do was to go to bed.

In the later part of 1941 the Americans were worried about the Japanese being sympathetic towards the Germans and they were busy building up its forces. Most Americans were against getting involved with the war in Europe but there were a few government intelligence officers having suspicions that Japan were getting ready to attack them but they didn't know where or when the attacks would take place.

At the beginning of December the Americans were gathering more intelligence that appeared to confirm that the Japanese were ready to attack but they still didn't know where or when. One of the intelligent officers mentioned that it could be Pearl Harbour but this was ignored by the Army and business went on as usual in Hawaii, but on Sunday the sound of fighter planes flying over Pearl Harbour began bombing and shooting at the battle ships moored in the dock. It was all over by 1.00 pm but it left chaos with approx. 2403 dead Americans and 188 destroyed planes and a crippled Pacific fleet that included eight damaged or destroyed battle ships.

Jessica and Me

America announced that they were at war with Japan. This was to become the most violent war the Americans would experience and lasted for four years.

Isabella kept in touch with her brother Charles in America and one day in his letter he wrote saying that his Grandson had been injured while on duty on a ship docked in Pearl Harbour. The injury wasn't serious but he was being sent home after coming out of hospital to convalesce and the wounds were bad enough to stop him serving in the Navy. Charles also wrote that he was pleased that America was at war because he could see that this would bring it much closer to ending the war although this wouldn't be for some time yet. He was very concerned about his relations being part Jewish and he had heard that the Nazi party were trying to annihilate the Jews in the concentration camps although some Americans didn't believe it was happening.

Jessica and Me

Chapter Seventeen

In 1942 the Americans were engaged in a horrific war because the Japanese were proving to be very hard to beat. The war was still raging in Europe, Africa and the Middle East but at home with the Blitz over and the Enemy kept at bay the living conditions were becoming more bearable but life was still grim in the bombed out areas and a lot of people moved out to the country where they could grow vegetables to make themselves self-sufficient. Both families in Barnes were coping and Jim was making himself known in the pubs.

Although the plot in Marlow was more or less a field it was a place to get away from the everyday drudge and Isabella along with Jessica and her baby would stay their during the week and their husbands would join them at weekends and William would visit them as well to give a hand in cutting the grass. Everybody enjoyed themselves going to the local pub and having a sing song and joking with the locals trying to forget the war. Yvonne didn`t go to Marlow because she didn`t like going to the pub and seeing people drinking too much.

Yvonne and Richard liked Barnes because she had a large kitchen to cook in and he could go to the pub and entertain people singing to them while they had a drink. He was in his element telling jokes and clowning about but when he got home he was a different person being serious and not talking much. He seemed to be two personalities depressed one minute and playing the clown when he was with his mates. Ivan would spend precious moments in the den on the top floor messing about with his inventions that would keep him occupied until he went to bed exhausted.

Isabella and Vivien were always at loggerheads with each other because Isabella would interfere in the kitchen where her daughter-in-law was preparing dinner. Jim didn`t get to hear about this because he was always in the pubs or gardening.

Charles grandson was home in America feeling much better but was bored because he couldn`t get involved with his hobbies due to his wounds he suffered in Hawaii. Charles paid for him to be treated at one of the best hospitals to get him fit again but it was a long job and

Jessica and Me

his grandson didn't help because he was always signing himself out and going to parties where he would dance the night away until the wounds started to bleed through the bandages and undoing all the work that the doctors had achieved in the ward.

In January 1942 the Americans arrived in Britain. They were to be known as `GI`s and they would transform some of the villages and towns bringing food and clothes especially nylons and chocolates and their unique entertainment that had become popular in America. They danced to big band music especially by a guy called Glen Miller. The yanks were crazy about his unique music that was easy to listen to while they were in their bunks in the camp or going to dance at the local hall. The Yanks loved dancing the Jive which was very fast and athletic. They would organise dances on their camp and invite the local girls on a Saturday night. At first the girls couldn't believe what they were watching when they saw the jive in full swing but they soon picked it up and couldn't get enough of it as they hadn't had so much fun for a long time.

Jessica would go to the dances with Robert in tow but he stayed in the back ground because he was shy and felt awkward dancing such quick dance like the jive. He didn't mind dancing to the slow dances but they were few and far between with the popular Jazz jiving.

As a teenager Ivan would play his records in his room and he liked playing Rhapsody in Blue by Gershwin and the loud speakers were set up such that you felt like being in the orchestra. Later in his middle twenties he would get involved in Ballroom dancing but in his teens and early twenties he concentrated on qualifying as an Engineer.

During 1942 Britain and America were beginning to step up the pressure on how the war should be conducted. The Germans were still bombing the Cathedral Cities but the RAF was giving as well as they got by bombing Cologne.

A General called Eisenhower came to London from America and his presents would have a great effect on the outcome of the war.

In El Alamein General Montgomery was having success.

At last people were beginning to see a turning point in the war and the Germans weren't in complete control although they were still a

Jessica and Me

force to be reckoned with. It wouldn't be easy to overcome the occupation in Europe but this could be the beginning of the end of this most disastrous world war that had claimed so many lives.

After a few months in England General Eisenhower (nick named Ike) began putting together a strategy to put forward a plan to liberate Europe by crossing the Channel and begin pushing the Enemy out of France and make them retreat back to Germany. This was a very ambitious plan in 1942 and it had the backing of the Prime Minister but even he recognised that it wouldn't be easy at this stage of the war. Ike said 'If we don't start planning the invasion now then it will create problems that will delay the outcome of the invasion and more people will die because of it.' Churchill gave the go ahead and made Ike Supreme Commander of the forces to enable him to bring all the Generals together to organise the plan called 'Overlord'. This would take three years to come to fruition.

Jessica had a tough time like everybody else during the war years apart from the occasional break in Marlow there wasn't much entertainment except for listening to the radio such as programmes called Bandwagon and Itma and listening to the news which was mainly about the war. Although TV had been invented it wasn't being broadcast. Going to the theatre or cinema was dangerous because of the blackout and the bombing. Everywhere at night time was in darkness with the Home Guard checking if the blackout rules were being kept.

Robert and Richard were kept busy fire watching during the night and working by day. Everyone tried to keep cheerful but it was difficult because at times the news broadcasts were full of disasters. The food, drink and clothes were being rationed and travelling was restricted. It was fortunate that Jessica lived in Barnes which wasn't affected by the bombing.

A lot of the population living in London especially the Docks in East London sent their children to the country to be safe from the bombing.

Young girls left school and went to work on farms to make up for the shortage of men being at war. These were called 'Land Girls' and

Jessica and Me

they were given a uniform which was hard wearing to stand the rigours of farm work.

Vivien stayed at home when Jim went to Marlow for the weekend to make sure everything was alright on his plot and he got to know some of the land girls near the farm. He would meet them in the local pub on a Saturday night and had a good time especially when the GI's were there. Jim didn't get too involved with the girls because he loved his wife but it didn't stop him having a good time having a laugh and a joke but that was as far as it went.

The GI's liked Jim and they would drink till the early hours of the morning when he would make his way back across public foot path to his plot and fall into bed sleeping till late Sunday morning before going to the pub again to sober up with a stiff drink and then make his way back home.

One of the land girls really liked Jim and took every opportunity to spend time with him on his plot and it was then that his old girl friend saw them together and she took him to one side and said 'People will talk and it may get back to your wife.' Jim wasn't worried because Vivien never went to Marlow and besides it wasn't serious between him and the girl. Jim always said 'I prefer younger women because their looks will still be good when I am an old man.' Jim took after his father who was a womaniser but he didn't gamble because he knew how it ruined him leaving him without much money.

In 1943 the Allied forces were beginning to make the Germans retreat from Tunisia, Stalingrad and Tripoli but the 'U' boats were still destroying the merchant ships in the Atlantic and at one count they had sunk 27 ships. The Nazis were attacking the Jewish resistance in the Warsaw Ghettos. This was worrying Isabella's brother Charles in America because there was more evidence being gathered by the Intelligence forces that suggested that the Germans were accelerating their efforts to liquidate the Jews in the concentration camps. Charles had lost touch with his relatives and feared the worst thinking they had been killed by starvation or put in the gas chambers.

Jessica and Me

The Jews were not the only group to be targeted by the Germans. Others were Gypsies, people with learning difficulties, people who were disfigured in some way, Prostitutes and resistance/spies. The amount of people that were killed amounted to millions. After the war it was discovered that 6 million Jews had been starved or gassed to death by the SS forces.

Music played a big part in boosting moral and the most popular big band was the Glen Miller orchestra and he decided to join the army to create a band from musicians that were already in the service. One day the Generals came to listen to the band play its unique swing tunes and they were very impressed and came up with the idea that Glen should take his musicians to Britain and play for the troops.

Jessica managed to get tickets to go to see the band play in London and she took Ivan. When they arrived at the venue the band were playing in the open air in Piccadilly Circus. During the opening number the air raid siren sounded but Glen kept the band playing as the audience cheered as the planes flew overhead dropping bombs in the distance. It could have been worse if the spitfires hadn't been able to fire at the enemy planes and put them off their target. Next morning the newspapers showed pictures of the band with the head line saying 'It would take a lot to stop Glens music.' When they got home everyone wanted know what happened and Jessica said she wouldn't have missed the experience of listening to Glen and see the action going on in the sky above them.

Glen's band toured all over the country and his music could be heard on the radio and in the cinemas and even the Germans listened to it much to Hitler's displeasure. The Nazis decided to create a band in the same style but they couldn't really produce the same sound.

In September the British intelligence had broken the code the enemy used to communicate with the 'U' boats to enable them to find and sink the merchant ships in the Atlantic. Once this was discovered it enabled the Navy to find the submarines and destroy them and this forced the enemy to suspend operations which allowed the ships to

Jessica and Me

reach Britain and supply the nation with much needed food and clothes.

Also in September a meeting was held between Churchill, Roosevelt and Stalin which would have far reaching effect on the outcome of the war.

Mussolini was arrested and eventually the Italians surrendered in September. Although the Germans did manage to rescue him, this would not help because his own people re-captured him and stoned him to death.

Some Jews were able to escape before they reached the concentration camps because the resistance were able to attack the trains and Charles through his contacts in Europe managed to find out that some of his relations had been amongst the ones that had escaped to Switzerland. An English woman who was part of the resistance was very successful in getting them off the train while the guard's attention was elsewhere. Charles decided to try and reach them with the help of the resistance and bring them back to America. This wasn't going to easy but he had friends in the American Air Force and was able to board a bomber travelling to France where he met the group that could get him across the border. He was in his seventies but very fit for his age and handsome with thick wavy white hair. The women was in her thirties and very beautiful but with her plain clothes she appeared to be a bit dowdy but Charles who was attracted to her saw past the down at heal looks. He thanked her for all work she had put into the rescue plan that had put her life at risk. Her code name was Andorra and she was also attracted to Charles with his rugged looks and over six foot frame he was a handsome man.

The group made their way to a safe house to stop overnight and have a meal before travelling on the next day. Being a farm house there was plenty of food which surprised Charles because he thought it would be similar to the rationing going on in Britain. They enjoyed the meal before retiring to bed. During the night Andorra crept into his bed and they made love. She was very good much to his surprise but

Jessica and Me

being widowed for several years he hadn't felt this way for a long time.

The next day the group made their way through a forest to avoid the patrols searching for any resistance fighters and as they reached a clearing Andorra told everyone to stay out of sight. She and Charles went to see if it was safe to carry on. They came to the edge of a road and saw Lorries full of troops and officers walking up and down. Andorra decided to retreat back to the others and told them 'We have got to stay where we are for the rest of the day. ' This would make it necessary to travel by night to get to the relatives and make it easier to cross the border. The Germans had been tipped off about the rescue bid and they stepped up their search but they didn't know where the safe house was located and this enabled Andorra and the group to avoid being captured. They knew that people in the area were informants and they had to be careful as they made their way to the house. Fortunately the resistance was feeding the wrong information as well to the enemy making them go in the wrong direction and this helped the group get to their destination.

It was going to be difficult to cross the border but Charles said 'We have come this far and I will do anything to complete the journey.' The resistant managed to surprised one of the patrols and silently kill them all with knives to stop others from hearing them as they made their way across fields near the border. They waited until night fall to cross into Switzerland and they all danced with joy knowing they were safe at last.

Charles hugged and kissed Andorra for a brief moment before saying goodbye to his new love and promised to meet her again when the war was over. Charles and his relatives made their way to the nearest American Embassy. He had become an American citizen which made it easier to deal with the Embassy staff to arrange for his relatives to obtain temporary permits to get into America. They were all skilled carpenters and this made it easy to work in Charles factory. The relatives couldn't thank him enough and said 'We will be forever in your debt. ' They promised to pay him back as soon they could. Charles said 'I don't want your money all I want you to do is for you

Jessica and Me

to work hard in the factory.` They said `We will give you 110% to the business.`

Andorra had given Charles details of her family in England and he kept in touch with them to follow her progress through the war although there wasn't much information coming from France because of the secret nature of her work. Charles hoped she would survive so that he could keep his promise to meet her when the war was over.

Andorra's real name was Brenda and she came from a very rich family. Her efforts in the war were top secret and even her family didn't know the extent of her work in the French resistance entailed. They were very surprised when Charles contacted them to tell of Brenda's exploits although he couldn't say too much as his girlfriend had sworn him to secrecy before he left her in France.

The family was very pleased to know that their daughter was still alive and said to Charles that he was most welcome to visit them when the war was over.

Jessica and Me

Chapter Eighteen

As 1943 came to a close everything was beginning to come together for the Allied forces. General Eisenhower's staff were working on the battle plan for the `Overlord` project that would see the invasion of the German forces on the shores of France. The main problem was to try to fool the enemy into thinking that invasion would take place in Calais when the area would most likely be on the Normandy beaches where they were light on the ground and have trouble stopping the Allies from fighting their way through France to liberate Paris and the rest of Europe. This was going to prove more difficult than originally planned.

Christmas time in 1943 was the best one for a long time for Jessica and Yvonne's family because like everyone else they realised this could be the beginning of the end of the war in Europe. Everyone listened to the radio for the latest news about the war effort.

Roberts's younger brother was called up to serve in the army and after training he was shipped out to Italy where he spent the next four years. He was ten years younger than Robert and was a healthy young man but when he came home and married his girlfriend the couple both landed up in hospital suffering from `TB` which was a common illness in those days.

Roberts other brother married an Australian girl and after the war they moved to Sydney and he got a job as a supervisor in a large store later to be known as a super market.

In 1944 the Russians were beginning to make great gains advancing on Poland and relieving Leningrad after 900 days siege and also liberating Crimea. The Soviets also began an offensive against the Finnish front.

The allies were attacking Italy in Anzio, Monte Cassino and Rome. With Allies having the command of the sky they were able to bomb the industrial heartland of Germany. In March they dropped 3000 tons of bombs during an air raid on Hamburg. The air raids were relentless and the newscast showed the destruction, after the war everyone was shocked to see such devastation.

Jessica and Me

Hitler was in a defiant mood saying he would fight every inch of the way and the German nation would never surrender but some of his top officers could see the end of the war coming and started to suspect that Hitler was going mad. They began discussing in secret how to bring about his down fall. There was one high ranking officer who said `Hitler should be assassinated. ` Others were not too sure favouring surrendering to the British and American forces. They all agreed that it would be a disaster to surrender to the Russians. Being afraid that Hitler's closest aids would shoot them if they deserted, they eventually agreed that the best way to get rid of the Fuehrer would be to assassinate him. This would not be easy but a plan was put into place to leave a small bomb in one of the meetings that Hitler attended. All that was left was to wait for the right moment and make sure that it was kept secret so that whoever carried out the operation was above suspicion. All the officers involved realised that good planning was crucial and it would take months to organise because of the tight security surrounding Hitler.

General Eisenhower and Churchill were busy organising the `Overlord` plan to invade the French beaches to enable the liberation of Europe. They were working towards the months of May or June for the Allied forces to land on the beaches of Normandy. This was not going to be an easy task because the weather would be a deciding factor as to when the ships could set off across the Channel and also keeping the enemy guessing where the invasion would take place.

Eventually it was the month of May that Ike and his Generals were preparing the way for the allies to cross to France for the invasion. They had successfully fooled the Germans into thinking that Calais was the landing point. All the Generals aiding Churchill were geared up to go when the weather forecast changed. This made it impossible for the parachutist and amphibious craft to make it safe to get ashore. The `D-Day` plan was called off and everyone wondered if it would happen at all. The weather was still holding up plans in early June. A sudden break in the cloud formation and the drop in the wind helped the invasion to begin. The amount of men and equipment trundling

Jessica and Me

down the county lanes was incredible especially when they boarded the ships to cross the channel.

When the news broke of the invasion everyone cheered and had a party to celebrate. There was no doubt that this was the beginning of the end for Hitler and the German war machine. The euphoria didn't last too long because the enemy showed they weren't finished yet by sending `V-1` Rockets over London and the country side. They proved to be a nasty weapon because nobody knew where they would land. The only suspicion of any warning came when the rocket engine cut out and went silent before dropping out of the sky and exploding on impact. Anything in its path caused untold damage and killed people in the buildings.

When Isabella moved in with her son she gave up renting the house in Fulham which was making things awkward for Vivien because she didn't get on with her mother-in-law and this didn't make the atmosphere in the house a happy one. Jim set about looking for an alternative accommodation for his mother. There wasn't any room where Yvonne lived and anyway Isabella wanted to live in London which made it expensive to rent apartments. She insisted and Jim gave in to her demands and eventually found a flat in Kensington. It was a nice flat on the first floor not far from the shops and buses. Isabella was not the type of person to use London transport because she always relied on her son to take her in his sidecar. Jim was very worried about his mother living in Kensington and persuaded her to return to Barnes on a temporary basis.

In July a German high ranking officer attempted to assassinate Hitler. He attended a meeting in a wooden hut and managed to leave a bomb in a suit case under the table but someone moved it further away from Hitler. When it exploded some of the officers were wounded but the Fuhrer escaped with minor injuries. The officer involved was hunted down along with others suspected of organising the coup and shot by a firing squad.

The Allies pushed further into France and by August managed to liberate Paris much to the delight of the Parisians who showered the conquering troops with flowers and the girls ran up to them kissing

Jessica and Me

them as they drove by. Everyone was in a party mood and it went on for days after the troops entered the City.

Andorra (Brenda) was delighted by the news and managed to contact the Americans as she entered Paris. She was able to contact her family in Britain and Charles in New York to tell him she was safe and well. Her escapades being over she stayed in Paris for a while to soak up the atmosphere before she got a lift back home to meet her family. When Charles heard the news he arranged to meet her in London. Being a widower for some years Charles wanted to get to know Brenda better. She was free because she had split up with her boyfriend before war broke out because he didn't agree with her joining the secret service. When their eyes met they realised their feelings for each other hadn't changed and they booked a room in a small hotel where they drank champagne and ate chocolate while making love. The pair were ecstatically happy and although Charles was much older than Brenda for the moment this didn't worry them as they were very much in love. When they weren't making love they discussed her exploits during her time in France and both realised that she had been very lucky to have survived the ordeal. The couple spent several weeks together and when Charles started saying `I want you to come to America and live with me. ` Brenda realised things were becoming serious. Brenda was tempted by his offer but she said `The war would have to come to an end before I could make any decision that would make such a change in our lives. `

Jessica and Me

Chapter Nineteen

Towards the end of 1944 the allies were winning the war as they steadily forced the Germans to surrender. The town of Aachen was the first to capitulate and the last use of gas chambers was in Auschwitz. The Allies were getting closer to Berlin but the Russians were making the most headway into the heartland of the Reich.

Life in Britain was still on a war alert and rationing was still being used because of the shortage of food and clothing. Yvonne and Jessica were managing to keep feeding the family and they also made their own clothes. Yvonne made a velvet suit for Donald and Richard made a toy lorry for him as well. It was a make do and mend society.

Ivan managed to get hold of some 78 rpm records by a guy called Bing Crosby and a relatively new singer called Frank Sinatra. Bing was still popular with the older generation and Frank being that much younger appealed to the young girls who were nicked named `Bobby Soxer's` because they wore white socks up to their knees and their hair was done up in a ponytail. When Frank performed on stage the girls would scream and become hysterical and some of them would faint. This was unprecedented in America and the girls in Britain were just as bad when his films were shown in the cinema.

The young men liked film stars like Betty Gabel and Bette Davis but there was also singers called Ella Fitzgerald and Peggy Lee and many more. In 1944 Glen Miller went missing while travelling to Paris. His plane had taken off in dense fog and disappeared over the English Channel. Everyone was in shock and wondered if the band would carry on but they kept to the plan of playing in Paris and they were a great success.

Jessica and Me

Chapter Twenty

By 1945 the war was finally coming to an end. Most of Europe had been liberated and all that was left was to conquer Germany which wasn't easy because Russia wanted to occupy the whole of Berlin but the Americans and the British wanted part of the city as well. In April the Nazis were surrendering as the Allies entered the towns. Adolf Hitler didn't make things easier as the Russian closed in on Berlin and on thirtieth April committed suicide. President Roosevelt also died in April.

On the seventh May the Allied forced the Germans to an unconditional surrender and by the eighth May Churchill named it VE Day and street parties were created to celebrate the day war ended.

Jessica's family went to the pub leaving Yvonne to look after Donald who was 4 years old. Everyone had a good time at the party and when they eventually came home the little boy who knew his mother had been drinking became very upset and cried saying `You have been drinking and you are all drunk.` With that he hid in his bedroom.

With the end of the war in Europe it was left to America to force Japan to surrender. The Japanese proved to be a difficult enemy to deal with because their President told his people to fight onto the very last man and this left the new President of America Harry Truman little choice to drop a horrific bomb on Japan. This was Atomic and to be known as the A-bomb. As expected the blast caused devastation in the City of Hiroshima and when a second bomb was dropped the Japanese surrendered on 14th August. The Americans celebrated VJ day on 2nd September.

Brenda contacted Charles and agreed to live with him as soon as she could get a flight to New York. Charles was pleased that his girlfriend was coming and arranged for the decorators to work on the house that had become dowdy and dusty since his wife had died. He was also pleased that the war crime trials had begun in Nuremburg. His long lost cousins that had been killed in the gas chambers would finally be laid to rest in peace and he would see justice being carried out with those closest to Hitler being sentenced to death. For those with a lesser crimes were put in prison for life. Charles could see life

Jessica and Me

getting back to normal with the added bonus of having Brenda with him supporting him in his old age having a quality of life he thought he would never have again; he would love Brenda for the rest of his life.

Jessica's husband wasn't happy sharing the flat in Barnes with Yvonne and he began looking around for another place to live. A workmate said he should get in touch with the Council in Fulham. They were allowing people who had been bombed out of their house to move back to where they lived for the same rent they were paying prior to the war. Robert got in touch with the Council and they confirmed that he could return to Fulham but it would have to be in the flat next door. This was good enough for him because he would be close to his mother including the rest of the family and where he worked as well. The only thing stopping him was Jessica who was happy living in Barnes and when Donald was told he had to leave his Aunty Yvonne he asked his father 'Why do we have to move?' Robert was surprised at his son being upset as he was only five years old and wondered why his son should have an opinion at that age. Robert didn't give a reason but said 'We are moving and that is that.' Donald had started going to school in Barnes and he would have to start all over again in Fulham. The new school was called Peterborough near Parsons Green but that was a temporary measure as Jessica wanted her son to go to a school nearer to where they lived. After a few months she managed to get Donald into a school at Langford Road which was walking distance from their flat.

The flat was an odd shape on the ground floor because it was located on a corner of the street. It appeared that it had been squeezed into a plot that had been only available because of the curve in the road and the building was very close to the pavement. There were two bedrooms with a back and front rooms plus a scullery with an outside toilet. The people above were the Landlords and were an odd couple. The husband was always away leaving his wife and little boy to fend for themselves. She liked listening to Al Jolson and

Jessica and Me

let the music play very loud all day and the boy would run across the room stamping his feet as he went. Jessica complained to the woman about the noise but she took no notice. It wasn't just the noise that upset her it was the fact that she didn't like Al's voice.
   After suffering the noise for about six months it suddenly went quiet and Jessica discovered that her Landlord had absconded the flat because they couldn't afford the mortgage. The council took possession of the house and eventually found another buyer. They came from Spain and worked as chef's in the Grosvenor Hotel. The couple had originally fled from Spain because he had fought against Franco. After the war they became displaced and hunted they managed to escape to Britain as refugees and couldn't go back to their native country for fear of being put in prison or shot.
   The couple were much quieter as they were always out at work. His English was ok but she could only speak broken English. Her name was Marbella and she called Robert by his second name Carlos (for Charles) and every time he went upstairs to pay the rent she would give him a Spanish liqueur. When he came back Jessica knew he had been drinking because he had a silly grin on his face.
   Robert was coming up to 40 and he was working very hard on the building sites mixing sand and cement and carrying bricks plus helping the plasterer. By the time he got home all he wanted to do was have his dinner and fall asleep in front of the fire with the radio on. This was very boring for Jessica and when William came to stay he would help her with the chores and they would fool around as they washed up. She resisted at first but he kept trying and she began to enjoy his affectionate ways. She told him not to go any further and he respected her wishes but when he stayed over she would get up in the middle of the night and lay with William for part of the night before going back to her own bed. Robert would be still snoring away because once he was sound asleep nothing would wake him. Jessica didn't look at it as a love affair because she thought she wasn't making love but just fooling around and that wasn't wrong in her eyes.

Jessica and Me

William proved to be a good friend because he owned a car and would take Jessica and her family to the sea side on Sundays usually to Hayling Island. This was good for Donald as he suffered with bronchitis and the sea air suited him. He would be ok for the rest of the week until they went to the coast again.

William was visiting every Wednesday as well as the Weekend and Donald knew him as Uncle Wills although he wasn't a relative. He helped with the chores around the house. The landlord Anton bought a new car and asked Robert to build a garage at the rear of the house to park the car off the street. Robert and William set about digging out the ground to create a concrete foundation to support side panels and a roof. They also built double doors and a single side door to complete the garage. Anton was very pleased with the building and invited the pair upstairs to have a drink to celebrate the completion.

One day Jessica was shopping and an acquaintance came up to her with a puppy in her arms and offered it to her, she couldn't resist and took the puppy home. She called it Bobby and told her son to look after the dog.

Donald was too young to take the puppy for walks because it was highly strung and strong for its age. The only exercise it got was chasing after cars when he was let out of a morning and Jessica had to search the streets looking for the dog before she went to work. Obviously this made her late for work and the dog would get a good spanking.

School days were a bit of a blur for Donald at 6 to 7 years old except one day he was walking home with a so called friend who live in the same street, as they walked along a few cars passed by and the boy dared Donald to throw a bottle at a passing car he refused saying it wasn't right but the boy took no notice and picked up an empty milk bottle and threw it at a car. The bottle landed just in front of the car. The driver was furious and jumped out and chased the boys but the other boy was very fast and managed to get away. Donald was running too although he hadn't done anything. As he turned to face the big man to say that it wasn't his fought the man was suddenly on top of him and the pair fell onto the pavement damaging Donald's

Jessica and Me

teeth with blood pouring out of his mouth. The man said `I am sorry; it's not you that I am after. ` Donald hadn`t been the culprit and he took him home. The driver apologised to Jessica and after he had gone she went round to the boy's mother and told her what had happened. The mother didn`t seemed worried saying `Boys would be boys. ` This made Jessica very angry and she told the mother to control her son and Donald was banned from seeing the boy.

From that day Donald was frightened of men in the street especially if they were big and heavy, he would walk on the other side of the street to avoid being near them and this would go on for a year or more.

The weather in 1947 was very bad with heavy snow falls making it difficult for people to get to work. Donald had a great time playing in the snow but he didn`t like clearing it from the front yard. When the snow cleared the River overflowed causing a great flood throughout the Thames Valley area. The water spread across fields and into houses causing a lot of damage and some of them had to be knocked down and rebuilt with the ground floor level above the flood level to stop it happening again.

In London there was still a lot of bomb damage making the buildings unsafe but this didn`t stop the children from playing amongst the rubble and the fire brigade were kept busy rescuing them when the buildings collapsed trapping the kids and hurting them in the process.

Ivan completed his apprenticeship and he received his call up papers from the army. This was the last thing he wanted to happen and although the war was over there were places that were dangerous and needed the presence of the army to keep the piece. Ivan was not a pacifist but he didn`t like being in the army either. Anyway he said farewell to his parents and reluctantly travelled to Salisbury. Army life didn`t suit him and he was getting more attacks of migraine and the food was upsetting him giving him diarrhoea causing piles. He had to see the army Doctor who wrote to his commanding officer recommending that he be discharged from his unit and sent home immediately. Ivan was pleased to be out of the army and resumed working as a tool maker with his original

Jessica and Me

employer. They were glad to see him because he was very skilled at his job.

Jessica and Me

Chapter Twenty-one

In 1949 the plot in Marlow was still a field and none of the family seemed to be interested in going to stay there so Jim decided to sell the land and one day he spoke to the neighbour about getting rid of the property and much to his surprise he made Jim an offer. After some haggling they agreed a price of £1500. Jim was pleased with himself as he could put the money towards bribing the authorities to enable him to adopt a baby boy who lived in Ireland. Vivien was thrilled to have a baby in the house because she had recently found out that she could not have children.
Her relief would soon turn to disappointment because the baby would turn out be a little horror as it grew up, especially when he found out that it had been adopted.
By June 1950 the Korean War began and carried on into 1953. The war was a military conflict between the Republic of Korea supported by the UN and the Democratic Republic. It was the first significant armed conflict of the Cold War that was taking place during the 1950's.
Charles' grandson volunteered to go to fight in Korea. He was a fun loving boy but when he came back from the war he was physically unscathed but he suffered from depression and looked much older. He would have to attend meetings with a councillor for years to come Meanwhile back in England Donald's Uncle Richard was the nearest relative that Donald could relate to as being something like a Grandfather. He didn't know his mother's real father and his father's father had died before the second world war in his mid-forty's. So Richard took Donald to people running on the track just as he did with Jessica when she was a young girl. He also taught him tap dancing and one day when he thought he was good enough he dressed Donald up in top hat and tails. The pair danced for Richards relatives when they came up from the country. The Aunts were very impressed

Jessica and Me

with the show and said `Donald you should go to drama school so you could try and make it in show business. `

Donald was also good at drawing but he could only practice when he was ill and spent his time in bed all day. He would copy some of the characters from the comics that Jessica bought him. William helped by taking the family to the seaside during the summer especially to Hayling Island that had the sea air that suited Donald and helped him to fight the bronchitis and spend more time at school.

Jessica bought a second hand bike for her son and although it was a ladies bike he was pleased with it because he was able to cycle to Barnes to see his Aunty Yvonne at weekends and school holidays plus it also helped him get away from Fulham as much as possible. Donald liked cycling with his friends to the areas where there were blackberry bushes and he would give them to his mother to make jam and pies which saved her money. One day Donald went to Chessington with his friends and they picked blackberries again. As they went through the forest they were pestered by flying ants buzzing around them, Donald picked up a branch to fan the ants away. Next day he went to his friends to ask them out to play but when they answered the door he could hardly recognise them because they had been bitten by the ants making their face swollen from their bites.

Some children formed gangs in Donald's street to fight other gangs by throwing stones at each other. The children said `Look after the cash of stones. ` So he put them in a hole and sat on them and when the rival gangs passed by he looked so innocent that they took no notice of the boy.

St. Marks College was a secondary school for boys at 11 years old. It was just over the border in Chelsea and the football club was just across the road. This was where Donald would spend two years after he left the junior school. He was beginning to understand the reason for going to school but he failed to pass the exam to go to grammar school this was because of being ill so much with bronchitis keeping him off school but when he was 13 years old he took a another exam to go to trade school. Donald passed this exam and his cousin Ivan

Jessica and Me

was pleased and said `You should go to Paddington Technical College. ` He had been their when he was a boy. The trade was engineering which at the time was a popular industry to be in. Donald decided to apply for an appointment at Paddington. He had to sit a test and go for an interview with the teachers before being accepted for a place in the college. A few weeks went by before he heard he had been accepted. The school was very strict about a uniform so Jessica had to buy a cap and blazer for her son and also a holdall bag to carry his football outfit and gym shoes. Donald realised this was a much higher standard of education than he had been used to and he enjoyed every moment of his time at the school. He liked playing football but after a while the teacher left and a history teacher replaced him. He didn`t like the game and if the ground wasn`t suitable to play then the children would have to go cross country running. Donald wasn`t happy running across fields because of his bronchitis but after a while the exercise helped him build up his strength to overcome his breathing problems.

There was a workshop in the basement for the children to work on lathes and milling machines etc. One day the teacher said `I want all the class to work on the lathe. ` He warned everyone to avoid having a dry centre point connected to the metal bar that would be worked on. Donald couldn`t have been listening because soon after starting machining the bar a burning smell and smoke came from the end of the bar where the centre point was fixed. He quickly switched off the lathe and realised the bar and the centre had been welded together because of the lack of coolant. The teacher knew what had happened and said `Donald don`t get upset because you have learnt your lesson and you won`t do that again. ` The first year at the school the teachers were very good and Donald was doing well in all the subjects and passing the tests but he took a letter home that said that part of the school would be shut to make way for day students from apprenticeships.

The children would have to attend another school for two days a week. The teachers at this school were not as good as the ones at the old school which made it very difficult to study for the exams at

Jessica and Me

the end of the year. Some of the pupils were leaving when they reached 15 years so they weren't interested. This upset the boys that wanted to do well in the second year. When they needed to get good grades to allow them to enter an exam called the `National Certificate`. Donald was entered into an exam called the `City & Guilds course'. This course wasn't respected as much as the National exam although it was more difficult to take because none of the teachers or the boys new the questions until the night of the exam. This was unlike the National exam where the teachers set the questions and they would leak them to the boys making it easier for them.

Jessica and Me

Chapter Twenty-two

Jim was still driving his motor bike in 1954. One day while he was on holiday in Torquay he went to start the powerful engine when the action of the kick start hit is leg breaking his ankle. Being a tough character he decided to bandage the leg and ride all the way back to London before attending a hospital for treatment.

When the new school was built it became a comprehensive education system but this didn't stop Donald studying engineering. One of the teachers organised a group of senior boys to be prefects and Donald applied to be one of them. He thought it would help keep the boys in the class to behave themselves so that he could catch up with his studies.

Ivan was taking more interest in helping Donald to make his way into manhood. He took him on holidays in his van and they toured around Cornwall and got as far as the Lizard Point which was the furthest he had been from home. On the way back they stopped in a pub for a drink. The barman asked Ivan 'Is your boy old enough to have alcohol.' He said 'He isn't but old enough to be in the pub at the age of 14.' Therefore he could have a soft drink. They also went to a posh restaurant that was silver service. Ivan suggested that they should be dressed for the occasion. Donald grudgingly agreed and when they went in the pair of them could see that everyone else was well dressed including the waiters.

Ivan worked on an old second hand motorbike built in 1929. In those days because of its age it didn't need to have a speedometer and fixed front suspension. It was a powerful 500cc engine and could reach 70mph which was good for its age. One day Ivan could see Donald admiring the bike and he decided to show him how to drive it. The back yard where Ivan lived was ideal to drive up and down and after the first lesson Ivan said 'Try the bike out but to be very careful.' Donald gingerly got a stride the big beast and kick started it and carefully opened the throttle and the clutch and slowly drove up the path without stalling the engine. When he came back Ivan was surprised how his cousin had managed to control such a powerful

Jessica and Me

bike and said 'You are a natural rider.' The young boy was only 13 years old but from that moment he took every opportunity to ride the bike up and down the yard,

Donald's uncle Richard had begun to teach him the art of boxing which was good because the school also began to teach him as well. At the end of the first year the teachers arranged boxing matches between the boys in the ring. Donald was told that he would box a boy in his class and he turned out to be school bully that the boys were afraid of and no one gave Donald a chance of beating him. When the boys got in the ring all the boys were cheering on Donald to help him give the bully a good fight. To his surprise the first round was even with Donald giving as good as he got which was making the bully furious. When he came out in the second round he rushed over to Donald pushing him against the ropes to try and knock him out. Donald saw him coming and stuck his fist out and punched the bully on the jaw which hurt him because he was coming onto the punch. He staggered back and for a moment it appeared that he was going to be knocked out. Donald tried to move closer to the bully to finish him off but the boy recovered enough to stay away from Donald's fists and survived the round. The third round saw the bully having more respect for his opponent and despites Donald's efforts the bully managed to win the round and the judges awarded the fight to the bully on a 2 to 1 result. Those days at school and spending time in Barnes were very happy days for Donald and he could see this was the beginning of his adult life.

Jessica and Me

Chapter Twenty-Three

In 1955 Isabella was 85 years old and living alone in a ground floor flat near the Fulham road and Putney Bridge. Jim had found the flat because he was worried that she might have an accident if she was still in her first floor flat in West Kensington. Isabella had not been in her new home long when she slipped and fell injuring her hip. When Jim came to call he found her on the floor, he called a doctor who said `Your Mother has broken her hip. ` Somehow Jim managed to convince the Doctor that she should stay as a long term patient in Tooting Bec Hospital. Although it suited everyone that Isabella should be in that hospital, it was not very good for her because most of the people in the ward had mental problems. One day Donald's mother took him to see his Grandmother. He wasn`t happy going to the hospital when he sat near Isabella's bed an old lady a few beds away suddenly walked towards them. She was blind but it seemed that she was aware of them and tried to get nearer to the bed but the nurse quickly ran over and stopped her getting any further. Donald was frightened and said `I do not want to go there anymore. ` Isabella stay in the hospital lasted a few years and in 1957 she had a heart attack and passed away. Isabella's life had been a mix of being very rich during her early years to rich/middle class in later life and then having to rely on her family to support her through to old age with little money to speak of although when Jessica helped Jim clear out the flat they found a stash of money hidden in various rooms but they missed the mattress because it was thrown away before they could inspect it.

   One year later Jim retired to live in a rented property in Devon. The council bought the house in Fulham and he sold the lease on his house in Barnes so he wasn`t short of money which would support him during his retirement. The house was in a small hamlet in the heart of Devonshire country side and used to be the Post Office about 50 years ago. It went back about 300 years and was part of the country estate owned by the local Squire who also owned most of the surrounding farm land as well. The garden hadn`t been touched for about 20 years and Jim set about making a flower and vegetable

Jessica and Me

patch which was hard work for a man in his mid- sixties. By the time he got the garden into shape with a lawn, flower beds and vegetable plot he had been living there about a couple of years. Then he set about building a green house. Donald went to see him during this period and marvelled at the amount of work that had been achieved in such a short time.

Donald had saved up enough money to buy a 125cc BSA motorbike which he earned doing chores for his Aunt Yvonne and when he was 16 years old Ivan said `Lets go for a ride on your bike.` They both set off on the Saturday morning from Barnes to travel to Marlow. They reached Winters Hill just outside Marlow and when they were half way up Donald said `I have got to stop because I am exhausted. ` He was also frightened the bike might go over the edge of the hill. After a rest they continued to the top to see wonderful views overlooking the Thames and Marlow. After being out all day they eventually arrived back in Barnes and Ivan said `We have travelled over 100 miles. `

Donald was pleased to have ridden the bike without any mishap and began using it to get to work in North Acton where he had started work as an apprentice. It was a small Company that manufactured Paint Spray Equipment for painting various objects like cars and household goods. The Firm was a Family concern run by four brothers with the eldest being the Managing Director, the second being the Technical Director, the third being the Sales Director and the fourth had mental problems but was assigned to Research & Development department.

Most of the workers were related to each other in some way or other. The Factory Manager was married to the boss's daughter. All the Foremen were related to each other being brothers, cousins and nephews. Everyone got on well together because nobody knew if they were talking about someone's relative in a nasty sought of way so nobody criticised each other.

It was a good company to work for and Donald gained a lot experience working in the factory. The first job was working on BSA Automatic machines where the guy operating was virtually blind and Donald wondered how he coped but when he said `You can change

Jessica and Me

the settings.` He realised that to change the cams it was carried out by feeling your way because they were under a ledge and you could not see what you were doing.

After three months of working on the auto machine Donald was becoming bored and his boss noticed this and said `I want you to work in the drawing office.` Donald was surprised to find himself working their but was glad to be there. He made good progress adapting to drawing on a large board and using gateway paper which was much better than the cartridge paper used at school. After being in the D.O. for nine months he said `I want to work in the factory because it would help me understand what I am drawing.` Donald spent six months in each department and was able to use the experience when he went back into the D.O. One day he was talking to someone in the sheet metal shop when he noticed that the foreman was looking at the side of the spray booth and he walk over to switch the fan and pump on and as he passed by one of the welders said `Watch out I think the panels are electrified.` The foreman ignored him and grabbed hold of side panel with both hands and as he did so his whole body began to shake. Donald realised he was being electrocuted and shouted to everyone `Switch off the electrics.` The workers ran in all directions and one of them said he couldn`t find the switch and Donald told him `Try again and hurry the man's life is at stake.` Fortunately all the electrics were switched off in time to enable a first aider to give the foreman the kiss of life and he eventually came round. When the Managing Director heard about it he told Donald `You saved the man's life thank you for your quick reaction.`

In those days the company would take the employees on a works outing and this was usually on a Saturday. Donald was surprised to discover that it would be on a Wednesday and also they would get paid plus 15 shillings spending money. At first he thought it was a trick because he couldn`t believe it to be true but one of his work mates said `Wait and see.` Sure enough when the coaches arrived there was the wages clerk giving out the money in brown envelopes. The coaches stopped half way to Southend-on-Sea everyone got off

Jessica and Me

and went to the pub. Then it made its way to a hotel on the seafront to have lunch. This enable those to spend some free time in the afternoon before going back to another hotel for a dinner and dance in the evening. Everyone had a good time including the families who knew each other because they were all related in some way.

The atmosphere in those days was dirty and heating in the factories and houses was Coal fired which created a lot of smoke polluting the air to the extent that it created dense smog that made driving very difficult. When Donald was driving home on his motorbike through the smog he could hardly see. He nearly crashed into the kerb but at the last moment he saw a white line and followed it which was just as well because it was a roundabout. The next day when he drove past the roundabout he noticed that car tyre marks showed that they had driven straight over it.

The drawing office consisted of six draughtsmen and a Director called Jim Ware. He was a jolly dapper type of man with handlebar moustache resembling a RAF Pilot. Don found that if he thought of an idea to solve a problem or make an object more efficient the Director would put it down but about six months later it would become his idea.

Don made good progress in the D.O. and when he completed his apprenticeship he became second in charge of the office although nothing was made official but everyone treated him as if he was. One day the Chief Draughtsman went on holiday and left Don in charge but one of the drafters who came from Poland wasn`t happy and when Don told him to correct the mistake on his drawing he refused to carry out the request saying `I won't take orders from a boy.` When Jim found out he spoke to the Pole and told `Obey the request.` It made no difference and after a second warning he was called into the office and told `Pack your things and leave.` Don was upset about the decision but realised that it had to be carried out.

Jessica and Me

Chapter Twenty-Four

When Don was sixteen his cousin suggested that he should take up dancing lessons to enable him to mix with people of his own age. Ivan said `Let go to a dance school round the back of Olympia Exhibition hall. ` When Don arrived outside he looked for Ivan but he was nowhere to be seen so he waited. When he eventually arrived Ivan asked `Why haven`t you gone in. ` Don replied `I don`t know what to do. `Anyway he was too nervous to go in alone Ivan said `Don`t be silly.` The school didn`t look much from outside but when they went in the first thing Don noticed was the sprung floor. He soon found out that it was one of the best in London and most of the professional dancers practiced there. Everyone was very friendly and Ivan introduced Don to the head teacher whose name was Belinda (Bell). She said `I will soon get you dancing. `Bell introduced him to other beginners.

Don soon got rid of his nerves and began to enjoy himself learning the basic steps to allow him to dance with girls of a similar standard. Later on he would pay to have lessons on a Saturday afternoon with a teacher called Samantha. She was very good, as light as a feather to dance with and she helped Don get rid of his inhibitions. After some months Sam said `You are good enough to dance in front of judges to be awarded the Bronze Medal. ` When it came to the day Don was a bag of nerves and when he began the routine he shook so much that the teacher said `I could hear my bracelet rattling. ` He finished the dances and was surprised that he was awarded the medal.

While Don was at technical college he got to know a boy a year younger than himself. His name was Ted and because of the age difference he lost touch with him. One night when Don went dancing who should be their but Ted along with a friend called Alan. They had known each other since they were children when they lived in Barnes. Don and Ted recognised each other and got talking and when Alan mentioned that they lived in Barnes all three of them were surprised that they had been living there at more or less the same time. This

Jessica and Me

was the beginning of a long friendship between the boys which would see many changes through the coming years.

Living conditions near the Power Station for Jessica and her family were becoming unbearable with the dust coming from the chimneys. When the wind blew it created mini whirlwinds getting everywhere. This didn't help the health of the family in particular it wasn't very good for Dons father because in addition to the smoke from the chimneys his father was smoking about a packet of cigarettes a day.

By 1959 the problems between the South and North Vietnam had escalated into a full blown war. The Americans had been drawn into the conflict because they wanted to stop the communist from taking over the area including Laos and Cambodia. This was going to be a long drawn out war lasting until 1975 when the North Vietnamese Army eventually captured Saigon and this marked the end of the war.

Don bought a second motorbike using his savings and paying the rest on HP because being a new bike it was expensive. It was an Ariel Leader 250cc luxury type with side panels like a scooter but the rest was a proper motorbike. It was ahead of its time with a very powerful engine. It had the power of a 350cc engine and also there was the Ariel Arrow racing bike that was stripped down version of Dons bike which was very successful in its day. Don was happy riding the bike because it was fast and side panels protected his clothes. During the summer he and Ted decided to go camping using the bike. They packed everything they needed for the holiday and set off to travel to Devon. The young men were well built and along with the camping gear the bike was carrying a heavy load. About half way through the journey the bike suddenly came to a halt and despite Dons efforts it wouldn't start. After a while an AA man came along to help them get started, Don mentioned that he had changed the spark plugs to no avail but they put the old plugs back and it suddenly started. They carried on and finally reached a camp site in a place called Ladram Bay near Exeter. As they entered the camp site passing a row of tents Don noticed a blonde girl and realised Ted was looking at her. Ted was tall and muscular with looks to match and the girls liked him and the blonde was no exception. Don knew the way

Jessica and Me

they looked at each other that they would get together. The next day after a good night's sleep in the small tent Ted went off on his own to meet the blonde and for the next few days they became good friends. In the tent next door were two sisters and the oldest had gone out for the evening leaving her sister alone. Don had also gone for a ride on his bike and when he got back he noticed the youngster sitting outside her tent. He couldn't leave her all alone and said 'You had better sit in my tent to wait for your sister. ' As they waited he got into his sleeping bag. Soon the sister returned and thanked Don for protecting her young sister.

Don and Ted decided to go to a dance but when Don tried to open the carrier to get to his suit he realised he had mislaid the key and they didn't go dancing that night. Ted stayed a week before going back to the RAF cadet school. When he reached 18 years old he joined the RAF proper and stayed in for 12 years.

Don carried on going camping and one holiday he went to stay at Corfe Castle camp site. He went to the local pub and got involved with the locals playing pontoon dominos for pennies. There was one guy who was very good and always won but this particular evening Don could do no wrong and got into a winning streak and how ever well the guy played he couldn't get the better of Don and eventually he gave up. Don came away with a lot of money and after that the locals didn't encourage him to play. When Don settled down for the night in his tent the wind began to blow against the side of the tent and when he looked outside he noticed he was the only tent in the field because the storm had blown all the other tents down. Don decided to leave the camp site the next day and drove to Poole to meet his parents and as he was driving along the narrow street a lorry coming the other way beckoned him to come past but as he did so a van came from behind the lorry. As it over took Don had to steer away from the oncoming vehicle but the bikes wheel got caught in the tram lines in the road and he fell off the bike which carried along the rails before falling over on its side, Don was sliding along on his side looking at the bike and worrying if it was getting damaged rather than if he was hurting himself. Fortunately both the bike and himself were

Jessica and Me

ok but it was a frightening experience that he wouldn't forget for a long time.

Don carried on going to the dance hall and got to know various girls to dance with. He especially admired the dancing ability of one of the girl called Julie. She was a natural dancer and she was as light as a feather but she ended up marrying a guy that couldn't dance. There was another two girls called Lizzie and Jackie who were always together and they liked Dons dancing and sense of humour but they found other boyfriends. The dance school continued for about five years until it became too expensive to learn the dance routines and other places took over such as the Hammersmith Palais and Streatham Lacarno. There was another popular place called the Richmond Castle by the Thames. On Saturday night it became very crowded with both its dance halls heaving with people.

After riding two motorbikes from the age of 16 for six years Don was ready to give it up and learn to drive a car. He mentioned this to Ivan who said `It is a good idea. ` One night he called on Don at his home in Fulham with a surprise. He had bought Don a three wheeler car called the Bond Mini. Don could not believe what he was looking at. It was a two seated soft top with two wheels at the rear and one at the front. Ivan said `It needs a bit of work but I think it will be just what you need, it does not have a reverse gear and you can drive it with a motor cycle licence.` To start the engine the bonnet had to be lifted to enable it to be kicked started. Don was not too sure about driving this kind of car but he went along with it to please Ivan. The pair set about restoring the car which needed a lot of work such as a new windscreen, tyres, engine overhaul and a leaver to be fitted in the cab. This enabled a cable to be connected to the engine to be able to start it in the cab. Don with the help from his mother had to spend a lot of money on the car to make it road worthy. It was eventually ready to use but unfortunately the car kept breaking down. Don thought there was a jinx on the car so he decided to put it up for sale by advertising it in the local paper. After a little while Don was surprised to hear from a person in a place called Flint in Shropshire. When Don saw who was interested in buying the car he couldn't

Jessica and Me

believe seeing that the man was disabled. He didn't think it would suit him but when the man saw the car he seemed very interested and wanted to drive it down the road. To Dons dismay he didn't have any difficulty using the leaver to start the engine and it started first time. He was very pleased with the car and gave Don a deposit saying `I will pick the car up in a few days. ` Sure enough the man returned and paid the balance and with the paper work he drove off back to Flint. After a few weeks Don received a letter saying how pleased he was with the performance of the car.

Don decided to buy a normal car and took driving lessons for a licence. It was Christmas and the weather was fairly mild until Boxing Day when it began to snow. Usually it wouldn't last but this time it went on till March, the weather didn't deter Don as he carried on with the lessons in very poor conditions on the road. He thought that because he had been driving motorbikes it would be easier driving a car but it proved to be difficult especially with the bad weather. Reversing round corners was very difficult. It wasn't until he was taking the test that the driving instructor positioned a matchstick in the rear window that helped him to do a correct manoeuvre. During the test Don thought he had failed but he had been right to turn at a tee junction when everybody else had been wrong.

Passing his driving test opened up a new world for Don and he immediately began looking for a car. There was an Austin A4 car but it was expensive for a second hand model. He thought that a new Morris Mini would be better value at £488-00. When he saw what he was getting for a basic car he went for the deluxe model which cost an extra £50-00 which was better value. It included the carpet, heater, back window that opened windscreen washers and better upholstery. Don decided to buy the new model and he part exchanged the motorbike for £75-00. The garage completed the paperwork and polished the car to enable the car to be driven home. Don parked it outside and as he went inside to have a cup of tea somebody knocked on the door to tell him that the windscreen had been smashed by a stone from a passing lorry. Fortunately he was insured and the screen was repaired the next day.

Jessica and Me

Don was able to drive to the dance halls without changing out of his motorbike gear and also take girls in the car to their homes after the dance.

Alan invited Don and Ted to go to a wedding of one of his friends in Barnes. Don met them at the church and afterwards his friends along with their girlfriend went in the car to the reception but when they arrived nobody was there. After hanging around for a while Don decided to take his friends for a ride in the mini and although it was a small car they were all able to get in but it was very crowded because the young men were tall and heavily built. Don was able to keep the car going although he had to stop and get the men to swap places to help the steering. Alan directed them to drive through London but he didn't know where he was going and they kept going round in circles, going through the underpass at Hyde Park they all had a good laugh at the antics of Alan and were pleased they hadn't gone to the party.

Ivan wasn't that happy that Don had bought a Morris Mini describing it as a car for girls but Don wasn't worried because he didn't see his cousin as much as he used to because he was building his own life and besides he liked the car and was happy to be in the dry when he was driving in rain. There was a 17 year gap between Don and Ivan and the older Don became the more independent he became.

Ivan wasn't married and lived with his parents in Barnes. His father had to retire early because of ill health and his mother wasn't too healthy either. This wasn't a good time for Ivan and he became a bit of a recluse working in his den.

Don built a tape recorder connecting a tape deck, amplifier and a speaker and building a box around it, when Ivan saw it he said `I will build one myself.` When he finished it was a larger version than Dons with 12 inch spools. When he switched it on the spools flew off the deck hitting the ceiling making a mess on the floor and with that Ivan lost his temper and threw it all away.

When Jims step son was twelve years old Don took him on a camping holiday in Cornwall. He warned Alistair that if he misbehaved he would cut short the holiday and take him back home. Alistair got

Jessica and Me

the message and behaved himself and the pair had a good holiday seeing the sites.

Jessica and Robert along with William decided to travel to Devon to see her brother Jim. William bought a second hand car and they drove down to the hamlet for a holiday. The house was large enough to sleep everyone and William took them to the local villages where they went to the pubs that Jim frequented.

The cows from the farm would pass by Jim's house and one day Jessica and Vivien went for a walk along the lanes when suddenly the cows came out of the field and trotted towards them. Jessica was petrified at the sight of the heard and panicked when they gathered round her to the extent that she was surrounded. Vivien laughed at the way Jessica was panicking but she stayed cool and was able to move them away with the help of the cowgirl. Jessica never forgot that time in the lane and kept away from cows if they came too close.

Don went to stay with his Uncle Jim when his brother and his family came to stay over the Easter holiday. Frank and his wife reached the house before their son and his wife and daughter arrived later that day. The brothers wanted to go to the pub and Vivien asked Don to take them in his car. She said `Don't let your Uncles drink too much. ` She was hoping everything would go well when they all arrived for lunch. Everything went well to begin with as they chatted in the pub quietly enjoying the beer until Don made the mistake saying `There is only half an hour to go before we should get back. ` With that the brothers began emptying their glasses as quick as possible to the extent that the barman couldn`t keep up with them and Frank started helping himself to the drinks behind the bar. When Don managed to get them out of the pub in a drunken state Vivien told him off for getting them in such a state. Don said `I am sorry but it was too late to stop them.` He realised he had made a mistake when he told them that it was time to go back and that was when he lost control of the pair.

In 1963 President Kennedy started to be elected for a second term and he decided to visit the state of Texas although his advisors warned him against going. But he ignored their advice and went with

Jessica and Me

his wife Jackie and flew into Dallas to join a motorcade to drive in an open top car to greet the people crowding the side walk. When the cars reached Dealey Plaza shots rang out and hit the President as he waved to the crowd. The motorcade drove quickly to the hospital but he was fatally wounded and doctors confirmed he had been assonated. The news was flashed around the world and everyone was in shock and couldn't believe it had happened. John F Kennedy was a popular President and the way he was killed would be debated for years to come.

Meanwhile life went on in England with families still seeing each other in pubs and going on holidays. Jessica had always kept in touch with Yvonne in Barnes but this was coming to an end because of her bad health including Richard because he was diagnosed as having a brain tumour and in those days the treatment wasn't so advanced although after retiring early he managed to carry on living for two years before dying from a bad stroke. At the same time his wife had a bad ulcer in her ankle which made it difficult to walk. Her son didn't help because he let her wait on him by cooking and doing the house work although he tried to stop her but she insisted on carrying on as usual. After struggling on for two years she eventually collapsed and was taken to hospital, she wasn't responding to the treatment. Before she died Don went to see her but being so ill she told him off accusing him of seeing too much of her brother. This was unusual because she adored her nephew and he realised that she didn't know what she was talking about and soon after she passed away.

Ivan was left alone in the flat above the butchers but the landlord wanted to rent the property to another family and forced him out by charging exorbitant rent which he couldn't afford. Ivan moved into a small caravan round the back of the firm where he worked. Ivan took Don to see a small motor boat that he wanted to live in. When Don saw it he was surprised how small it was and couldn't understand why his cousin wanted to live in such a cramped space. After that Ivan used to go to see Jessica to get a cooked meal and he would sit talking all night but Don would become bored. He would go out dancing and when he got back his cousin would still be in the flat

Jessica and Me

chatting away. He would keep Don up till the early hours of the morning. Eventually Ivan got the message that he wasn't welcome and gradually stayed away and went to see his other relatives.

Jessica and Me

Chapter Twenty-Five

Don went to Hammersmith Palais two or three times a week where he saw some of the girls that had been to the dance school. He also met three lads a similar age to himself this was because one of them had a sister that had been out with Ted. He wanted to know why he had given up seeing Christine, all Don could say was `Ted had joined the RAF and would be in for another ten years.` Don and the three lads became good friends meeting each other at the dance halls or going to the local pubs. The lads were called Larry, Kevin and Bernard plus Chris who would go with them when he wasn`t going out with his girlfriends. Chris had two or three girls at the same time and Don wondered how he kept the girls apart.
   Most of the time was spent dancing or drinking in the pub but Larry said `We should go on holiday together camping. ` Everyone agreed and decided to go to Dorset to an area called Blackpool sands near Kingsbridge. Don met the lads at the site and they all erected their tents by the side of their cars. They all went in the sea and the local pub in the night time. As usual Chris got to know some girls camping nearby and asked them to go to the local dance. Don and his friends also went dancing but most of girls were already with their boyfriends so they danced with the girls from the camp site.
   When they got back to London they carried on going to the Palais trying to meet girls but it was difficult because they were shy or choosy who they danced with. Some girls would go with older men making it very frustrating because the young men had the best intentions when they only wanted to get to know them. Over the years the lads did get girlfriends except Don who made friends with the girls but it never lasted. Alan who was a good friend of Don wondered whether he would find a steady girlfriend but he kept going to dances trying to find the right girl believing that one day she would come along.
   Ted found a girl where he was billeted in Kent and after a few years he asked her to marry him. She was very much in love and didn`t

Jessica and Me

hesitate saying `I will marry you.` They began arranging the wedding, Don was asked to be the best man.

Jessica and Me

Chapter Twenty-Six

By this time Don was beginning to give up ever finding the right girl but one Saturday night as he prepared to go to the Richmond Castle dance hall he sensed that this could be the night to meet someone. The Castle had two dance floors, one larger than the other. It was very popular place getting packed out on the dance floor and it was very difficult to get to dance properly, most couples were just shuffling around. If you came off it was impossible to get back on especially on the large floor so Don went to the small floor and he saw two girls sitting by themselves. He went to ask one of them to dance, just as he got their one of them was asked to dance leaving the one he wanted to dance with alone. Don quickly made his move he said `Can I have this dance. ` They were quickly in each other's arms dancing, he couldn`t believe he had found her and realised she was the one for him. Her name was Diana with a slim build and beautiful and they danced the rest of the evening. Don realised he had found the girl he had been looking for a long time. She had a lovely smile and sense of humour to match. Diana introduced the other girl as Jenny who was her cousin and they both liked Don. When it came to say good night the girls went outside Don said `Can I give you a lift home. ` Diana said `My mother and father are waiting across the road in their car to take us home. ` Don was surprised that her parents were picking them up as most girls went home on their own but he went along with the situation and asked `Could I see you again?` They arranged to meet each other at the Castle on the following Saturday. He couldn`t get Diana out of his mind that week and wondered if she would turn up on the night.
   When Saturday came Don made his way to the dance hall filled with trepidation about how the evening would turn out as he waited for Diana to show up. After a while he was just thinking that she wouldn`t come when she suddenly she appeared tapping him on the shoulder saying `Hello Don. ` She greeted him with a big smile. This time she was on her own. Diana was exquisitely dressed in a tight skirt which showed off her figure as they danced the night away. Towards the

Jessica and Me

end of the evening they went to the bar for a drink and Diana went to the ladies room to freshen up. When she came out Don noticed that there was a long slit up the back of her skirt. He said `There is a problem with your skirt.` Diana took one look at it saying `I had better go back to the ladies room to fix it.` They had a good laugh about it as it wasn`t that bad and they were able to carry on dancing after she had put some pins in the skirt.

The following weeks the couple went out together most nights dancing or going to the cinema. The first film was called MadMad World which was a funny film with a lot of top comedy actors taking part. Don laugh all through the show and although Diana liked the film she didn`t laugh as much as Don but they had more or less the same sense of humour and enjoyed it very much. When they came out of the cinema and got in the car they both noticed a strong smell. When he looked at his shoes he said `I have trod in some dogs mess. ` They both giggled and got out of the car to wipe off the mess before going to Diana's home.

When they arrived outside the house Don kissed Diana goodnight which turned into a cuddle for about a quarter of an hour. There was a bush that hid the car from the house and the mother couldn`t see what was going on so she told her husband to trim the bush. Diana's mother was very protective and domineering towards her daughter as she was the only child and she thought Don was trying to take her away from her dominance. Diana was 19 going onto 20 years old and hadn`t known many boys and Don hadn`t been steady with girls either although he had known a lot of girls through his dancing.

Every time the couple came home after going out to the cinema or dancing at about 11 o`clock Diana's mother would always be waiting up for her daughter much to the annoyance of Don who thought the mother was being over protective and treating her daughter like a little girl. Part of the reason that made her mother act that way could have been her upbringing having a very strict mother who would stand no nonsense from her daughter but when she grew up she went against convention and rebelled by marring a boy who was her cousin which infuriated her mother and they didn`t talk to each other for years. It

Jessica and Me

was only when the mother reached old age and needed her daughters help that brought them together but it was a delicate relationship that could fall apart at any time.

Don had arranged to visit his uncle in Devon over the Easter holiday and Diana was going with him but she became unwell a week before they were due to go. When the Doctor saw her he said it was yellow jaundice and she had to stay in bed for two weeks to get over it. Don had already made arrangements to take his cousin James and his family to Devon and Diana told him to honour his arrangement even if she couldn't go. Don was not happy leaving his girlfriend but he could see he had no choice in the matter and went to see his Uncle. When he got back he went to see Diana and was pleased to see that she had recovered from the illness.

In June the company asked Don to go to Paris to attend an exhibition to look at the spray guns that were used on print machines to stop the paper sticking because the ink hadn't dried fast enough. The company wanted to know if any of their competitors were at the show. It was very short notice and Don had to rush to get a Passport to stay in Paris for two days. This was a completely new experience and he was excited to see Paris for the first time. When he arrived at the huge exhibition hall he soon found that none of the machines had any of the spray guns on show let alone the competitors. When he asked why he was told that the manufacturers were only interested in showing their machines. It appeared that it was a waste of time but Don was able to see the city of Paris and enjoy the atmosphere and the architecture which was very grand and left London in the shade.

While he was their one of the Directors came out to meet him and he wanted to find a restaurant for an evening meal. They walked along the river Seine without seeing anywhere suitable to eat until they reached the Eifel Tower. To their dismay they found that it was in the middle of a park and the only place to eat was on the first floor of the tower. They managed to get a table and ordered a two course meal and a bottle of wine which was very expensive. When the bill arrived the Director took one look at it and was amazed how expensive the meal was. He asked Don not to tell anyone back home.

Jessica and Me

Don told his boss that none of the print machines had any of their spray guns on show but he had made a sketch of them which would make it easier to design fixing bracket to support the guns in future. From that day Don fell in love with Paris and vowed to go back again when he got the chance.

When Don flew into Heathrow Diana was waiting for him and when they met she ran up to him nearly knocking him over as she hugged and kissed him saying `I forgot what terminal you was using and also where your car was parked.` She had got very worried thinking she might have missed seeing him and was in tears now that she had found him. From that moment the couple became inseparable and were very much in love.

The longer Don spent seeing Diana the more he thought about the future. When his mother asked him if he was serious about her he made up his mind to propose to her. He decided to ask Diana when they were at the dance in the evening but when they were shopping in Putney high street he summon up the courage to ask her to marry him. When they got in the car behind the cinema he popped the question. It wasn`t very romantic but he couldn`t stop himself. Diana immediately said yes and they kissed each other being overjoyed with their love for each other.

Later that evening the couple went to a pub in Esher to celebrate and talk about their future together. Don said he would like to buy a house and have two children. Diana agreed but she was worried about the lack of finances but he said that he had some money in the bank and Diana had some too. If they saved they would have enough money to put a deposit on a property. In those days the building societies were very selective about lending money and they wanted to know if you were credit worthy and how long people had been employed. Most of the societies only took the man's salary into consideration and in Dons case this was not enough but they managed to find the Co-Operative Society who would take the couples salaries and provided they had a large deposit they would lend enough money for a mortgage. This was ok but now they had to find a suitable property so the search began.

Jessica and Me

The couple stopped going out to save money and they visited friends and relations and occasionally going dancing with Alan and his girlfriend Karen at the Hammersmith Palais which would make a welcome break for the pair.

Meanwhile one of Dons friends Larry had proposed to his girlfriend. She said yes so they set a date to get married. The couple set about organising the wedding and part of it was to select a best man and although Larry had a selection of friends he could ask the couple couldn`t agree who to ask until the girl friend suggested asking Don. Larry thought it was a good idea and went to see his friend to ask him to be the best man. Don was taken by surprise because he hadn`t known Larry that long but he was delighted to be asked and said he would be glad to accept the position. Don had to think up a speech which he had never done before but when the day came he managed to overcome his nerves. Everyone was pleased with the way he organised the reception. After the wedding Diana told Don that her parents were going on holiday and had asked them to go with them. The father liked going on driving holidays. They went to the Lake District staying at bed & breakfast guest houses as they travelled around the Lakes. The week's holiday made a good break for Don and he enjoyed it because he had never been on holiday in the north of England.

When Don got back from the holiday his friend Ted told him that he was getting married and asked Don if he could be the best man. The wedding was going to take place on the other side of London and Don took Diana. There were a lot of people that he didn`t know but it didn`t worry him when it came to the speeches. Everyone congratulated him on how well he organised the reception. Ted and his new wife Jackie went on their honeymoon before going back to a house in Bournemouth that was owned by the RAF.

Another year passed and another friend Alan invited Don and Diana to their wedding which wasn`t a grand affair like Ted had but it went very well, everyone enjoyed themselves. The newlywed's went on honeymoon to Cornwall in a hired car because Alan only had a motor bike at the time and they didn`t fancy going all the way on that.

Jessica and Me

Chapter Twenty-Seven

By 1965 Diana was 21 years old and her mother arranged a party for her at local hall. The party also became an engagement celebration as well. Everyone bought presents which were on show in the hall and it was a great success with relations and friends on both sides dancing to the live band. Diana's Uncle and his son came over from America. He was a financial advisor making money advising a rich doctor and his family and this helped him build contacts with other rich clients. The Uncle was named Edward and he had been living in America since 1917. Edwards cousin lived in the USA in the early 1900's. He wanted his brother to work with him in New York but he couldn't make it so Edward went instead, working as a shoe shine boy in the same hotel. He just had enough money to live on which was a struggle and his Uncle said `It would be good for you to improve your education by studying at night school. ` He decided to take a course in finance. After staying up till the early hours of the night and working during the day he eventually qualified. His cousin worked in the hotels where he had contacts in the business world. He introduced Edward to rich families to help them deal with their finances. A director and his family kept him busy to enable him to set up as a financial advisor.

In the 1920's America was the place to live if you was in business and Edward found it easy to get work. Clients were happy to part with their money to enable him to invest it in lucrative shares and business dealings. The money kept rolling in allowing him to become very rich and ride the Wall Street crash in the 1930's but even then he found it tough going and at one stage considered returning to England. He couldn't stay for long because he had become an American citizen so he had to ride out the financial storm. The reason he had to give up his UK status was because he had to get a work permit and it automatically qualified him as an American which he didn't realise at the time so it meant that he could only stay in Britain as a tourist for six months at a time.

Jessica and Me

With the help from his clients and a rich Director, Edward managed to survive and keep going along with his German/Jew wife and his young son.

Just as Edward thought he was over the worst the second World War was looming and having a German wife didn't help although living in America was the best place to be and his financial expertise would be a great help in seeing him through the war years.

By the time the 1950's Edward Waters was a wealthy man. The Director had died leaving a considerable amount of money in his will to him. He continued to advise the wife until she died and he received more money from her will. Edward acquired properties in New York, Boston and a ranch in Texas.

Everything was going well for the Waters family until Edward's Daughter Jane in her early twenties met an older man while she was on holiday in UK. Her relations knew him and contacted Edward saying that her boyfriend did not have a very good family and Jane should stay away from him. Edward was very upset about the news and decided to fly out at once to confront Jane about the relationship. When she confirmed her father's suspicions Edward tried to stop his daughter from seeing him especially because he already had a daughter from a previous affair with another woman.

Jane was in no mood to placate her father and they had an almighty row about her liaison with an older man. When Edward's wife found out about Jane's indiscretion she fell ill suffering from anxiety attacks.

Edward returned to America to be with his wife. When she recovered he went back to the UK to talk to his Daughter and try once more to stop the relationship but when he arrived he found that they had already got married. Another row broke out between them but the father realised it was too late and rushed back home to look after his wife who fell ill again. She never properly recovered after that suffering from ill health for long time. To add to Edwards problems he found out that his son-in-law had a drink problem that would become worse over the years and despite Edward's advice about how alcohol could attack his liver and brain he carried on drinking. Eventually he had to attend alcohol anonymous to help him get over his addiction

Jessica and Me

but although he was able to stop drinking he would always have a problem with the amount of alcohol he could consume.

Jane managed to get a transfer with the American company that had offices in England and the couple decided to live near her relations in Surrey. After a few years Jane, managed to get her parents to grudgingly accept the marriage. The couple moved to America to live and work in New York near the parents. By this time the couple had two children and tried to build a new life together putting the turbulent past behind them.

Jessica and Me

Chapter Twenty-Eight

It would take about 18 months for Don and Diana to save enough money to put a £1000 deposit on a house. They decided to look for a home around the Sunbury - on- Thames area. This proved to be an expensive area especially near the river. The couple went to estate agents to gather information on houses and told the agents the price range they could afford. Soon enough leaflets came in thick and fast through Dons letter box. A lot of the details were beyond their price range and all they seemed to do was to tear up leaflet after leaflet before they found anything near the properties that were suitable. Then when they saw the houses they didn't turn out to be any good.

Don began worrying if there were any houses that would suit him and Diana but they kept trying and finally came across a nice road with bungalows for sale. They went inside one of them and liked what they saw but the owner said it had already been sold. As they came away Don asked if there were any other bungalows for sale in the road and to his surprise they said that there might be because their friend was due to put his property on the market in about six months' time.

When Don and Diana went in September to see the people selling the bungalow they were only too happy to delay selling the property until the couple were ready to get married. Don said they would probably get married in May the following year. This would co-inside with the results of the exams to qualify him as a draughtsman.

Over Christmas Don said he and Diana had been invited to go to a party on boxing night. They were visiting her uncle & aunt in Kings Langley near Watford during that day and when they said that they were leaving to go to the party Diana's mother disappeared into one of the bedrooms. When the couple got into the car, Don looked back to see the mother looking through the window crying because her daughter was leaving her. She made a big thing out of a simple thing that her daughter was doing something that she couldn't control.

Don went back to work in the new year in the drawing office. He was asked to prepare a layout showing the arrangement of the company's

Jessica and Me

products on a stand that would be at the Finishing Exhibition at Earls Court. He noticed that the amount of equipment on show would take up two stands where as the competition had only one stand. When Don visited the show he noticed that the companies name was blazoned across the top of the stand making it look as though it was a large company and people flocked onto the stand asking questions about the equipment and getting the reps to give them quotes for supplying spray booths and air compressors. When the queries reached the drawing office the draughtsmen became over loaded with the enquiries to the extent that they couldn`t handle so much work. The customers had to wait a long time before they were sent the quote.

The job involved travelling to factories' to measure to decide where the spray booths and ducting would be positioned. He enjoyed the work because he was able to see how other companies ran their business. One occasion he had to fly up to Newcastle to measure a building to enable an installation of a spray booth and ductwork. The plane was a propeller driven Britannia. When it came to land the rivets on the wings were shaking as it came down shuddering and vibrating and the passenger next to Don said that once again it was a controlled crash landing. This didn`t go down well with Don as he wondered what the flight back would be like.

Don was picked up and driven to the factory to carry out measuring the site to finalise the layout with the client and had a meal before going back to the airport. When he reached the terminal it was very windy and he decided to insure himself prior to getting on the plane. This time the plane was a Viscount and as it took off Don noticed how smooth it was realising he need not have worried because it was a perfect landing.

After a lot of work revising for the City & Guilds Don had to sit the exams in the evening and as usual he was very nervous because he had failed before but when he saw the questions he knew everything would be ok because he recognised most of the answers and completed the exams feeling confident that he had passed the tests.

Jessica and Me

Being a Draughtsman in those days wasn't just about creating a drawing but involved running a Project such as issuing a quotation along with the layout drawing to the client and when the order came in the equipment was ordered such as fans, pumps and pipework plus electrical controls. Once everything was in the factory a drawing was issued to the workshop to enable manufacturing to begin and then another visit to site would be required to instruct the fitters to install the equipment. It was a very interesting job but one day Don realised he wasn't being paid very well for all the work he was doing. This came to a head when he was trying to raise enough money to put a deposit on a house when he was getting married.

When it came to setting a date for the wedding it wasn't that easy because Diana's parents couldn't agree with the date. The couple wanted to wed in early June. The mothers brother-in-law couldn't attend the wedding until a week later because he was working. Don could not believe their attitude but to keep the peace a later date was settled and the couple managed to buy the bungalow prior to their marriage. They set about redecorating the rooms to suit their taste.

When the couple went to see the Vicar to finalise the ceremony they discovered that the Vicar was ill with shingles and a stand-in was found to step in to marry them which was a bit disconcerting but apart from the cloudy day and the atmosphere between the couples parents things went smoothly. Everyone gave them a good send off with usual cans attached to the car clanking along as they sped down the road. The honeymoon was split in two with the first week spent in the bungalow doing the odd jobs that needed to be done and then the second week staying in a pub in Corfe Castle in Dorset. Don knew this area well having camped nearby when he was younger with his motorbike on holiday.

The honeymooners went out for days in the surrounding country side and they also went to the sea side at Swanage and Weymouth. It was while they were in Swanage that Diana got sun burnt. They had taken a pederlo out to sea and although it wasn't hot the wind and the sun shine burnt her arms. She spent the rest of the day lying on the sand covered with Dons vest and shirt to protect her from getting

Jessica and Me

burnt any more. Diana didn't like getting hot and was happy sitting in the shade.

The two bedroom semi-detached bungalow was just right for the couple and they were happy with the large garden. Don had always wanted a garden because he had never had one when he lived in Fulham. Diana had been brought up with gardens. Her grandmother had a large plot with room to grow vegetables enough to supply her through the winter months. Diana would stay with her when she was a child on school holidays and helping her with the gardening.

The Sunbury area in the 1960's was a good place to live being on the edge of greater London it was still country fide but this was going to change with the enlargement of the roadways to cope with the ever increasing traffic jams caused by people buying cars to travel to work and going out weekends. More people were living out of town. The railways had been cut therefore more people used their cars instead of the public transport.

Jessica and Me

Chapter Twenty-Nine

Jessica and Robert continued to see her brother Frank and his family on Saturday nights in the pub and William would tag along too. Everyone thought he was Roberts's friend but the truth was that he was Jessica's friend but she said `He is my husband's friend. ` She hoped this would stop people talking.

Roberts family knew about William and weren't happy with the arrangement but none of them did anything about it except for Roberts younger brother who would bring up the subject whenever he saw Jessica but she said `Mind your own business, any way nothing untoward is happening between me and William. ` Her brother-in-law accepted the explanation but he carried his suspicions through his life and would continue to bring up the subject every now and again much to Jessica's annoyance. William didn't help the situation by continuing to stay close to Jessica. Robert didn't say anything because if he knew about their friendship he either ignored it or he didn't believe his wife liked William in a sexual way. It was very convenient to keep William as a friend because he took Jessica and Robert everywhere they wanted to go in his car. They would go on holidays together. Also going with them was Frank and his family. The threesome went regularly to see Jim in Devon.

Jim was well off using the money from his pension and the compulsory purchase of his property in Fulham and the sale of his lease on the house in Barnes. His wife didn't need to work and therefore was able to look after her step son Alistair in the cottage in Devon. The family wondered how Jim managed to arrange the adoption because he was in his late 50's when it happened. Jessica wondered if he had lied about his age because when he wanted something he always resorted to bending the rules. This enabled him to find a way to get what he wanted. He would regret ever adopting the boy because when he was young and even into his teens he was terrible towards his step parents.

Alistair was bored living in Devon in his teens and he used to hitch a lift to travel up to London getting involved with drug users to get his

Jessica and Me

kicks. There was a writer who was investigating a group in the drugs world in London when he came across Alistair. He said `If you could get some information from your contacts to enable a Television programme to be broadcast then you would be included in the show and I will pay you a £1000 for your trouble.` Alistair dully obliged providing the information for his part in the documentary. When Jessica found out about the TV programme she told everyone that Alistair was going to be on TV not knowing that it was all about the misuse of drugs. The writer held nothing back involving the stepmother and father making them out to be bad parents. They were blamed for letting their stepson get hold of drugs. The real story would have shown that Jim and Vivien had treated their stepson very well making sure that he was brought up in the best possible way although in some ways they over did it with all the clothes and toys they gave him. The TV show didn`t pick up the evil side of Alistair who had a twisted view of life. Instead of being grateful to his parents he behaved very badly towards them. He blamed them for taking him away from his real parents when in fact the opposite was true. When he went to Ireland to see his family he found that they didn`t want to know him. The mother and father had split up long ago because the father abused the wife when he was drunk.

Jessica and Me

Chapter Thirty

Don realised he wasn't going to be able to earn enough money staying in the drawing office and had a meeting with the Managing Director with a view to try for a different career. He sympathised with Don and offered him a job as a sales rep. When Don told his wife about the offer she said. `It would be a waste to give up all the studying as a draughtsman and a reps job wasn't that secure anyway. ` After giving it some thought he decided to turn down the offer and get a job nearer home Don had been ten years with the same company and was sad to leave but he found a job with a company only three miles away from home as a chief draughtsman. Everything seemed to be ok until the boss called him in to tell him that the company had been taken over and the position was already filled by the parent company and he would have to let him go. The timing couldn't be worse because it was Christmas and the couple's first one since their marriage. Luck was on Dons side because in the New Year he went for an interview with a company in Slough and was offered a job as a contract draughtsman. Don said `The money is a lot more than the old company had been paying me. ` His wife agreed with him that it was a good offer. This company was based in Uxbridge but they were due to move to new offices in Slough High Street. This was a much better journey because the traffic was lighter coming out of London. They manufactured heating and ventilation equipment which was different to the work that Don had been used to but some of it was similar such as the pipework and the ducting that were part of the spray booth layouts so he was able to use his experience to cope with the other different parts of the job.

By this time it was 1968 and Don had been driving his Morris Mini for five years, he had covered 77000 miles. It was a good car but he decided to buy another one. Diana had been talking to a workmate who had heard that there was a Hillman Imp for sale. The couple went to see the car and decided to buy it because it seemed in good order and had only one owner with low mileage. Don managed to sell the Mini to a local garage and decided to go on holiday to Cornwall

Jessica and Me

with the Imp. It was a long journey and Don was pleased with the way the car performed, it was slightly larger than the Mini, making it a more comfortable ride. The couple rented a room in a house for £20 for the week in a village called Column St. Minor a few miles away from Newquay. The weather was good until the last Friday when it rained all day. The couple decided to go to the local cinema to a musical called Funny Girl starring Barbra Streisand and Omar Sharif. They enjoyed the show because the romance between Barbra and Omar was very touching with their on/off relationship and the music suited the singer's voice which was very strong and tugged at the heart strings. By the end of the film Diana was in tears because the story was very tragic all the way to the end.

In those days a group called the Beatles were all the rage and everywhere the couple went in Cornwall they heard their records playing and although they were good Don still liked listening to Frank Sinatra. He did not mind being slightly out of step from the latest craze that the Beatles had created in those days. He still liked the big band music of the 1930's, 40's and 50's which would follow him into old age.

Jessica and Me

Chapter Thirty-One

By the 1960's the song & dance type of musical film was on its way out with only a few films of its type being shown compared to the block buster films in the 1930's to the 50's.

The Beatles type of music changed the way the teenagers and older people would listen and dance for decades to come.

In the late 60's going abroad for holidays was becoming more popular and Jessica and her husband along with William flew for the first time to Jersey and stayed at a hotel in St. Helens for a fortnight. Jessica paid for a lottery ticket and forgot about it until one of her friends reminded her to check the numbers. When she read out the numbers to Robert said. `It appears you have won a prize. ` First of all she thought it was £350 but when she went to collect the money it turned out to be £700. Jessica was overjoyed with the win and phoned Don to tell him the news and said `I will give some of the money to you. ` This would help pay for their holiday. It was one of the best holidays Jessica had enjoyed; she even met a popular singer in a cabaret show on the island where he signed a photograph for her.

Dons job in Slough didn't warrant any travelling that he had been used to in his old job but the manager called him in and said there was a contract at Battle Hospital in Reading and he wanted him to work on site to prepare layout and pipework drawings. Don liked the offer and agreed to work on site but he wanted travel expenses which the manager agreed to. It was a longer journey to the site but it was going away from London so there were hardly any traffic jams. The contract went through the winter and into the summer the following year. It was very hot and dusty and conditions in the hut became unbearable. Although the site huts were basic, Don enjoyed working on site and was able to learn more about heating and ventilating. It was winter time and very cold but the huts were cosy and warm.

It was that year Diana told her husband that she was pregnant. The couple were overjoyed about the news and they told their parents who were thrilled to hear the news.

Jessica and Me

One day Don was making his way home when he noticed the engine was over heating and he stopped at garage in Ascot which was half way home. He opened the bonnet at the rear of the car where the engine was housed and steam was coming from the radiator. After a while Don decided to unscrew the cap but unlike most cars it wasn't positioned on top of the radiator because there was no room in the compartment and therefore the cap was turned at a right angle pointing out from the engine which made it dangerous to handle. Don realised this and put one of his white coats over the radiator to protect him from any hot water spilling out. He gently unscrewed the cap but left it partly undone to enable the pressure to drop and make it safe to take the cap off. When he thought it was safe. He removed the cap but it hadn't released the pressure causing the coat to blow off and a huge amount of steam and boiling water to splash onto Dons chest burning him in the process leaving him in agony. The garage owner saw Don in pain and rushed out to see what he could do but when he undone his shirt and saw the burns he immediately phoned for an ambulance to get him to Wexham Hospital in Slough.

The doctor examined the burns and said Don would have to stay overnight for further checks. Don thought he would be there for a short while but when the doctor spoke to Diana he said it would be at least a fortnight before the burns would heal. When Don heard the prognoses he was surprised and was concerned on how Diana would cope especially being pregnant but both parents said they would help. William took Jessica and Robert to see Don but they were unable to speak to him because he was in an isolation ward to protect him from any germs infecting the burns.

The time spent in hospital wasn't very good because after the first week the chest became infected and the doctor decided to cover up the burns with gorse and bandages. Every day Don would have to get in a bath of warm water to allow the nurse to peel off the gorse and change the dressing. This was not good because peeling off the gorse pads was painful and the first day he nearly fainted in the bath. It was only the sister shouting at him to get out which brought him to

Jessica and Me

his senses that stopped him sliding further into the bath and going under the water.

Each day the burns began to heal and towards the end of the week Don was looking forward to getting home. One day he went as usual to remove the gorse and noticed that it was a different nurse who had a trainee nurse with her. She took off the dressing showing the young nurse the procedure and then she put the new gorse on. As she did so Don nearly fell off the bed in great pain because the nurse had used a whole sheet of gorse and he then realised why small pads had been used.

During the time spent in hospital one of the engineers from the office came to see him bearing fruit and flowers and a book to read. Don was very surprised at the company's attitude and they also paid him while he was ill. After two weeks the burns healed sufficiently enough for him to come home.

The couple decided to look for another car because the Imp was dangerous and they set about looking for a larger car. On the way to work Don saw a garage in Wraysbury that had Vauxhall Victors for sale which was large enough for the two of them plus the baby when it arrived in November.

Don asked the company if he could work in the office because during the summer the site was very dusty and the heat in the huts was unbearable. The manager agreed much to his surprise.

At the beginning of November Don was working in Slough he received a message from Diana that she needed to go to the hospital because her waters had broken and her labours had begun. He rushed to their home to take his wife to the local hospital and Diana was omitted straight away. Don was present at the birth and when he saw that it was a boy he immediately thought it looked like his father. Don was overjoyed and went into the local pub to calm down and have a pint of beer to celebrate before he told the new grandparents who were also overjoyed at the news.

The grandparents came to see the baby and were shocked to see the amount of hair he had and Don was able to give him a parting in his hair. The couple named their new born son David and when he

Jessica and Me

was only a few weeks old they went into a Chinese restaurant with the baby in a carry cot to have a meal and he slept all the way through much to their delight.

The people at Diana's office gave her presents for the baby and said she could carry on working for them at any time but she didn't go back for years to come.

When David was nine months old his parents went on holiday to the Isle of Wight staying in a guest house in Ventnor. He was a good baby and everyone in the hotel's restaurant were amazed how good he was and if he did get a bit restless during the meal time Diana would feed him with bits of bread while they waited for their meal to come.

When they went for walks it was like going on safari with all the gear they had to take with them as they walked to Shanklin and Sandown. The guest house was owned by one of Dons work mates father. He had been a plumber but retired to buy a bed & breakfast place and never regretted it. The owner next door died and his widow offered her guest house for sale to the plumber for £9000 as a going concern. All he did was knock a hole to create a doorway between the two buildings to enable the houses to become one concern and he carried on letting the two properties.

Jessica and Me

Chapter Thirty-Two

By late into 1971 Diana was pregnant again and in April 1972 she gave birth to a baby girl and the couple called her Julie Samantha. Her middle name was going to be Elizabeth but just before Don went to the registry office he heard a song on the radio by Bing Crosby called Samantha. This was one of his favourite songs and he decided to make that his daughter's middle name.

With two children Don decided to add another bedroom to the property and he used the loft space to create a main bedroom so that the children could have a bedroom each on the ground floor.

The couple chose a contractor that had been recommended by a work mate and although he had done a good job for him things didn't go well on the work in the loft because he was a one man builder. He didn't put in a full day's work; one day while he was working in the loft Diana heard an almighty crash. She rushed from the kitchen to see what had happened and saw the contractor's legs dangling through the ceiling. This was one of many problems that happened during the building of the room and in the end Don had to tell the contractor to finish up to enable him to complete the decoration himself. Eventually the bedroom was finished just before Diana gave birth to her daughter and during the birth the nurse noticed the cord round the baby's neck and told Don to leave to let her take action urgently to remove the cord to enable the birth to take place.

In 1973 Don decided to go on holiday to Swanage. They had been there before and they mentioned it to Jessica. She said could they come. Don's car was large enough to carry all the family. On the Saturday morning in August they all squeezed in the car which was at its full load. They set off for the holiday. Don was worried about the load in the boot and stopped at a shop to buy a roof rack to spread the load to make it easier to drive. When they reached the out skirts of Bournemouth the car wouldn't pull away from the lights. Don discovered the half shaft had broken making it impossible to carry on. An AA man towed them to a garage where it could be mended but it couldn't be carried out straight away so they hired a taxis to get them

Jessica and Me

to the hotel. The receptionist gave them the keys to their rooms. When they began unpacking Jessica said the leg of the bed was broken Don told her to tell the manager. When he arrived she was surprised to see that he had some bricks in his hands and even more astounded to see him remove the leg and replace it with the bricks. Meanwhile Don was unpacking when he opened the wardrobe door to see a brick on the floor, he bent down and picked it up and as he did the whole wardrobe began falling towards him so he quickly put the brick back. This was just the start of the experiences at the hotel.

When the family went down to dinner Don noticed an atmosphere with people whispering to each other saying they were unhappy with the food. When they went to the bar after putting the children to bed he also noticed people commenting about the service and the manager/barman wasn't always at the bar and people were helping themselves to the drinks. When they went down to breakfast the baby daughter didn't like the food and Diana said `Could my daughter have an alternative.` She was told that she should have ordered the day before because they didn't cater for changes in the menu. Diana wasn't happy and complained to the manager but he took no notice. A couple nearby said this was typical of the attitude and they said `It would be better to get food elsewhere.` When Don was in the bar that night he overheard the manager saying to his friends that he didn't understand people coming back each year.

Don collected the car the next day and took the family out for a ride but it broke down again. When the AA man took one look at it he said the half shaft had broken again. Don took it to another garage to repair it again and obtained a report to enable him to get his money back. At the hotel people were making friends talking about the way the place was run with all the problems that kept cropping up. This was prior to Fawlty Towers TV show and although it was said to have been based on a hotel in Torquay Don thought the problems with their hotel would have also been used in the programme. The owner wasn't worried because he owned a farm and was using the hotel as a hobby.

Jessica and Me

Chapter Thirty-Three

Ten years after Don had left his first company the chief draughtsman rang him up offering him a job. Don was surprised and told him that he wouldn't mind going back to work for him but the reason he left was because he wasn't being paid enough. Now he had two children to support and therefore the money situation was even more of a problem and if the company could match or even give him more than he was earning at the moment then he would consider taking up his offer. After some thought the chief said he couldn't give any more money. Don thanked him for thinking of him and said goodbye.

During that year Don was working for a consultant as a supervisor for heating & ventilating projects on building sites. His job was to oversee contractors installing pipework and ducting designed by the consultant.

Don had to check layout and detail drawings supplied by the contractor and then visit the sites to inspect the work and attend site meetings to liaise with the client and the architect. He also had to agree payments to the contractors as the work progressed. He was running seventeen contracts on the mechanical side of the job. Don was working alongside an electrical supervisor named Fred who knew what he was doing but he would always turn up late for the site meetings. He had an excuse ready when he was late but nobody believed him. Don used to avoid going with him to site so that he could be on site early to inspect the work prior to the meeting. This helped answer any questions that would crop up and not take him by surprise. Usually the architect ran the meetings but sometimes Don would take over which gave him a lot experience in later life. Part of the job meant that Don had to inspect the contract once the job had been completed and one day he was sent to a luxury block of flats that were ready for occupation. It was on a Friday afternoon and usually there was a care taker on the premises but this time he had gone to see his sick wife in hospital so the place was empty. Everything went ok until he walked into an airing cupboard to inspect

Jessica and Me

the controls on the hot water cylinder which was at the back of the cupboard. As he got to the pipework the door swung closed leaving him in the dark. He turned around to grab the handle to let himself out but there was no handle. Don was locked in with no one around to let him out. Once he realised there was no escape he began to shout for help and kick the door to try to force it to open but to no avail. Don began to panic because he could see himself being trapped in the cupboard over the weekend until the caretaker came back on the Monday. Fortunately an electrical contractor was working in the flat above and heard Don calling for help. The contractor followed the noise and when he got to the cupboard he was able to open the door and Don fell out and couldn't thank him enough.

When Don got back to the office he told them about his ordeal and although some of them sympathized others thought it was funny and had a good laugh about it. They had an annual party to enable the north and southern offices to get together. When it came to the evening do, the northern lads put on a show and it was all about Dons ordeal in the luxury flats but included jokes about how funny it was that he was locked in and how he reacted to the experience. Don went along with the jokes but at the same time he said. `It was serious ` because an inhabitant could have the same problem with the door. He also said that the luxury apartments shouldn't have doors without handles.

Soon after the party the management called in Fred to tell him that they no longer needed him and he would have to leave. Don carried on for about six months on his own until he too had to leave the firm. He put it down to the lack of work in the building trade because everyone was suffering at the same time.

Don saw an advert for a job as a chief draughtsman and went after the interview he was offered the job. He noticed that there was only one other draughtsman in the office and he was told they would be getting more people in to make the D.O. larger. As he got more involved with the job it wasn't very long before the other draughtsman left leaving him alone to do the work. Once again Don was in a job where he was doing more than originally intended. Not only was he

Jessica and Me

doing more work he realised he wasn't getting paid much either. The only perk was when the contractors gave the director whisky etc. at Christmas time. They gave it to Don because they didn't drink. After being in the job for about a year he decided to ask for a raise but it was turned down. This was not good enough and Don decided to look for a job.

Jessica and Me

Chapter Thirty-Four

In 1976 Don and Diana decided to book up a holiday in the Isle of Wight at the same hotel they had been to when David was a baby but this time it was more expensive. Never the less Diana booked a holiday in August. The guest house had become a hotel because the owner put in a bar and had a liquor licence but soon after he sold up and retired. By this time Diana had put a deposit on the holiday. Just before the holiday Don saw a camping shop and said to his wife that those were the days when he used to enjoy himself camping. He wished he was still doing it, to his surprise Diana said she would be happy to go camping provided they had all the equipment. The couple went into the shop and bought a six birth tent and all the equipment.

Diana contacted the hotel owner to cancel the holiday but they wanted the full amount because it was too late to give them any money back. The couple decided to try and sell the holiday by advertising it in the local paper. To their surprise they sold the booking by splitting it into two separate weeks and were able to use the money to buy the tent. They also paid for a placing on a camp site a short distance from the hotel. That year it was very hot making it ideal for camping. Don was surprised that Diana enjoyed herself because she had never been before but she said it was because they had the right equipment making it a luxurious camping holiday.

The next job was nearer to home and it involved measuring pipework and vessels that were used in manufacturing dye for cosmetics like lipstick and food stuffs etc. The work was interesting but very dirty because the powder used for making the dye got everywhere and was a health hazard. Don was sent up to the Yorkshire factory to measure a plant room for pipework modifications. He took three sets of clothes including shirts with him, one for the factory, one for the office and one for the hotel.

The factory was in the middle of the country side adjacent to a farm with cows grazing in the fields. While Don was measuring the existing building he noticed that the workers were dressed in heavy overalls and they wore balaclava type head gear with only the front of their

Jessica and Me

face showing and this looked as though they had been smashed in the face with a beetroot with blotches of deep red. He carried on with his work and towards the end of the day when he had finished he went to the toilet and looked in the mirror and saw that he was covered in red blotches as well. Don said `Where can I get rid of the dye.` The foreman said `Use the shower.` The dye washed off and he changed into his second set of clothes before going to the hotel. He changed into his third set of clothes in the room including his best shirt to go out for the evening but just as he started to leave the room he looked in the mirror and noticed a red stain around his shirt collar. He told the manager who said `You used hot water when it should have been cold. ` This would have stopped him sweating and stopped the dye from getting into the pause. The story that was told to Don was that when the cows in the field nearby ate the grass and were milked it came out pink because the field was polluted. When Don got back to the office in London he claimed for a new shirt. The manager was very reluctant to agree to provide the shirt asking the age of the shirt and how much did it cost, Don got the impression that it wasn`t going to get any money but he insisted and eventually the company paid part towards a new shirt. This didn`t go down well with Don and he started looking for another job. The site was made up of separate sheds to house the dye plant and one day the management shut down one of the sheds and put the plant into mothballs. When the union asked why this had happened the answer came back that the same plant in America had also been shut because it was feared that the dye could cause bowel cancer in workers that came into contact with it. The official communiqué was that the action taken was only a precaution and the workers shouldn`t be alarmed because their hadn`t been any problems with the dye in the UK. The union investigated the type of dye being used and discovered that the cancer could lay dormant for twenty years before people were found to be infected making them ill and possibly die from the decease. The union also said `That if there was no problem why had the management let the plant operate for ninety nine years before

Jessica and Me

shutting it down.` There was no answer to that question but the shed was shut and the doors locked to stop anybody getting in.

The site was divided into two areas of wet and dry dyes. In the dry area, bags of powder were tipped and mixed into drums without any containment, making it easy to escape into the atmosphere. Don said `Why the powder couldn`t be passed through ducts in a sealed arrangement. ` He was informed that it would waste powder which was very expensive. The company didn`t seem to worry about the pollution that was being caused by an out of date operation. It was like stepping back in time which wasn`t very good for the environment.

The wet dyes were just as much of a problem because if the operators stood over an open vessel and then looked in the mirror his tongue would be bright green. Depending on the colour of the dye the powder and fumes would get into the offices and it would get onto peoples clothes and into the pause of their skin so when they had a wash it was difficult to remove.

Don only stayed working on the site for eighteen months before he found another job and he was pleased to get away from such a polluted factory. His clothes would be cleaner and when he had a bath the dye would stop coming out of his pause.

Jessica and Me

Chapter Thirty-Five

By the time of 1977 Dons Uncle Jim was eighty three years old and age had court up with him. Up to a few years ago he had been in good health but he began suffering with thrombosis in his legs and he wasn't eating that well. He had always liked a drink and the amount he had consumed over the years it was a wonder that he had lasted so long. His constitution must have been very strong with hardly any fat on him. He was short with a slim stature but very strong. The climate in Devon suited him very well and he kept himself busy in the garden and socialising in the pub. Since his retirement he had given up driving the motorbike but he always managed to get a lift to and from the pubs that he frequented. He also made his own wine and beer. He had a vegetable patch to supply him with fresh potatoes and broad beans etc. All this helped to keep him fit but his illness was getting worse and even he couldn't carry on the life style he had been accustomed too over the years and one night he passed away in his sleep.

After the funeral Vivien carried on in Devon until her sister who lived nearby suddenly died. Being completely alone she decided to pack up and live in Ireland near her relatives. She was able to get a sheltered bungalow from the council and after selling off some of the furniture she took the ferry across the Irish Sea and moved into the bungalow.

Also in the same year two huge stars in America died. They were the crooner Bing Crosby and the king of rock and roll Elvis Presley. Bing was in his late seventies but was still active and it was when he was playing golf that he suffered a heart attack and died before he got to the hospital. Elvis was 44 years of age and had been taking drugs prescribed by his doctor but he must have taken an over dose because he also had a heart attack and died despite desperate attempts to revive him. For years afterwards people would not accept that he was dead and they flocked to his house called Grace lands to pay homage to his memory. His ex-wife created a museum and it was

Jessica and Me

said it made more money than when he was alive although the rumour circulating said he was in financial difficulty prior to his death.

A few years passed and Jessica decided to visit her sister-in-law with Robert and William. They stayed in Dublin and also a short while with Vivien. Everyone was friendly and gave them a good welcome and they enjoyed travelling around the country and drinking the Guinness.

Don found a new job just down the road from where he lived and it was a soft drinks manufacturer. He hadn`t been their long when the engineers took him out for lunch in the local pub. Don said he didn`t want much to eat but there was no such thing as a small meal and although the lunch was egg and chips by the time it was served it became eggs ,sausage, and a plate full of chips. The engineers were drinking pints of strong ale and Don decided to have the same. When he got back to the office he knew he had a lot to drink and it was only the huge meal that kept him feeling ok. One of the engineers would go out drinking every day and everyone knew he had too much to drink because he would shout a lot and want to pick an argument with anyone that got in his way. Friends wondered what sought of work a draughtsman would do in the soft drinks business but there were a lot of site and conveyor layouts to be drawn and Don was kept busy because he was the only draughtsman. There were three factories that needed to be updated with new projects. The factories were in Wandsworth and Manchester that Don had to travel to and take details for creating layouts to enable the updating. The workers varied from being very efficient in the north and not so great in the south. One of the reasons that southern factory was under performing was because they were always being threaten with closure and therefore moral wasn`t very high. The atmosphere in the Wandsworth factory was very negative and Don was aware of this as he walked round the plant. He was told to design a guard around the labelling machines and when he showed the drawing to the factory manager he was accused of slowing production down. Don said `If the machine was maintained properly then it would help rather than hinder production.` He also arranged for the same guard to be fitted in the Manchester

Jessica and Me

factory and when he saw the installation the workers were just watching the machine rather than getting in amongst it as the workers were doing in the south. Don said `What is the difference between the two factories. ` The engineer said `Look again at the operation. ` Don noticed that only two out of three labellers were working compared to three in the south. The engineer explained that they kept one clean while the other two ran so that the cleaning kept the machines running efficiently and didn`t need so much attention.

The department that Don worked in was called Central Engineering. There were five engineers plus two secretaries and Don. One of the engineers was working in the Manchester factory. He was called Ben and when the new department was formed the manager said that he should move to be local with the office in the south. The company help Ben with cost of moving. He sold his house in Manchester and bought one in Woking. Ben and his wife settled into their new home but after a couple of weeks he was called into the office to be told that there was a problem in the northern factory that had to be sorted out. He had to oversee the new arrangement of the conveyor layout. He spent the next five years travelling to Manchester leaving his wife to cope in their new house where she had to make new friends.

Ben was a very experienced engineer and he had been a prisoner of war in Italy for five years. He was forced to work on laying railway lines. He put himself in danger because the gang he was working with didn`t fix the lines properly. If he had been found out he would have been shot as a saboteur. He was a very brave man but he didn`t talk about it much.

Everyone worked hard in the team visiting factories to oversee the maintenance on the bottling lines including the services such as the soft drink from the syrup room etc. Don went to survey the sites to carry out modifications to the bottling plants and the services. It was a very interesting job and the manager was pleased with Don. He told him to layout the syrup room at Sunbury to install a blending unit to feed lemonade and squash to the lines.

The blender was built in Germany and was delivered in pieces on the back of a lorry. When the blender arrived it was discovered that the

Jessica and Me

legs were damaged. It had to be propped up in the syrup room. The manager left Don in charge to see it lifted in position. Don warned the contractor to be careful because the centre of gravity made it awkward to lift. He left them to get on with their work while he met the insurance company to discuss claiming against the manufacturer for the cost of the damage. No sooner had he began the meeting when the foreman rushed in to say that the blender had been dropped making more damage. The contractor denied responsibility saying Don had instructed him on how to lift the machine. Don was surprised at the attitude and said they were the people that were experienced at lifting and they should have known how to lift the blender without any instruction from him. Don had only warned about the unsteady arrangement of the machine.

Jessica and Me

Chapter Thirty-Six

Don had lost touch with Ivan and all he knew that he had moved to Henley-on-Thames. He had attended a University to qualify as a Professor. This came as no surprise to Don because he knew that Ivan was a very clever person but eccentric, but he was surprised to hear that he had married and possibly had children. Don had also lost touch with Alistair and all he knew about him was that he had parted from his girlfriend and her baby but still worked in a jewellers shop.

Dons friend Ted was due to leave the RAF after completing twelve year service as a motor mechanic. He then went to live in Bournemouth and much to Dons surprise he gave up being a mechanic and went to work in the building trade working on site as a plasterer in his own business.

Ted and Alan were married with two sons and along with Don kept in touch with each other over the coming years.

During 1980 Don and Diana decided to go to France in a caravan. They took the ferry across to Dieppe and drove to a town called Tour where they collected a caravan and towed it to a sea side resort called St.Jean De Mont. It was an organised site with shops, toilets/shower and an area where a circus could come and entertain. It also had a private beach which the children loved but it was too hot for Diana but the family travelled to local towns to see more of France. The French were very helpful especially when Don tried to take the caravan off the hook on the car and before he knew it the French came and managed to release the caravan to place it on the site that had been allocated. Don's daughter became friendly with a French family who invited her to a birthday party. When they offered her champagne she declined saying she wasn`t allowed being too young to drink alcohol. Towards the end of the holiday Don heard there was a strike by the ferry operators and he decided to leave a day early and got back to Tour to stay overnight in the caravan before handing it back. The family made their way back staying in a hotel for one night where they bought a cooked chicken and took it back to the room to eat. They eventually made it back to Belgium to catch the

Jessica and Me

ferry in Oostende. When they got back they found that the strike had ended and realised that if they had waited then they would have been able to catch the ferry in France.

Jessica was 66 years old in 1980 and had been semiretired for six years but she kept working as a cleaner in the houses in Fulham where there were mansions. The people could afford nannies to look after their children and cleaners keep the rooms clean. Jessica was working in three houses during the week. One of the clients was a divorcee and had a title because she had been married to a Lord. Lady Harrington didn't pay much but like all aristocracy she gave presents instead like winter coats and drink for Jessica's husband. This arrangement went back into the eighteen and nineteen century where the servants lived in the big houses where the Lords and Ladies of the Manor gave them gifts to supplement their income.

Most of the people that Jessica worked for were very good to her but others felt that she should be treated like a servant and were very strict on how she should behave which made her feel that she had to know her place in the house.

Jessica's husband Robert had a mild stroke in his mid-50's. He had to give up working on the building sites because it was too strenuous. His younger brother managed to get him a job in MOD as a messenger in the Earls Court office. The stories he told about the money that was spent on new offices and furniture when people were promoted or were employed from outside was tremendous because they all wanted new carpet and desks which was expensive and the existing furniture was thrown away creating a lot of waste. This happened all the time with staff coming and going in various changes of management or when the Prime Minister had a cabinet reshuffle. Robert carried on working until he was in his 70's to get a better pension.

Jessica's friend William was still around but he was getting old and grumpy plus he was smoking a lot. This got on Jessica's nerves because Robert had given up smoking to help him improve his health so William had to go outside to smoke which made him unhappy but because of his love for Jessica he put up with it.

Jessica and Me

Chapter Thirty-Seven

When Dons daughter was ten years old she loved dogs and kept asking her mother if she could have a puppy. In the past Julie was told she was too young but now her parents decided she could have a puppy but she had to accept that she should look after it like taking the dog for walks. Diana began looking at adverts for a suitable breeder and also to decide the type of dog that would be suitable for a ten year old girl. They eventually decided that a small dog like a Yorkshire terrier would be ok and Julie agreed that she would be able to cope with that type of breed. Diana found a breeder in Crawley and the family went to see the dogs. When the owner showed the puppies they were so tiny that she was able to hold them all in both hands. Julie picked one of them to enable the owner to hold onto the pup for seven weeks prior to handing it over to go to a new home. Julie couldn`t wait for the day to come before picking up the pup which she named Mindy and when the day finally arrived to bring the pup home she immediately went to toilet in the hall, Don said she was marking her territory. Mindy was a tiny dog but she became very fiery terrier and made a good guard dog protecting the house and when Diana held her in her arms if anyone came near she would growl and be very aggressive. Don wondered why she was like that but thinking about it he realised it was because his wife held the dog so tight that this gave a signal to Mindy that her mistress needed her protection and nobody was going to hurt Diana. Mindy was a tough little dog and Don said that she thought she was as big as a German shepherd showing no fear. Yorkshire Terriers were a long living dog and Mindy was no exception and she lived to fourteen years of age albeit towards the end she suffered with diabetes and she became blind but she coped very well and the family were very sad when the end came.
    Don was still working for the soft drinks company and was kept busy re-arranging layouts of the bottling lines including the mechanical and

Jessica and Me

electrical services. He was also acting as a trouble shooter dealing with problems that occurred when things went wrong with the conveyors/services. Solving the problems would help the plant to run more efficiently. It was difficult to convince the factory managers to agree to carry out the work required to improve the efficiencies of the plant because they weren't engineers but qualified chemist. They relied on information from the factory engineers who in turn had a limited budget to run the plant and they were against the idea of having a department like the Central Engineering telling them how to run the bottling lines. This made things difficult for Don but he pursued his aims to do the best he could in his job and was very good at dealing with people to persuade them to do the right thing. Don's manager backed him when the managers tried to stop the work that was required to help improve the efficiencies.

    The job didn't get any easier because the owners decided to merge with another soft drinks company and instead of three factories another six factories were added to the work load. There was a change of management to deal with as well. The technical manager called everyone to see him on a Monday morning. The staff wondered what the interviews were about as they went in one by one to see the boss. They soon found out when the engineering manager came out of the meeting to say he was finishing and would leave at the end of the month and then the engineer John who liked to drink went in and after a short while came out and he also said he was leaving and he picked up his case and walked out. Everyone was in shock but they needn't have worried because they were told that their jobs were secure and there would be a new manager to run the department. The two men were sacked because John was fiddling his expenses and overtime hours and his manager couldn't control him so he had to go too. All this was after they had been warned about it some months ago. Although the engineering manager had his faults generally he was technically a good manager and with technical drawing background. Everyone thought that Ben would be the next manager but he was overlooked because of his age being that he was due to retire in a few years. The top brass decided to choose a

Jessica and Me

slightly younger man as manager. The rest of the engineers and Don were surprised at the decision because of his lack of experience in engineering. The new manager's name was Colin and he had been a service engineer in his previous job where he supervised men who maintained bottling machinery abroad. He looked after their expenses and their accommodation. His engineering skills were average but he could talk a lot and Don called it having the `gift of the gab. ` During this time Don would find it difficult to work with the new manager because of his lack of understanding when it came to reading drawings and not allowing enough time and money to enable Don to do his job properly. Whenever Colin had a meeting to discuss an up and coming project he would begin talking to the contractor but when it came to explaining the details shown on the drawing he would get into difficulty. He would have to call Don in to explain how the modifications should be carried out relating to the layout drawing. This was not because the drawing was wrong but it was due to Colin being inexperience at reading drawings. He hadn`t worked in the drawing office when he was a young man but as a trainee in the service industry. Don ended up having to take over the meeting and although he could cope with this arrangement he didn`t get the praise he deserved in getting his manager out of trouble. Some of the Directors realised his short comings but let him carry on because the rest of the staff were working in such a way that the department was able to run ok despites the manager's inadequacies.

Colin got in touch with a friend who lived near him and he worked as an engineer in the coffee industry but he wasn`t happy. He came for an interview and Colin offered him a job. His name was Paul and when he joined the department he was full of complaints about the company finding fault in how it was run and comparing it with his old company. He said `I was better off where I had come from. ` Don listened to Paul complaining and thought to himself that maybe it would be better if he went back. Sure enough after six months had gone by Paul put his notice in and went back to work for his old company. This wouldn`t be the last of Paul because after a few years Colin got in touch with him again and once again he said `There was

Jessica and Me

a position to be filled.` Paul gave in and came back to work in the office alongside Ben who was the senior engineer. It wasn`t long before Ben found out that Paul was a grade higher and earning more money than him. This infuriated Ben because he had been trying to be up graded for years but the personnel had always come up with some excuse to find a reason why they couldn`t give him what he wanted. Now they had to give in and grant his wish to be upgraded and adjust his salary to suit. Ben told Don it left a nasty taste in his mouth and continued to resent Paul but he wasn`t the type of guy to hold a grudge and got on with his job travelling to Manchester where he got on with the workers and they helped him keep the factory running efficiently. Don's attitude towards Paul was that he always seemed to be looking over his shoulder trying to protect himself from being blamed if there were any mistakes being made that he might be part of. Don said Paul was so busy protecting his back that if he wasn`t careful he would bump into lamp posts in front of him.

When Don was in the factory measuring the floor area for placing some machinery, Colin told Paul to see if Don needed any help. When he asked if he could help Don said he could by holding the end of the tape but when he turned round to give him the tape Paul was not there, it was as though he had disappeared into thin air. Dons only explanation was that Paul didn`t want to take the responsibility for measuring the area in case he was blamed if anything went wrong.

Colin liked going to the Brewing Exhibition in Birmingham and he would encourage everyone in the office to go to see the bottling machinery on display to see if they could be incorporated into the layouts in the factories. It was a two day affair so it meant an overnight in a hotel usually in Stratford-upon-Avon. On one occasion Don went with two electrical engineers Chris and Dan. Chris was younger than Don and liked to drink and when they visited the stands the reps would get Chris drinking. On this occasion Don wasn`t staying overnight and said `I want to see as much of the machinery as possible before going back to London by train.` He left Chris and Dan saying that he would meet up with them before leaving for

Jessica and Me

London. After a while he went back to find his work mates and when he eventually found the stand he discovered Chris in a drunken state with Dan trying to stop him doing anything silly. When Chris saw Don he put his arm round him saying `You are just the man I want to see.` He thought Don knew the name of the hotel he was staying at that night. Don did not know what he was talking about. Chris said `I can't believe you don`t know.` He thought Don knew everything. Don said `I will ring the office.` He asked Ben because he would know the answer. During the phone call Chris started messing about playing with a fire extinguisher nearby and winding the hose round Dons neck. Dan managed to stop Chris making a fool of himself Ben found out the name of the hotel and Don told Dan `Control Chris.` He didn`t want him to drive to the hotel in such a drunken state.

Apart from going to exhibitions the company would take the staff away on two day seminars staying in a hotel to carry out lectures to enable the management, supervisors and engineers to be informed about the financial performance of the company. Also what was expected of everyone in the coming year to keep up efficiencies and help the company make a good profit.

The secretaries and accountants would also go to the seminars and the exhibitions and gossip was that the bosses would have affairs with the secretaries.

In the engineering department there were two women, one was the accountant and the other one was a secretary. The accountant was named Christine and the secretary was an Italian woman named Gina. Don took no notice of the gossip and didn`t link Colin with Christine as an item until some years later he saw them meeting each other at a local supermarket. He also began to wonder about Gina and was told that she was having an affair with Dan. Her husband found out about it and divorced her and he went to live in America.

Colin's wife was ill with cancer and Christine's husband had a heart attack so the pair of them had to be careful when they saw each other out of working hours. Going away on company business was a perfect cover for the affair and the couple felt that they weren`t hurting anyone with their liaison.

Jessica and Me

Now Gina was alone with her grown up sons it was easy for Dan to visit her at home pretending that it was to do with business when her sons were around but when the sons were out they would make love in her bedroom. The sons became suspicious of Dan and kept watch on the couple and soon found out about the love making. The sons confronted Dan and their mother accusing them of deceit and when they confessed the sons were very angry and chased Dan out of the house telling him never to see their mother again. Gina was broken hearted and went back to Italy to stay with her parents leaving the sons behind. When Dan found out where his lover had gone he decided to follow her to Italy and try reconciliation with her and ask her to marry him. Gina was pleased he asked her and said `I will think about it. ` She did not want to make the same mistake again.

In the following years the company was going through upheaval in its business and was shutting down factories one by one. Don was kept busy because the management needed to save money so they told him to create layouts to enable some of redundant machinery to be installed in the factories that were still open. He had to visit the sites that were going to shut to measure the equipment which was very political and Colin told him not to say what he was up to at the factory. When he arrived to carry out the work some of the workers became suspicious and would guess what Don was doing, others would know and even the cleaners would know exactly what was going on. After a while Don was fed up trying to keep his visit secret and if he was asked what he was up to he would tell them and he found that most of the time the workers were very helpful. One day Don went with the Production Director to the Manchester factory and the union leader confronted the Director saying that he had heard rumours that the factory was closing down in six month time. The Director denied that the rumour was true but Don knew it was true although he didn`t know exactly when and within three months it did close. Don was sad at the deception because the people in that factory were very hard workers and they kept the efficiencies up but it didn`t make any different.

Jessica and Me

Over a period of seven years the management closed seven factories leaving only two to carry on with the production of soft drinks.

Jessica and Me

Chapter Thirty-Eight

By 1985 Dons father was in bad health and one Sunday the family were at a get together in a local pub when Robert became ill with pains in his chest. Don took his parent's home and told his mother to get in touch with the doctor. On the Monday Robert was taken to the hospital with a heart attack. He was put into intensive care for over a week and it was touch and go whether he would survive but after ten days he recovered enough to be taken out of intensive care and was transferred into main ward but Don wasn't happy with the situation. The nurses said he was doing fine but he wasn't walking that well. Despite Dons reservations Robert came out of hospital after fourteen days. The doctors said he could go home and as long as he looked after his diet and took short walks each day he would be fine. He came out of hospital on the Monday but despite Jessica's efforts to look after him he had a massive heart attack on the Thursday morning and she called for an ambulance and he was taken back into hospital. Don was at work when he heard the news and his boss said `Go to the hospital now. ` By the time he arrived and met his mother he was told by the doctors that his father hadn't got long to live and in the afternoon Robert passed away. The doctors carried out a post-mortem and discovered that Robert had a diseased heart. Don wondered why they hadn't found out about it while his father was in hospital in the first place, the hospital didn't comment. At the funeral Don and his mother were very upset and everyone gathered round to support them in their grief. After the funeral William was hanging on trying to comfort Jessica but she told him that she wanted to be left alone and told him that he shouldn't see her any more. William was upset but respected her wishes and said goodbye. It would be a long time before she saw him again. She would try to make the best of her loss alone.

 Don tried to see his mother as often as possible but he lived twelve miles away. To make things worse the landlord upstairs had sold out to property investors and they wanted Jessica out as well. Things started happening outside the house. Jessica began hearing strange

Jessica and Me

noises and she saw a stranger next door in the back yard where nobody had been before. The other neighbour didn't help by saying that there were burglars about. The man came again and this time he climbed over the fence to get into a neighbour's house. Don decided to get his mother out of the house and find her a place nearer to where he lived. He spoke to the new landlord who said there were properties in Sheen and Twickenham area that he could look at.

Don and Diana took Jessica to see the properties. The first one was in Sheen above a shop but it was more suitable for a family so they went to the flat in Twickenham. As they entered the one bedroom flat they all agreed this was the one that Jessica could live in although Don had reservations about the path leading up to the front door which was in need of repair with large cracks in the concrete making it uneven. The flat was part of a group with its own path way and it didn't have any lamp post, the only lighting was local to the front doors. There was a garden at the back of the property which helped Jessica make her mind up to agree to have the flat because she had never had a proper garden and this one was just the right size with a small lawn and borders to grow flowers. Beyond the garden was a nice outlook over the common with large trees and an open field to the edge of a road that led to the town. There was a bus route that she could catch or walk into the shopping area.

Most of the neighbours were ok and were out at work through the day except for a couple next door that were a bit odd and Jessica called them the 'odd couple. ' After she had been living there for a few months the people upstairs decided to move away. The new occupants were related to the old tenant. When Don saw them he wondered if they were going to be suitable because their dress code was in the style of 'punk rockers.' Usually these type of people were loud and rude and could be violent to people around them but this couple couldn't be nicer, very polite and they talked very well. This couple would be very good to Jessica doing her shopping if she needed it and generally keeping an eye on her and letting Don know if there were any problems.

Jessica and Me

Jessica liked the area saying it was much better than Fulham. She was able to go shopping in Twickenham by catching the bus and if it was late she could walk to the high street, this wasn't bad being that she was in her seventies and exercise was good for her.

Jessica had a new lease of life and Don encouraged her to go to the community centre where she could make friends and play bingo being lucky winning prizes like bottles of wine or food hampers. She liked the small garden where Don bought some roses and flowers to grow and she could sit and read her books. The last time she had anything near a proper garden was in Barnes during the war when Robert grew vegetables and a few flowers. They did manage to grow flowers in a small plot in Fulham but it couldn't be called a garden. William was the one who looked after the roses etc. in that small area.

Where Don lived he had 50ft frontage and 70ft back garden. He grew mainly roses and he counted fifty roses in the front and back garden. He was surprised that anything grew because he classed the earth as being a mixture of gravel and clay. When it was dry the ground became very hard making it impossible to dig and one day the ground was so hard that when he tried to dig it with a fork it bounced off not making any impression in the earth, but the roses seemed to grow very well in that type of soil.

Don liked gardening and decided to apply for an allotment about a half a mile from where he lived. His son said `I will help. ` When they went to see the plots David persuaded his father to have two plots saying he would look after the extra ground. Don agreed but he wasn't surprised when after a couple of weeks his son found it hard going and gave up trying to plant anything on his plot leaving his father to carry on by himself and compared with the small amount of time he spent on the plot it was very successful. Don was able to grow a variety of vegetables like runner beans, broccoli and sprouts etc.

The company went into another merger but this time it was different because it was more of a takeover and new management were biased towards there company. They wanted to keep their staff and

Jessica and Me

let the old management go. Don counted himself lucky because there was still a position for him in the new set up although the other draughtsmen were using CAD to do their drawings.

The manager gave Don two chances either he leant to use the computer or leave and find another job. Don was in his forties and' wasn't confident that he would find another job so he accepted the challenge to work on the computer. Fortunately the other draughtsmen were happy to help him operate the drawing system and within the time frame of three weeks he mastered the operation of doing drawing on the computer. Although the management accepted he was good enough to work for them they weren't that happy because they had hoped he would have failed so that they could get rid of him but he stayed with them for three years. Don realised that the management were friendly enough towards him but they were only too happy to stab him in the back if any mistakes were attributed to him. He didn't like that kind of hypocrisy but he had to put up with it if he wanted to stay working for them.

The new company had eight factories but like the old regime they began closing them down one by one as they became uneconomical. Their aim was to close all the small factories and create two large ones in the south and north of the country. When the management approached various towns with a view to building super large bottling halls they were all worried about the amount of water that would be required to feed the plant. One of the towns said it would be ok provided the company built a new reservoir to hold enough water just for the new bottling and canning lines. Although it was a good idea it was very expensive and they hadn't allowed such huge project in their budget. The company eventually found a forty acre site near Leeds. This would become the northern plant. Don got the job of preparing the layout and although the production area was huge it only took up a third the size of the site which allowed for expansion in the future.

The production of soft drink was the fastest in Europe but Don thought that it would never reach its full potential because of the speed being so fast that if anything went wrong the lines would lose

Jessica and Me

production which would be huge and affect the efficiency. Don attended a lecture about the soft drinks industry and the consultants were showing typical layouts of bottling and canning lines which were a copy of drawings that Don had prepared and when the lecturer noticed him in the audience he acknowledge him saying to everyone that he had worked with Don in creating the layouts and he should be the person who should be speaking.

One of the factories that stayed open was in the north of London and there was a problem with the crate conveyor and Colin asked Don to prepare drawings to replace the conveyor. When he investigated the problem he told his manager that it would be very expensive. The bottles were falling out of the crates as they changed direction going towards the decorator. The manager said he wasn`t worried about the cost and told him to get on and do the job to replace the arrangement. When costs came in from the contractors it proved to be very expensive as Don had warned and the modifications were dropped. After a short while Don had to visit the factory and he found time to look at the crate conveyor in action which he had never seen before. When he saw the bottles falling out of the crates he said to the maintenance engineer that he wanted to see the drive arrangement. He discovered that the sprockets were the wrong way round making the conveyor speed up instead of slowing down and when they were changed it cured the problem.

Jessica and Me

Chapter Thirty-Nine

A year after Dons father died his father-in-law passed away after suffering from various strokes and heart problems. Diana's mother Mary was very upset but she was a strong woman and managed to overcome her grief and carry on living in the same house that she had been in during her marriage. She was able to drive her car that she had been doing since passing her test when she was 60 years old. Everyone was surprised that she was able to drive without having an accident because she couldn't see too well and drove the car in the middle of the road. One day Don and his family including Mary drove in their own cars to Brighton. Mary was following in her car and when Don looked in the rear view mirror he could only see half a car because she was so far out in the middle of the road. Cars coming towards her were honking their horns to make her move over but she wondered what they were doing saying she didn't understand because she didn't think she was doing anything wrong. The longer Mary carried on driving the more dangerous she became and one day she was taking Dons mother home and as she was driving along the by-pass Jessica noticed she was driving on the grass verge that separated the two roads on the dual carriage way. After the journey Jessica told her son that she didn't want to go in the car with Mary because she felt she was too dangerous. The mother-in-laws driving came to an end when she was driving through Kingston entering the roundabout and as usual she was in the middle of the road but as a lorry over took on the near side it caught the wing of, it was lucky that it didn't right the car off. This accident shook her up and she vowed never to drive again but she still thought it wasn't her fault. Don used to call her Mrs Mcgoo after the TV cartoon character Mr Mcgoo who blamed everyone but himself when he had a mishap.

Dons son David was sixteen years old when a group of so called friends had a school leaving party at one of their houses. It seemed innocent enough but when David failed to get home by 12 o'clock, Don and Diana began to worry and they gave it another half an hour and were just about to ring the police when the mother of one of the

Jessica and Me

group phoned to say that she had just got home to find the party in disarray with everyone drunk especially David who had fainted and was laying in his own sick. She managed to clean him up and put him to bed in the spare room. She said it would be better to leave him until the morning before picking him up. Don was relieved to hear the news but angry with his son for getting in such a state. When he question his son on how he got so drunk it appeared that the kids played a game of cards and whoever lost had to down a measure of strong alcohol to allow the game to go ahead. The trouble came when the group arranged the cards to make David loose more often than the rest therefore he had the most alcohol. Don said to his son `Never get in such a state again. ` Although David heeded his father's warning he knew he would get drunk again although not as bad as he was at the party. This was what Don hoped would be the case but from that moment he was never too sure how his son would react when he went to a party with other friends. Don couldn`t understand why his son drank so much but when he thought about it he realised that in the past some of the family did drink a lot like his Uncles Jim and Frank plus Diana's Grandfathers. When Don was in his twenties he would go to the pub with his Uncle Frank and his son's family along with Jessica, Robert and William. The drink used to flow but Don was a slow drinker and after talking for a while he would notice that a lot of glasses of lager had lined up for him to drink. He would say that he couldn`t drink that much as he was driving but really he didn`t want to drink that much anyway. Franks family couldn`t understand Dons attitude because they had been brought up with parents that were heavy drinkers.

Jessica and Me

Chapter Forty

During the 1980's Don and his family went on holiday to the South of France. Don decided to drive through France but stop overnight about half way through the journey. He came to a town called Vienne and parked the car to look for a hotel. After a while Diana saw a sign showing small bed & breakfast guest house but known as pensonnes in France. When the couple went to see if there were any rooms they found it was in the bar and there was a land lady behind the counter. Don tried to speak French by asking for a chambre (bed for the night). She found it difficult to understand and spoke to Dons children instead. Eventually the land lady understood what Don wanted. She gave him the key to see if the room was satisfactory. She also asked him if he wanted a garage for the car. Don said he didn't need it because the car was parked outside in the street. That night the family settled down in their beds but Don could not settle and decided to see if the car was alright. When he got in the car he noticed he had left their passports inside and thought it was just as well he had gone to the car. It was 10-30pm and just as Don was getting out of the car a voice from above called out asking 'Do you want a garage. ' It was the land lady calling and it surprised Don because it was late but he called back saying it was ok and when he reached the bedroom and told Diana they had a good laugh and wouldn't forget it for a long time.

The following year the family went to the South of France again and once again they stopped at in Vienne. This time Don said he wanted a garage and was directed to a huge barn full of cars except for one space and as he was reversing the land lady was saying gauche. Don didn't understand her but his son said 'She means 'left' to go into the garage.' Once again they all had a good laugh at the way the land lady acted because it appeared she was doing everything in running the guest house.

Other holidays were in caravans in the south west towns called Argerle-sur-mer and also in a resort called Agay near Cannes. Both holidays were very enjoyable except for the forest fires that raged

Jessica and Me

near the site in Agay. The site was high up overlooking the fires and they could see planes flying over the forest dousing the flames with huge amounts of water and it appeared to work because soon after the fires died down and when they drove through the area the next day everywhere was black it was like being in the middle of a coal field.

Despite the general view in Britain about the French being nasty and treating the British as being ignorant and rude. Don found the French people to be most helpful and friendly. He thought it was because he tried to speak the language and they appeared to respect his attitude. A lot British people didn't speak French and expected them to speak English and the French felt that this was very pompous and showed their anger at people who wouldn't try to speak their language. Don adopted the attitude with the saying `When in Rome do as the Romans do. `

Jessica and Me

Chapter Forty-One

During 1985 Dons father had passed away but prior to that Diana had book a holiday and Jessica said. `You should still go on the holiday because that would be what your Father would have wanted. ` In early September Don and his family went to Menorca. Diana had found an advert in the BP newspaper showing a small villa for rent. When they arrived they were surprised to see how nice the area was. The villa overlooked the estuary and it was great to see the ships passing by to moor in the harbour in Mahon. This harbour was the second deepest in the world with the first being Pearl Harbour in Hawaii. Therefore the port could take large ships such as cruise liners and battle ships. In the early hours of the morning Don could hear small fishing boats going out to sea to catch the local fish. They were fairly quite except for the put-put noise of the engines. In the future this sound would change to a loud droning noise due to the ships becoming much larger to enable more fish to be caught.

The first time Don and his family went to the villa they discovered it was up for sale and when they enquired how much it was going for they were surprised at the asking price of between £25000 and £27000. In those days it was a lot of money, Don felt that it would be a good price to pay and said to his wife `We should be able to afford to buy the property' but Diana wasn't too sure. Don said. `We might not make any money for the coming year but I couldn't see us losing money either especially if we carried on renting it out, we would probably come out even. ` Diana still said. `I do not want to take a chance. ` She feared that people who rented would damage the villa and Don would have to keep going there to keep an eye on the place but he said ` The site has a management arrangement that would look after the property and the garden' but Diana was still worried about things going wrong and persuaded him to drop the idea. This would prove to rankle with regret about not buying the villa for years to come.

By 1989 Don had been working in the soft drinks industry for twelve years and was fed up with the politics and the company said they had

Jessica and Me

changed the rules regarding the ten year loyalty payment and they also didn't give a decent pay rise he decided to look for another job. If he had been working for the old company he would have received a week's pay and extra holiday pay plus a lapel badge for being there for ten years but Don overheard a conversation by the chief draughtsman saying that he hadn't got the same treatment so he didn't see why Don could get the award, it was then that he realised he didn't stand a chance of getting any deal.

An employment agency told Don that there was a job working for a company producing stout beer on a worldwide scale but he had to be on a contract arrangement. Don was not happy with being a contract draughtsman but as this was the only offer he was glad the pay was much better than his previous salary he decided to take the job. Originally there were two draughtsmen and a supervisor but when he began in the office one of the men had already left and the other one was working on the drawing board leaving Don to work on the CAD system. After six months the remaining guy left leaving Don to work on his own. The supervisor called Tim asked for the same computer but the management said no because Don appeared to be doing all the work that was required. This annoyed Tim but he let Don carry on with the job but he trained working on the computer with the idea that he would take over the work at the most opportune moment. The engineers liked working with Don especially with his positive attitude but Tim was negative in dealing with the staff so much so that they would wait for Tim to be away or on holiday to load Don up with work. Although Tim seemed to be friendly enough there was an element of jealousy in his attitude which would get worse as the years passed by.

The work was very interesting because it involved preparing layouts for bottling halls in Africa. The factories were in Ghana, Nigeria and Cameroon. Don never went to these factories but some of the engineers did. When they came back and gave Don the information to prepare the drawings, they would tell him stories that made him glad he never went to those countries. One story was that if a white man came across an accident while he was driving he was advised

Jessica and Me

not to stop to help because the locals would attack him throwing sticks and stones. They would probably end up killing him. So the advice was keep going even if it meant driving over the body. Another story was that there was a strike in one of the factories and the engineer had forgotten some paper work in his office so he decided to go back to the factory to retrieve them but as he neared the gates the strikers threw bricks at his car because they thought he was trying to break the strike.

Most of the engineers respected the African workers but there were a minority that treated them as though they were slaves in the old colonial days of the British Empire. Don tried to tell one of the engineers that his attitude was wrong because it would be better if he got the workers to be on his side because he would find that they could help him with the work that needed doing and they would respect him plus he would get more work done in a shorter time. He would have none of it and carried on in his old tyrannical way.

Jessica and Me

Chapter Forty-Two

By the 1990's Don and Diana decided to go on holiday in America. They took their daughter Julie and went on a fly/drive to Orlando in Florida where the Disney Organisation had a theme park called Disney World. Everyone went to it with their children because the area was full of other places like Sea World and night life which was very good. The restaurants put on shows like cowboy stunt shows and knights of old when the legendry King Arthur ruled. In the cowboy shows boys and girls sang country and western songs.

There were film studios such as MGM, Universal and Warner's that opened their sets to show the stunt men acting out scenes from popular films such as Raiders of the lost ark.

Julie loved America and after the first week Diana said she wanted to visit her Uncle Edward and his Daughter Jane who lived near Miami so they drove on six lane highway in their rented American car which was a dream to drive being automatic and cruise control for the long trip. When they met the Uncle and Jane's Husband they went to their four bedroom bungalow with its swimming pool overlooking a large lake. Don said to Diana 'If this bungalow was in England your cousin would have to be a managing director because it would be very expensive' American property was very cheap especially in Florida where people went to retire and the only work was in the tourist trade.

Diana's Uncle lived in a condominium with a shared swimming pool. The luxury flat was fantastic with its walk in wardrobe and large rooms. He was in his late eighties but seemed much younger and he was travelling back and forth to his flat in New York although he was trying to sell it but the neighbours had to approve the people who wanted to buy the property.

When the holiday ended Julie asked if she could stay in America with her great Uncle and he said she could stay with him for another week. Julie asked her father if she could stay and he said yes knowing she would be in good hands.

Jessica and Me

Don and Diana drove back to Orlando where the roads were wide and straight. Don thought there would be a lot of traffic on the Saturday afternoon but the roads were virtually empty except for the odd cars now and again. There was one car that Don was worried about because as he drove closer it appeared that both the girl passenger and the driver were asleep at the wheel so Don was very careful as he passed the car worrying that it may give the driver a fright making him crash but everything was ok much to the couples relief. When Don and his wife got back to Heathrow their friend Alan picked them up and he noticed they were on a high and they said it was because they had enjoyed themselves so much.

It took some time to get over the holiday because the living conditions in America seemed to be in a different world. It made England appear drab and the weather didn't help because of the persistent cloud and rain compared to the blue skies and sunny weather from where they had come from. When it did rain in Orlando it was very heavy down pours but it would only last about fifteen minutes and then the sky would clear and the sun would come out drying everywhere and within five minutes it was as though it had never rained. This happened in Fort Lauderdale when Don wanted to go on a river cruise on the intercostal waterway. When it began to rain he thought he couldn't go on the trip but no sooner had it started it stopped and the sun came out and dried everything to allow them to take the trip. It was good passing the mansions where the film stars lived although they were only their when they were on holiday for about three to six months at a time. Before returning the boat moored at an Island where there were alligators in a pen and everyone got off to see a man amongst them prodding the alligators to wake them up and he opened their jaws while striding over their bodies. At first the alligators hardly moved but one of them did and everyone gasped with fright at how fast he moved making the man jump out of the way very quickly. Everyone including Don took pictures before returning to the boat and they were impressed at how the man handled the alligators.

Jessica and Me

Towards the end of 1990 Diana wanted to move away from Sunbury because she was unhappy with the way the area was becoming run down and all the cars parking in the road instead of using their garages. Don took a time to understand how his wife felt. After taken more notice of the way neighbours lived like the guy next door who was constantly working on his cars leaving them unfinished and motorbikes riding at high speed round the roads, he began to think that Diana was right to find somewhere else to live.

   The couple began to search through the lists of houses in the estate agents in Staines although they didn't want to live in the centre of town. Eventually Diana saw a property for sale in Laleham and when they went inside they found that it needed a lot of work to bring it up to their standard so they carried on looking nearer to Staines. There were several houses but they were either too expensive or too small and the couple realised it wasn't going to be easy finding the property they really wanted to live in. While they were looking for properties just outside the town they saw a house up for sale and arranged to see it and turned out to be just what they wanted. They put an offer in and although it wasn't turned down straight away the people didn't seem to be interested and after a while Don found out that another offer had been accepted which upset Diana. She really liked the house but they had to start all over again. Fortunately another house nearby came on the market and the couple liked what they saw and put an offer in and after some negotiation it was accepted but their bungalow still had to be sold. This was a very stressful time because there were three sets of people interested and eventually they all pulled out but a widow with a small child saw the property and put an offer in that same day. It wasn't as much as they had asked for but Don said to his wife that he thought they wouldn't get the asking price and decided to accept the offer. It still took a long time to seal the deal and Don had booked a holiday in September and they decided to go because they couldn't see the contracts being signed until they got back from the holiday so they went to Menorca. While they were away Don rang the solicitor who said `I have not heard anything you should give up the deal. ` Don was furious with the solicitor's attitude

Jessica and Me

and rang the Estate Agent who was dealing with the sale of the house. He told him what his solicitor had said. The Agent told him to take no notice because as far as he was concerned everything was going through and by the time they got back contracts were ready to be signed and the family moved into the house at the end of September. On moving day the stress finally got to Don and he developed a very bad cold. It was so bad that as soon as the bed had been installed he went to bed the rest of the day to try and get over it. After the family settled in Don managed to shake off the cold and began inspecting the house to find out what needed to be done to be able to make living conditions bearable. As it turned out there was not too much to do to the inside but the back garden needed rearranging because the previous owner had a rockweiller living mainly in the garden. The patio had been extended so that the dog could wonder around and go to toilet in fact they wanted to pave the whole area but thankfully ran out of paving slabs even so Don decided to pull up large areas of the slabs to claim back the garden and he had to remove a fence round the existing lawn as well. Eventually Diana and Don managed to get the garden into shape where they could put flowers and bushes in place of the slabs and they also installed a pond to attract the wild life.

One day Don counted the number of birds coming into the garden and saw fifteen different varieties of birds. They even saw two ducks on the lawn due to being near the river Thames.

Don liked the area because he could walk into town and if he walked the other way there was an area where he could sit and watch the boats go by and feed various birds like swans, geese and ducks.

In 1992 Don decided take a fly/drive holiday on the west coast of America. Along with their daughter they flew to Los Angeles and rented a car to take a round trip taking in San Diego, Las Vegas and San Francisco. As soon as they got off the plane they drove a hundred miles to San Diego which was no mean feat seeing as they had flown all the way from UK on that day. When they arrived they spent a few days to rest then visiting Sea World where the whales and dolphins put on a show splashing people that close to the pool

Jessica and Me

and everyone had a good time especially the children. Being only there for two days they didn't see too much but it gave them time to relax before driving onto Las Vegas which was 400 miles away. As Don drove out of town the area suddenly turned into desert and he noticed that he was running low on petrol. The road sign showed that the nearest town was 57 miles away. He began to worry because being that he hadn't driven the car for long he wondered how much fuel was in the tank and Don spent the next hour watching the gauge to try and guess how much petrol was left. If it ran out they would be in trouble being in the middle of the dessert could turn nasty especially because they hadn't seen any traffic for a long time. Fortunately they came across a small settlement of mobile homes along with a petrol garage. When he got out to fill the tank he hadn't realised how hot it was because of the air conditioning being on in the car and it was the only time that he ran to the shop to get out of the blazing heat.

When they reached Las Vegas they found the hotel in the down town area although the standard was good and they enjoyed the food. It was when they walked through the casino and saw how people were gambling with pots of money. They realised how addictive it was because when they went to eat in the restaurant and returned a few hours later to find the same people operating the one arm bandits. When they came down for breakfast they were surprised to see the same people gambling. In the reception area Don saw an advert showing that Frank Sinatra was in town and he had a show at the Desert Inn. When he asked the receptionist about the show she said it was fully booked. Don felt he wasn't missing much because he thought that at the age of seventy six years old Frank would probably be past his best but he wondered why so many people still wanted to see him. The receptionist said he could go on standby if he really wanted to see his idol, Don said he would think about it and in the meantime he bought tickets to fly over the Grand Canyon in the afternoon.

They went to a restaurant for lunch and asked the waiter if they could have a quick meal because they were going on a flight over the

Jessica and Me

Grand Canyon. He said ok but he had a worried look on his face and when Don asked him if there was a problem he said no and everything would be ok with the flight and kept mentioning that they would enjoy themselves. Don felt that the waiter was trying to put them at their ease and thought no more about it.

When they arrived at the airfield Diana was surprised to see small planes dotted around the edge of the runway and as they passed the planes she kept asking if they were their yet because the planes were getting smaller the further they went. It wasn't until they reached a plane with eight seats that Don said that this was the one which was a big surprise to his wife. They boarded the light aircraft and it took off very smoothly and Don began taking photos but when it got to a certain height it hit an air pocket and dropped about twenty feet making the passengers tummy turn over. At this point Don was still taking photos as he sat next to the pilot but he turned to see how his daughter was coping and noticed she had her head in a sick bag. He quickly turn his head away but it was too late and he to grabbed a bag and was sick as well. Everyone was being sick except for Diana who was busy fanning her husband to keep him cool. Don looked across at the pilot and noticed a wry grin on his face and wondered if he had done it on purpose seeing as the rest of the passengers were Japanese and probably wasn't keen on them being on the flight.

After the gruelling experience of the flight they arrived back at the hotel and went straight to their room and lay on the bed to recuperate for a few hours. When Don awoke from a light sleep he suddenly woke his wife and daughter and said lets go and see Frank. They quickly had a wash and change of clothes and made their way to the Dessert Inn and when they reached the front door they saw a huge queue going round the block. Don asked someone where they should go for the standby queue and was told this was it. By the time they reached the front of the queue the theatre was filling up and they wondered if they would get in. When they were next to go in the doorman said `There are only two seats left. ` Don said `I need three seats to include my daughter.` The doorman went back into the theatre and had a word with someone and came out saying it would

Jessica and Me

be ok and as they went in Don noticed that they were the last ones and felt lucky to have made it. When they sat down the comedienne was doing his show and after thirty minutes he introduced Frank and he came striding out to loud applause and cheers. He went straight into a song and Don felt that Frank had shed at least thirty years with a performance that was as though he was back in the height of his career. All through the show the audience gave him a standing ovation at the end of every song. It was a fantastic atmosphere and Don said he would never forget it especially when Frank introduced the band and the leader who turned out to be Frank Jnr. Don was surprised to see that the son seemed to look older than his father going bald and having a stoop in his shoulders.

When the show was over it was 11 o`clock and Don was on a high trying to sing the song just like Frank but obviously not succeeding. They hadn`t eaten so they went to the adjoining restaurant hoping to see Frank and his minders but he didn`t appear. If Don had managed to see Frank that would have been the icing on the cake but it was not to be.

They spent a few more days in Las Vegas taking in the shops and the casinos and they took a taxi ride where the driver who was very talkative told them how the area was built up because the hotels were on existing granite making it easier to build on that kind of foundation. He said that everything was changing with buildings being demolished and rebuilt within six months and if they came back in a few years' time they wouldn`t recognize the place.

After seeing the sites they made their way to San Francisco. The journey was ok until they came off the motorway and hit the streets where they immediately lost their way and having to go into petrol garages to ask the way. Eventually they found hotel and the next day they drove into town to do some site seeing. They travelled on the tram which was an experience in its self and were crowded but great to ride down to the water front looking over the bay with the old Alcatraz island prison in the distance. They took a boat trip around the bay including going under the golden gate bridge which was an eerie feeling when the mist came down making it difficult to see the

Jessica and Me

shore but when they came away from the bridge there was blue sky with bright sunshine as though it hadn't happened.

Don was surprised at the amount of beggars about especially in the wharf area where the tourist were site seeing. Some of them put a busking show on. When they came out of the multi-storage car park exit a beggar jump out in front of the car making Don braked hard to avoid him. The guy had a notice hanging from his neck saying he had a wife and child to support. Don said to Diana 'If he is not careful it would be a widow if he was run over. '

On the way back to Los Angeles they stopped in a restaurant in Carmel where Clint Eastwood was the owner and they hoped to see him their but all that was said 'That is where Clint sat when he was eating'. Don said to the waiter 'That is what you say to everyone. ' The waiter smiled in agreement. As they were leaving Don thought he saw Clint in the distance but wasn't sure.

Although they weren't too keen on Los Angeles it did have all the attractions and Don and Diana took Julie to most of them including Disney Land, Universal Studios and the theme restaurants that put on a show such as the Knights of the round table and Wild West Cowboys singing the country and western songs. They also went to see Queen Mary Ship that was in dry dock. The Americans had turned it into a museum. It was interesting like walking back in time. They went down into the engine room and the guide said it was haunted by one of the engineers but there wasn't any evidence of a ghost. They also went on one of the board walks equivalent to our piers, there were Pelicans perched on the rails and flying around and diving into the sea for fish. There were supposed to be Dolphins but Don could not see any. They also sat on the beach but were wary about going into the sea because the current was very strong and some people got into trouble and had to be rescued by the life guards.

The only time Don realised that there was violent people on the streets was when he was watching the TV news and there were reports of gangs shooting at each other and a young girl was killed in

Jessica and Me

the cross fire and when the name of the street was given out, Don saw that it was the next street to where their hotel was situated.

Don had driven 2500 miles in 14 days on the round trip from Los Angeles to San Francisco and enjoyed every minute. It was a fantastic holiday and when they arrived in the UK it took them some time to settle back into the routine of living in England.

Don's friend Ted had an accident when he was driving along the M25. He came to a halt at a traffic jam when the car behind crashed into the rear of his car. It didn't do much damage but mentally it effected Ted and that night his hair turned white making him look much older than he really was. After a few weeks Don went to see his friend and when Ted appeared Dons mouth dropped with disbelief at what was in front of him. Over time his appearance improved although he never regained the looks of his old self.

By 1994 Don had left the brewing company and had a hard time finding another job. He spent most of his time working on short contracts. The longest job came when the agent asked him to work in their office as an inspector checking the drawings on a hospital project. He had to check twelve draughtsmen over a period of three months. Don discovered that there were three types of draughtsmen, those that knew what they were doing, those that thought they knew the job but didn't and those that were whiz kids on the computer but were useless at drawing. Don would cover the drawings in red ink but some of the youngsters didn't seem to care because the management didn't sack them although they were on a short contract and when most of the drawings were complete they would have to go. This was what happened to Don when the project came to an end

Jessica and Me

Chapter Forty-Three

By 1995 Jessica was the only one left out of her adopted family with the exception of her nephews family and they had moved to live near Margate and Jessica hadn't seen them since her husband's funeral in 1985. They carried on sending her Christmas and birthday cards and Jessica used to phone them now and again but that became less often as time went by. Basically the only family Jessica could call upon was her son Don and Diana and their children who were teenagers.

Jessica at 80 years old was very good for her age because she was able to cook for herself and potter about the garden and walk about a few miles every day shopping in Twickenham. She would go to the social club to see friends to play bingo. Don used to phone her every day and have her over for Sunday dinner along with his mother-in-law Mary who wasn't so healthy but she wouldn't admit it because she had a strong will power, because it was mind over matter.

Dons mother and mother-in-law hadn't got on that well in the past but the fact that they were living alone made them need each other. Don encouraged them to see each other and they became friendly towards each other with an uneasy truce built up between them when Jessica would stay with Mary at her house over the week end.

Don had more work in 1995 although he had become more uncertain about the future and wished he could retire early but when he approached the insurance company to find out how much he would get from retirement payments he found out that the amount of money he would get wouldn't be enough to retire on. The insurance company sent Don a letter asking him to let them know if he was satisfied with the private pension arrangement and he quickly wrote back saying that he wasn't happy with the set up. He complained that when he took out the policy he was told that he would get the same deal that he achieved if he had been with the company pension that he had given up in 1989. The insurance company said they would investigate his complaint but this would take over two years before he would hear anything. He managed to get some satisfaction

Jessica and Me

from the company, he thought it could have been better but an advisor said `This is the best deal that you could achieve and you should accept it. ` The deal meant that Don would get paid part of the pension when he was 60 years old with another payment when he reached 65 years of age so he carried on working for the time being.

The neighbour on the left hand side of Dons house said that he was going to build an extension on the side their house and this would also mean that a brick wall would be built to replace the fence. Don agreed with the build but with proviso that it was built on the neighbours side of his boundary and therefore didn`t effect Dons garden. The neighbour agreed but as soon as the builder began digging the foundations for the wall in the back garden, Diana could see that it was going to spoil the bushes and phoned Don at work to tell the builder to stop or move the earthwork. After consulting the neighbour the builder agreed to keep the concrete away from the bushes but he wasn`t happy and didn`t bother putting the earth back on the plants. There were other incidents such as telling them to keep the rain water gulley within their boundary and that was when the neighbour complained that he had lost three inches when he moved the wall. Don said `It is ridiculous because the wall is still within the line of the old fence. ` There was worse to come when the wall in the front garden was built. Because the bushes hid how the wall was being built Don had not noticed the line of the wall. He was very busy at work and the wall was being built at a bit at a time. When another neighbour looked at the wall from the road he told Don `Your neighbour has built the wall on your side of the boundary making it come over by as much as 16 inches. ` Don took measurements of the garden and compared it to a site ordinates map supplied by the government. It confirmed his suspicions but he hadn`t got a plan showing the dimensions of the boundary from the contractor who had built his house. Therefore he couldn`t prove anything if he went to court. The other neighbour said `I will back up your claim. ` He said `They would drag your name through the mud and I couldn`t allow that to happen. ` Although Don did send a drawing to the council and the neighbour, it was ignored and the neighbour accused Don of

Jessica and Me

building part of his front wall into his property which was absurd and from that day Don never spoke to his neighbour.

Dons son hadn't been with many girls but one day when he was out with his friends in a local pub he noticed a very attractive girl with some of her friends and when they looked at each other David knew that this could be the special one. They didn't get together straight away it took several visits to the pub before he got up the courage to talk to her. She spoke very good English he realised she came from another country and when he finally asked her where she came from she said `I am Slovakian. ` The girls name was Anna and she was two years younger than David but seemed a lot older. David thought that it was because Slovakia was a fairly old traditional country with strict rules in treating their children similar to how the British brought up their children in the 1950`s.

Although David liked being one of the lads he secretly wanted a steady girlfriend and Anna seemed to fit the bill but it seemed that she wasn't ready for a steady relationship but she was attracted to David. She tried to keep him at arm's length but the pair couldn't stop seeing each other and gradually they became infatuated with each other and after six months David proposed to Anna. She said `I will think about it and consult with my family in Slovakia. ` Anna had a work permit for a year and had a job as a waitress in a restaurant where she was hoping to become a chef. She attended night school to become qualified which was a long way off because although she already had Qualifications in Slovakia they weren't recognised in the UK so she would have to start all over again.

David introduced his girlfriend to his parents and they took to her straight away. They were pleased to see that he was finally going to settle down but were concerned that Anna's family would have something to say about the romance and wouldn't necessarily agree with it.

Don quizzed his son about the relationship saying was he sure about his feelings for Anna and what if things didn't work out. David in his usual laid back manor said he would work it out. Don said that was all very well but with Slovakia being a poor country his son would

Jessica and Me

have to save enough money because there wouldn't be any money coming from her side of the family.

In 1996 David and Anna said they wanted to get married but David hadn't saved enough money and Anna and her family hadn't any money either so it fell to Don to find the money to enable the marriage to go ahead. Don said to his son that he hoped it wouldn't be like this through his marriage because he expected his son to make his own way in the world.

Dons neighbours offered to help by making their garden free to erect a marquee to house the reception. They had empty rooms for Anna's relations to stay overnight but her mother and father stayed in Dons house.

The wedding went very well and Diana phoned a contractor to supply the food and drink. Everyone gathered in the marquee to wish the newlyweds all the best for the future plus the best man and Don made speeches before the disco began. Don invited the locals except for the neighbour that he didn't get on with, this helped to keep everyone happy about the noise from the party.

That evening David and his bride said farewell to the guests before departing on their honeymoon in Slovakia. This gave David the opportunity to get to know the in-laws and Anna's friends. The couple spent two weeks in a log cabin overlooking a lake near where Anna used to live in a small village where everyone knew each other. Everywhere the couple went people said hello and wished them well as if they had known David all his life. It was a mountainous area and David said he wanted to climb one of the mountains which he had never done before. Anna said they could travel to a mountain nearby that wasn't too high and fairly easy to climb. The next morning the couple set off. They went to a shop where they could rent mountain climbing gear and clothes to keep them warm as they reached the peak. The weather was ideal for climbing so they changed their clothes and made their way up the mountain. After an hour and a half they were within reach of the peak when the weather closed in and it became very cold as snow started to fall. Although the couple were well equipped their clothing wasn't that warm and they began to

Jessica and Me

shiver with the cold. They found a cave where they could huddle together to keep warm and wait out the storm. They managed to light a fire to dry their clothes and kept eye on the weather. The sky cleared and gradually it stopped snowing. After a while they could see the fields below and decided to carry on down the mountain although it was still slippery. They found a way down Anna lost her footing and fell onto the rocks before David could save her and when she tried to walk she realised she had sprained her ankle which was going to make it more difficult to get off the mountain. Fortunately David had a mobile phone and managed to contact the mountain rescue team and they sent a helicopter to pick them up. After a check-up at the hospital the couple went back to the cabin and went to bed to rest.

When the couple got back to England David searched through the papers and estate agents to find a flat to rent local to his parents.

After everything had settled down Diana said that the next occasion would be to see her daughter get married.

Don thought enough had happened during 1996 to last a while but by the time 1997 came along he was saying to his wife in the new year that he couldn't see his mother-in-law lasting much longer because there was so much wrong with her. She had given up eating despite Jessica's cajoling her to eat more and look after herself better and also Mary's will power to overcome her weakening physical state was beginning to wane.

Jessica and Me

Chapter Forty-Four

After the New Year Don was out of work but he kept in touch with the agents and in the next few weeks an agent rang to say there was a job in Woking. It was peculiar because when Don was working near Guilford he used to pass this particular company. Would think to it would be good if he could work there because the journey was closer to home and hear he was going for an interview. The company offered him a job as a contract draughtsman. Don accepted working for a young project engineer but the atmosphere seemed strange with some of the staff keeping themselves in a cliché tending to ignore Don although he wasn't worried and concentrated on his job but there was one guy who although he was reasonably friendly towards Don he didn't like contractors working in the office. He took every chance to drop him in it if any mistakes were found although Don was not involved this engineer would try to blame Don. This made life difficult for him and Don could not see himself lasting to long at the company. Finally the guy found something he thought he could pin on Don that would make the management take notice and sack him which was exactly what happened although Don felt he wasn't to blame. He accepted it because he didn't like the companies attitude and was glad to leave knowing that he would get another job but it wasn't going to be easy.
   As usual jobs came in drips and drabs but Don was able to survive albeit only just but he was earning enough money to think about going on holiday.
   The other casualty in Dons family was his pet dog who was getting old at 14 years of age. After suffering from diabetes for years which affected her eye sight making it difficult to see the end of life was very tragic. Don and Diana went to the supermarket for their weekly shopping and as usual left the dog in the living room with all the doors open. Their daughter was on her way home but before she arrived the dog somehow managed to bump into the door leading to the kitchen where she could get to the water bowl. The door closed trapping her in the living room stopping her from getting to the water

Jessica and Me

which she needed to help her survive. By the time Julie got home the dog was in a coma. She quickly picked her up and rushed to the vet. At the same time Julie managed to get in touch with her parents and they also rushed to the vet. When they met their daughter she said the vet was trying to bring the dog round to keep her in for observation, they were told to get in touch the next day. Don realised that the news wouldn't be good and tried to warn his wife and daughter but when the vet told them the next day that the dog had to be put down because she was suffering too much. The whole family were in shock and Don found that he couldn't stop crying which was unusual for him because he didn't usually show his feelings. The last time he did such a thing was when his father passed away. On reflection Don realised it was the best thing that could have happened because the dog had a good life and it would have been cruel to keep her alive with all the suffering she was going through towards the end. There was a song that was popular at the time being sung by Natalie Cole called Miss You Like Crazy that seemed to strike a chord with Don and Diana. Every time they heard it they would think of their pet dog filling them with emotion.

Jessica and Me

Chapter Forty-Five

The following month Diana and Don went to see her mother as usual on a Sunday afternoon. They knocked on the door but there was no answer. Diana used her door key to get into the house. Mary wasn't in the living room where she usually sat and when Diana went upstairs she found her mother on the floor in a coma. Apparently she had suffered a severe stroke. The couple phoned for an ambulance to take her to hospital but when the doctor examined her they didn't give her much chance of pulling through the stroke. Don said that if his mother-in-law did come out of the coma she would have a life of a vegetable and Mary wouldn't like that.

After a few days Mary was still in a coma. She was having to be fed through a tube but in her sub conscious mind she was still in control because towards the end she was pushing the tube away and the doctor said if Mary wasn't eating then there wasn't much they could do and later that day she passed away.

Soon after the funeral Don found himself out of work but after all that had happened he said to Diana 'We should go on a holiday.' Dons best friends Alan and his wife Karen said they wouldn't mind going with them so Diana booked a flight to visit the Czech Republic in a hotel in Prague. When the group arrived at the airport they hired a car and made their way to the hotel which was very good even it felt as though they were in the 1950's. The country had just became independent after years of Soviet Russian rule which had held them back from being up to date with other counties. The people were very friendly and the food and drink was very cheap. The architecture was very old world and Don was taking loads of photos of the buildings. They went on a tram which was also very cheap. Alan liked the tram system because there were plenty about making it very easy to travel around the city, if they needed to change trams there was always one coming along. As they were walking round the town Don said 'We should look for a restaurant for a midday meal' and just as he said it a man came out of nowhere saying 'I can show you the way to a restaurant'. Don was a bit wary but the man was similar age to them

Jessica and Me

and seemed to be respectable. The group went with him to a shopping area where he showed them to a basement. Don wondered what he let himself into but when they entered the restaurant the atmosphere was great. Don liked the back ground music of Frank Sinatra records being played. While they were eating a group of Germans came in and the waiter quickly found room for them to sit but one of the women wasn't satisfied with the seating arrangement. She abruptly walked out and all the rest of the Germans followed her. Don thought to himself that was how the second-world-war had begun with everyone just following their leader which at that time happened to be Hitler.

When it was time to fly back home the group packed up and got in the car to travel to the airport. As they made their way out of Prague Alan who was driving noticed the lack of directions but Don pointed out a sign showing the way but after that there were no more signs and they became lost going round in circles. By this time it was getting close to the time when they should have reached the airport. Eventually Don asked Alan to stop the car and he got out to stop a passing cyclist and with a bit of sign language made himself understood by showing them the way to the terminal. Every one sighed with relief as they eventually arrived at the airport. Alan and Don could not understand why there was only one sign post directing them to the airport. When they got over the trauma of thinking they were going to miss the flight they had a good laugh about it.

When Don got back home the telephone rang and an agent that he had never heard of was offering him a job in the Windsor area. Don was glad but bewildered because he wondered where the agent had found his name. Thinking about it he realised that the agent must have been in touch with other agents he had contacted in his search for a job. He didn't dwell on it too long and quickly put it behind him and went for the interview where he was offered the job and he started the following week. The work was interesting using Caterpillar Engines in sea and river boats plus fitting them onto generators for converting gas from landfill sites to electricity to be incorporated into the main grid making it become renewable energy. To prepare the

Jessica and Me

drawings meant that site surveys had to be carried out to enable a decision to be reached where to position the generators. Don had only been working for the new company for a month when the awful news came on the radio at the end of August. Princess Diana had been killed in a car crash in Paris. Everyone throughout the Nation were grief stricken as the Princess was very popular throughout the world and people couldn't believe she had been taken from them in such away.

The Royal family were on holiday in Scotland and didn't seem to share the sadness that everyone else were showing. The area outside Buckingham Palace was awash with flowers and notes expressing peoples sorrow, people were gathering outside the Palace being very subdued but beginning to become very angry at the attitude of the Royal Family. None of the national flags were at half-mast and no one from the family appeared because they had decided to stay in Scotland for the time being.

It took the action of the Prime Minister Tony Blair to send a message to the Queen asking her to comment on the Princess's death. The family travelled from Scotland to show themselves in London and witness the effect that the people were showing outside the Palace. Eventually the Queen and her family did arrive in London although it had taken five days for the Queen and her husband to see the huge amount of flowers outside the gates to get the message loud and clear and the Queen decided to go on TV to express her condolences for the Princess. She was showing the distress and sadness that everyone else had felt since the so called accident.

The police in Paris said the car crash was an accident but there was a general opinion amongst the public and Diana's friends that felt she had been murdered because of her relationship with her boyfriend Dodi. His father also was sure that the crash had been caused in suspicious circumstances.

The gossip in the newspapers showed that the Princess was going to become engaged to Dodi. The Royal family and the Arabs didn't want this to happen because the Royals didn't like Dodi and his

Jessica and Me

father. On the other hand the Arabs did not like a Muslim associating with a Western Princess.

The friends and the public felt there had been a cover up. It didn't help the situation when it was reported in the media that it took the ambulance over an hour to reach the hospital that night when it should have taken a matter of minute because the hospital was close by. Also by the next morning the scene of the crash on the road had been washed clean so any evidence had been lost.

The police said the chauffeur had been drinking and in their opinion caused the crash but it didn't convince anyone. The video showed him acting in a normal way prior to the crash when the group were getting ready in the hotel to travel to Dodi's flat on the other side of town. Experts said that if the chauffeur had that much alcohol in his blood then people would have seen the driver being unsteady on his feet and slurring his speech but this wasn't happening.

The media didn't help because when the Princess and her bodyguard left the hotel with Dodi they gave chase on their motorbikes to find out where they were going. The driver sped off but took a different route to the flat which seemed suspicious and as the car entered a tunnel. Witnesses said the car came into contact with a small white fiat which disappeared after the crash.

When the coffin was flown home from France accompanied by Prince Charles there was a huge out pouring of grief and a feeling of disbelief that she was dead. The funeral was shown on TV all around the world. Elton John sang a eulogy which was originally a song about Marilyn Munro but he changed the words to suit the occasion and her brother spoke of how he would miss her and blaming the press for causing the crash and at the end the people outside the Cathedral clapped and cheered. The dignitary inside clapped but only after the applause from outside. It was a very emotional day which hadn't been seen since Winston Churchill's funeral.

The coffin was carried onto the hoarse and it drove through the streets lined by crowds throwing flowers onto the car for miles until it reached the family burial ground where it was laid to rest on an island in the middle of the lake.

Jessica and Me

The speculation on how Princess Diana died would go on for years and a lot of witnesses disappeared or died during the investigation. There was one theory that a blinding light was shone in the drivers eyes which made him crash but this was discounted early on in the investigation. Over the years Dodi`s father wouldn`t except that the crash was an accident. He told his security personnel to keep on investigating to find evidence that would prove that his son and the Princess were murdered. It was difficult because the police were convinced it was an accident.

Jessica and Me

Chapter Forty-Six

As a teenager Dons daughter decided to go ice skating with girls from her school and at first she struggled to master the art of skating but the other girls had joined a class to learn skating on the ice and Julie went with them and although it was difficult to start with she soon caught up with the rest of the girls and began to enjoy skating and made good friends and they went to pubs and they also went on holidays abroad and had a good time. Being a teenager was a good experience for Julie because she overcame her inhabitations and became a much more confident person.

By 1998 Dons daughter had been out with a few boyfriends but none of them had lasted and she complained to her father about being lonely because she couldn't get a boyfriend. She felt unwanted because most of her friends had either got boyfriends or were married. Don gave the problem some thought and said `You should join a club to get to know people of your own age again. ` Julie said `I have given up ice skating and I don't know of any other clubs that are suitable enough and I am not that keen to go to one.` Don looked through magazine adverts and saw a rowing club just down the road where they lived. He said `You should try it. ` Julie still wasn't happy with the idea but Don didn't give up and said `I will take you to the club and I will stay around while you investigated it.` After a while Julie came out and after some discussion and cajoling by her father she agreed that she would give the rowing a chance. At first Julie was nervous getting into the boat but the girls were very helpful and eventually she managed to learn the art of rowing.

The social side of the club was good for Julie. Everyone was very friendly and willing to show her the basic requirement of rowing. Julie was glad her father persuaded her to join the club but she did complain that the rowing caused her to have calluses on her hands. It was a small price to pay because she had found a sport to get involved in. Despite her fears Julie began to enjoy the company of the crew and became good at rowing and slowly the calluses

Jessica and Me

disappeared after her hands became hardened with the handling of the oars.

Soon after joining the club Julie went out to a bistro with a girl friend called Lizzy. While they were chatting she noticed a group of young men across the restaurant and one of them kept looking at them. Julie thought he was looking at her friend but Lizzy said `He is looking at you.` and said `You should encourage him to come over to talk to you.` Julie who wasn't normally shy said `I feel awkward could you go and talk to him on my behalf.` Lizzy went over and brought the boy back and introduced him as Andy to Julie and to her surprise they hit it off straight away and spent the rest of the evening in each other's company and Andy asked `Could I see you again.` they made a date to meet each other the next week end.

From that night things began to change for Julie and she found that she didn't have any time left to go rowing so she gave up being a member of the club. She concentrated on building up the relationship with her new found boyfriend Andy. He told Julie `I broke up with my old girlfriend but it was some time ago. `. He had forgotten about her and said `It is you I want to see and get to know. ` As far as he was concerned it was love at first sight and he hoped it was the same for Julie.

The couple had been going out with each other for some time before Julie introduced Andy to her parents who were pleased that their daughter had at last found some one that she could be happy with and begin to build a lasting relationship.

Jessica and Me

Chapter Forty-Seven

During 1998 Frank Sinatra was Eighty Two years old and had retired from singing because he had fallen off the stage in his last show when he was Eighty years old. He hadn't really recovered. He was also suffering from kidney trouble. Earlier Don had read a book about the singer. He came to the conclusion if only half of what he had read was true then it was a wonder Frank had lived for so long. According to the book Frank had always drank a lot during his life. He had also been with a lot of women. He had been married four times with three children from his first marriage to Nancy and although he loved her, it was another woman called Ava Gardner that stole his heart but they were too much alike and it didn't last. He made a record when they broke up singing `I am a fool to want you` which was very poignant and touched many people who had gone through the same experience.

Toward the middle of the year Frank had been in and out of hospital and each time his fans thought he wouldn't make it but he was a tough character. He kept getting well enough to go home but even he couldn't keep going and in the end with all his family and friends around him he passed away.

When a vote was cast to see who the voice of the century it was Frank Sinatra who beat all the other singers including Bing Crosby. Nat King Cole came second.

It was all ways alleged that Frank was associated with the Mafia but he denied it but being born in Hoboken in New York it wasn't surprising that he should be linked with the Mob because that area in the early 1900's was steeped in crimes that involved the Mafia. Franks mother was involved in illegal activity carrying out abortions so he had been bought up in the middle of gangsters shooting each other. Toward the end of his life Frank was involved in a lot of charity work which didn't get much publicity because his fourth wife organised it while he was putting on shows in Las Vegas.

The shows in Las Vegas involved four characters called the Rat pack of which Frank was nicked named `The Chairman of the Board.

Jessica and Me

` Others in of the group were Dean Martin, Sammy Davis Jnr and Peter Lawford. They would entertain by clowning around and joking with each other and throw in the occasional song which the audience loved.

By 1999 Jessica was 85 years old but she was very good for her age pottering about in her small garden and walking into Twickenham to do shopping. Don would phone her every day to make sure she was ok.

A friend of Jessica who lived in Fulham used to go to see her in the flat and she also had friends in the social club. One woman she was particularly friendly with was in a wheel chair and they would have a good laugh but she was in ill health. Just when Jessica was getting to know her very well she took a turn for the worst and passed away. This upset Jessica very badly. She began to stop going to the club because she thought that if she got to know other people that well then they would probably die as well.

People were surprised when they discovered that Jessica was 85 years old because she didn`t look or act her age because of her face having a smooth skin. Her hair was grey it was curly and when she had her hair done at the hair dressers it looked very attractive. She was still walking very well. Dons friend Alan said `Jessica must have come from good stock. ` Nobody knew what the family was like on her mother's side. On her father's side of the family they seemed to have longevity but that may have come from her step mother because the father died when he was in his mid-forty's.

The fact that nobody seemed to know about Jessica's past intrigued Don. He said `I will try to find out what happen when you were born. ` If her real sister was still alive he would try to contact her. Don was busy at work and put off the search saying that he would begin looking for the sister and her family when he retired.

Jessica and Me

With the advent of computers being more affordable enabling people to buy and install them in their homes it was becoming easier to look into their families past. A lot of companies were springing up offering their services at a price to help search the computer to create a family tree. They also hunted for heirs that were entitled to money that had not been claimed because they had lost touch with their families or didn`t know that their relation had any money.

Jessica and Me

Chapter Forty-Eight

By year 2000 Julie's boyfriend proposed to her and she said yes. Andy introduced Julie to his family and they were surprised that he was getting married but liked Julie with her outgoing personality and welcomed her into the family. They would help organise the wedding but the couple said that they weren't short of money because they had managed to save from their earnings.

Andy and Julie arranged their own wedding by organising the cars and the reception in a local hotel and located a vicar in a nearby church where Don and Diana lived. There was one hitch in the arrangements which nearly spoilt the day when they found out that the chauffeur driven wedding car was a sham because the owner was fiddling the arrangement of the cars by promising to supply a classic 30's style. He charged extra money for it but when it came to the day he came up with an excuse that the car had broken down and he supplied an ordinary Bentley to take the bride to the church. It was found out later that the classic car didn't exist after the wedding the police became involved because one of the guests was a policemen and when he heard Julie complain about the treatment they received he decided to investigate and when the fiddle was discovered the owner was prosecuted and fined for deception. He was lucky that he wasn't sent to prison. Apart from the transport problem everything went well on the wedding day and everyone enjoyed themselves at the reception by dancing the night away and nobody got drunk.

The couple saved up enough money to put a deposit on a two bedroom semi-detached house in Basingstoke. To offset the lack of children they bought a puppy that needed as much care as having a baby.

David's wife announced she was pregnant half way through the year and she travelled to Slovakia to tell her parents who were over joyed with the news and they embraced David and celebrated by inviting all their relatives and friends to a party. Everyone made a toast wishing the couple well and wishing it to be a baby boy. Anna's family was large and she was the youngest among three sisters and three boys.

Jessica and Me

There were also a number of cousins and school friends plus the neighbours who made a huge gathering and the party went on for several days.

Everyone celebrated the year 2000 in their own special way. The Government had given the go ahead to build a Dome to mark that year. It was initially a success the organisation let it down because it couldn't deal with the crowds of people attending the big New Year party. There were queues outside waiting to get in which took hours to clear. The building soon became a white elephant falling into debt and despite efforts to find a use that would be sustainable it remained empty for a long time.

Jessica and Me

Chapter Forty-Nine

In 2001 suicide aircraft attacked the World Trade Centre and the Pentagon leaving untold injured or dead. The office towers being 1350ft tall were hit by the aircraft causing them to eventually collapse and were to known as ground Zero.
President George W Bush vowed to hunt down the terrorist and this eventually led to war known as the occupation of Iraq.
By March 2001 Anna gave birth to a healthy baby boy and the couple named him David. His father decided to look for a three bedroom house which was easier said than done because houses were very expensive in the South East of England. He hadn't saved enough money for a deposit although he had the flat to sell which helped but not enough to buy a decent home for his family.
After extensive searching the couple found a three bedroom semi-detached property that needed some work to bring it up to the standard that suited them. Don said `The house is too small. ` David went ahead with the sale after he had sold the flat. The family moved in but they soon found out that Don was correct in his assumption but David said `It has potential to be big enough for me when the garage is knocked down to make way for extra rooms. ` Don could see the point but realised it wouldn't happen overnight especially if his son was going to carry out the modifications. The couple did manage to install a new kitchen in the first year so at least that was one job completed. The rest of the modifications would have to wait because the cost of the kitchen was very expensive and their wasn't money left to do anything else for the time being. David went out for a drink with his friend who had been his best man at his wedding and after a few drinks his friend broke down and told David that he was having trouble with his wife because she was going with another man and although he still loved her he was thinking of leaving her. David tried to calm his friend down but it was difficult in the circumstances and the best that they could work out between them was to have a meeting between the friend and his wife and try to see if they could

Jessica and Me

come to some arrangement where they could still sort their problems out and stay living together.

In September Don decided to take his wife and mother to Venice for a holiday. They rented a first floor flat in a town called Treviso a few miles away from Venice and they also rented a car to enable them to drive into the outskirts of the City. Don liked the architecture and canals but soon realised it was a tourist trap with everything very expensive everywhere they went. One day it poured with rain and they hurried into a restaurant to get out of the rain and order a meal. The dinner wasn't extra special just pasta and a bottle of wine between them and at the end of the meal they were shocked to see how much it cost for the amount of food they consumed. Venice with its canals and great architecture was superb. Don was glad that the place was everything he thought it would be although he wished that he had chosen another place to stay because although the flat was very good as far as the rooms were concerned the one thing that let it down was the smell of drains in the bathroom was over powering and Diana had to put disinfection down the toilet and the basin.

This was the last time Don took his mother on holiday because although she was good for her age she would take the mickey out of people thinking it was funny but it was really embarrassing for Don and Diana and they agreed that enough was enough. The other reason was the worry over Jessica's age because if she had an accident abroad and landed in hospital then it would be difficult to deal with the problem and get her back to the UK.

In 2002 Diana was saying 'I don't want to go on holidays that involved driving a lot of miles.' The couple came up with the idea to investigate going on a cruise ship that would be good because the ship would take them to different ports. They could then travel by coach to places they wanted to see. Diana brought back some brochures from the travel agent and the couple agreed to go on a cruise line carried 2500 passengers. The ship cruised around the Mediterranean and they booked a seven night cruise to ports in France and Italy. At each port they booked an excursion to the various towns and cities where they hadn't been to before. It was

Jessica and Me

made even more interesting because there was a guide to show them different parts of the town and sometimes they visited wine tasting and museums etc. or just wandered around the town site seeing and shopping.

The people on the ship were very friendly and Don only had to ask if this was their first cruise and they would open up with their experiences. Sometimes they would chat for hours while they were at the dining table or in the Jacuzzi. This holiday was ideal because it gave complete freedom to choose how they could spend the time on the ship and when the couple went ashore.

The holiday was very successful and Don said `I will go again.` Some of the people on the ship had been on several cruises and it was becoming more popular with other cruise lines popping up increasing the choice of ships that people could go on their holidays. The competition between the cruise lines was very high and increasing the number of ships entering the ports more than ever.

The cruise line was a small company with ships that had their cabins converted to suit people on holiday, including other facilities such as a theatre and a gymnasium etc. As far as Don was concerned it was a good ship because he didn`t know any different. One night there was a storm which made the ship toss and roll. When he complained to the Captain about the ship being unstable he said `It is very safe and the weather for that time of year is unusual' Don and Diana must have been satisfied with the ship because they went on holiday three times. On the last occasion they made the mistake of being on the bottom deck at the rear of the ship which was very noisy and vibrated violently when it was manoeuvring to moor alongside port first thing in the morning. In future they would stay in cabins that were in the position of mid-ship and on the upper decks which wasn`t noisy although when the couple went on other cruise lines they were more up to date and therefore ships with a better design of stabilisers.

Jessica and Me

Chapter Fifty

From November 2002 to early January 2003 it rained nearly every day making the river Thames constantly run very high and threatening to burst its banks. Don's house was about 150metre from the river and just after the New Year they were woken to urgent knocking on the door. It was the early hours of the morning and as he looked out the window there were a group of people from the Thames Authority warning him about the river flooding the area. In fact it was already in their back garden and the water quickly began to surround the house. The officers gave sand bags to place around the house to help stop the water getting into the house. Fortunately the house was built on foundations that were above the flood level of 1947 when huge areas around Staines were flooded. This time the water flooded the garden and the garage but it didn't get into the house. The water level carried on rising for two days and although Don and Diana were safe in the house they couldn't get the car out of the garage. On the third day Diana phoned her daughter and asked her if they could stay in her house until the water subsided. Julie agreed to help by getting as close to the house as possible with their car but they would have to wade through the water to enable them to be picked up.

As a precaution Don and Diana re-arranged the furniture to a higher level. The couple put boots on and walked through the flood. Just as they reached the road Julie and Andy who had left their car about half a mile away were walking towards Don. At the same time a neighbour in a 4x4 car came along and offered them a lift to their car. Don thanked the neighbour as they reached the end of the flood they found the car to enable them to carry on to Julie's house ten miles away. Andy said `You can borrow my car to travel to work until the flood receded. ` After three days Dons neighbour phoned to say the flood had receded and it was safe to return to their house.

The flood covered a huge area and people were very angry at the damage it caused to property especially if they lived close to the Thames and the insurance companies were saying that homes weren't covered for flood damage especially when the Environment

Jessica and Me

Agency were saying that the flood was due to natural causes. Meetings were held in the local halls by the Agency to explain to the people why they had been flooded. When the locals heard that the Agency said the cause of the flood was due to heavy rain making the ground so wet that it couldn't absorb such a great amount of water fast enough to let the river flow as normal. This didn't go down very well at the meeting because no one agreed with the theory and called for an independent enquiry to be set up to investigate the cause of the flood.

In the past when the river burst its banks it mainly effected the area around Maidenhead where wealthy people lived by the river who were in show business and managing directors and they had a lot of influence with the local council and pressure was brought to bear on the Environment Agency to design and build a flood relief to stop properties being flooded. A by-pass river called the Jubilee was approved by the council to enable money to be allocated to the Agency to build a deep channel to run along as a bypass to the Thames. This seemed a good idea until the time came when the water began to overflow and burst its banks bringing the by-pass into action but it soon filled up which meant that there were now two rivers flowing at full bore into the river once it flowed passed Maidenhead. By now the water flowing towards the Windsor and Staines area was running very fast. The locks couldn't cope with the huge amount of water especially when it reached the old Chertsey lock which was acting as a bottle neck causing the river to burst its banks and spill over into the surrounding areas.

The area around Maidenhead was relatively flood free but this didn't help further downstream. What was really needed was a proper overhaul of the locks prior to Marlow and all the way down the river to include the Chertsey lock as well but that didn't happen because there wasn't enough money in the budget after the Jubilee by-pass river had been built.

The Environment Agency never admitted that they had got it wrong when it came to managing the flood and it took a long time before work was carried out on renovating the locks.

Jessica and Me

Chapter Fifty-One

After various negotiations and demands by the International community America pushed the UN to give the go ahead to invade Iraq and in March 2003 a multi-national force invaded the country after the UN Security Council passed a resolution calling on Saddam Hussein to completely co-operate with the UN weapons inspectors to verify that he was not in possession of Weapons of Mass Destruction. Saddam refused to comply and said that if his country was attacked then it would be the mother of all wars. Although WMDs could not be found the inspectors said that it could not verify that Iraq didn't have WMDs when the troops entered the country they found that there were buildings where the weapons could be built and this would have been carried out when and if sanctions had been lifted.

Towards the end of the year Jessica tripped and fell outside her flat fortunately a neighbour found her and called an ambulance. When she reached the hospital the doctor examined her eye and said she needed stitches to repair the cut over her eye. When Don reached the A&E dept. his mother had just come out of surgery. Jessica's eye was black and blue from the fall. There and then Don decided that he had to find a place nearer to where he lived so that if anything happened in the future he could get to her quicker than if she was still at the flat in Twickenham. Diana managed to get in touch with the council to find out if her mother-in-law could be able to rent a flat in a sheltered accommodation. To her surprise the council said they would be able to find a suitable place for Jessica but they needed to interview Don and Diana to find out what would suit Jessica to enable the correct flat to be allocated to her.

Although Jessica wanted to be nearer to her son and daughter-in-law she wasn't too happy about being in a sheltered flat because she thought it was like being in an old peoples home. She did not like being round so many old people even though she was old herself. Don had to talk to his mother for a long time before she came round to the idea to accept that it was the best place for her.

Jessica and Me

By the beginning of 2004 the council found two flats that Don could investigate the suitability for his mother to live in. One flat was too far away but the other one was only two miles away in Egham. Don and Diana took Jessica to see the flat and she was pleasantly surprised at the size of the rooms and was pleased that it was close to where Don lived. After some persuasion it became clear to Jessica that this was the only option to stay in the flat. Eventually she agreed that this would be the best place for her because there would be a warden on hand to keep an eye on her and she could go down to the main lounge and have coffee and play bingo with the other women in the flats.

A few months later the Warden went to interview Jessica to see if she was happy and also that he was happy with her health and attitude to live in sheltered house. Soon after the meeting the Warden informed Don that there was a vacancy in a first floor flat and advised him to see if it suited his mother. It had one bedroom a lounge, a kitchen and a bathroom. When Jessica saw the flat she said it was ok although she was concerned that it was on the first floor. She was worried about going down the stairs to the main lounge area. Don said it would be ok because there was a lift she could use if she couldn't use the stairs.

The building was in a very nice setting with gardens surrounding the building and Jessica could see the garden from the lounge window and she could walk around as well. The shopping centre was a half a mile away in an old worldly high street. Jessica was reasonably happy with the area and agreed to leave her home in Twickenham realising she would be closer to her son and daughter-in-law. Although Jessica was concerned about the people being old and some of them in bad health she was beginning to realise that she was a similar age to them but more active she got on well with some of the women.

Diana was nearly 60 years old and Julie decided to arrange a surprise party for her mother. She invited as many friends and relations as she could and told her father to keep the party a secret which was very difficult to do but Don managed to keep it from his

Jessica and Me

wife until the last moment. Fortunately the weather was good on the day of the party most of the guests were able to attend. It was on their shopping day and Don kept his wife away from the house as long as he could to let his daughter get everything ready by arranging the food and drink and re-position the furniture. Towards the time of the party Diana had completed the shopping. She told Don she was ready to go home but it was early and he had to delay his wife to enable them all to arrive to surprise her but some of guest hadn't arrived. There was still some time to go and Don was struggling to delay getting home and he slowed the car as he came closer to the house. Diana was now wondering why her husband was driving so slow and told him to hurry up because she wanted a cup of tea and begin cooking the evening meal. Don couldn't hold out any longer and eventually drove to the front of the house just as some of the guest were arriving. When Diana saw them she asked him 'Why are all the people going into the house,' Don mumbled some excuse and managed to keep Diana from entering the house until everyone got ready to surprise his wife. When she finally appeared all the guests shouted happy birthday and Diana broke down and cried with joy and thanked everyone for coming to make her day. The party was a huge success and the weather was sunny and hot to enable people to sit in the garden. Some of them Diana had not seen for ages.

Jessica and Me

Chapter Fifty-Two

In 2005 Don was working on a project that was on a site in London, there was only Don and a Senior Project Engineer working on the job which was too much for them to keep up with so the manager decided to employ another engineer to help spread the load. His name was Dave and he was introduced to Don to enable them to work together on the project. Dave hadn't worked for the company that long and he came into the middle of the project. Don brought him up to date with the outstanding work that was left to complete the contract. Dave was pleased to be working with Don because they got on well with each other. The information Don gave enabled Dave to continue and keep the job running smoothly and any problems that occurred could be dealt with in an orderly fashion.

Towards the end of the project Dave was diagnosed with cancer of the liver and although he was suffering from the decease he continued working. After a while the cancer was getting worse and it was effecting Dave's work but the management didn't seem to care. They carried on pressuring him to finish the project to the extent that Dave was making mistakes in handling the maintenance manuals. Don and the other people in the drawing office had to help finish the job. It was soon after that problem that Dave had a relapse and was taken into hospital and after a few days his cancer got worse. He passed away during the night. When Don heard the sad news he broke down with grief and the supervisor sent him home to get over the tragedy. Don was disgusted with the attitude of the way the Management had treated his friend and he began finding a way to retire at the end of the year.

Don's mother had always said she had a real sister. He began trying to find a way to look into the past and see if there was some way he could find the sister. He soon found that it wasn't going to be easy because the sister was born after the 1901 and that was when the census stopped. It seemed he would have to wait until the 1911 census was published. He decided to leave the search for a while but said to himself that when he had more time during his retirement that he would begin to search again.

Jessica and Me

As Christmas was a few months away Don informed the management where he worked that he wanted to retire by end of the year. They didn't want him to go and said `You will probably stay on because you won't know what to do with yourself. Don said `I will take up water colour painting. ` He definitely wanted to stop work because it was affecting his health. Meanwhile Don carried on working and once again the company involved him in a major project hoping it would keep him busy but Don worked very hard on the project. He asked the manager to let the other draughtsmen help him and he agreed. The supervisor let Don take over but was a bit scornful saying that Don was the boss now and it was down to him to finish the job. Don gave the details to the draughtsmen to carry on with the drawings. One of the worries was that when the supervisor did the drawings he wasn't very good. He would make mistakes and one of the drawings he managed to get the scale wrong making it difficult to fit on a layout. This was only one of the problems because he had a record of making minor mistakes which annoyed the manager. He used to complain to Don about the supervisors attitude but Don would say `He is busy working to be retired.` The management wouldn't agree so the supervisor kept on making errors hoping they would change their minds.

By July 2005 Terrorist planted bombs in London. As people went to work on the public transport two bombs exploded in underground trains and one blew up a double decker bus in Tavistock Square. The MI5 new that an attack was being planned but didn't know where or when it would take place. The explosions caused many deaths and the fire brigade took a long time to rescue the wounded. It was a dark day for the people of London and it would take a long time before the commuter's regained confidence in travelling on the public transport.

A week before Christmas the management arranged to take Donald to dinner to celebrate his time at the company and show their appreciation of all the work he had done in the past. They also bought a gift which was an easel to use when he was painting. Don was taken by surprise by their generosity because he was only a contractor and usually this sort of treatment was reserved for staff

Jessica and Me

members. On Christmas Eve every one gathered round to toast Don and wish him well in his retirement. Some of the managers made a speech about Dons achievements. They were still wishing that he would stay and carry on working for them but he thanked them all for their gratitude. He said `It is the right time to go especially while I am on top of my game. `

By March 2006 Don reached his 65th birthday and he was happy to be retired because he was keeping busy creating water colour paintings, going for walks and working in the garden.

Don was also looking after his grandchildren when Anna was working. He also had more time to look into his mother's past by finding information on the internet. He was also going to the local church where they had details on their computers and on micro films that went back to the nineteenth century. Don found a lot of information but not enough to find out about his mother's real sister. The lady in the church said he should go on a site called Rootschat.com to see if anyone could shed some light on finding the sister. Don managed to find the site on the computer and left a message asking if anyone could help him in his search for the sister and after few days a lady from Ireland left a message to say she could help if he sent a copy of the birth certificate of his mother and the sister. He got in touch with the births and death office and for a small fee they sent him the birth certificate for the sister. The certificate showed that she was born in 1910 and her name was Victoria and like Dons mother she was born in Fulham.

After Don sent the information to his contact in Ireland she came back saying that the sister had married when she was eighteen years old and moved to the other side of London in Essex. She had two grown up sons. Don decided to write to her family to request a meeting. The husband replied saying that `I will meet you on your own because I do not want my wife to get too involved. ` Don asked why and was told that the reason they moved to Essex was to get away from Victoria`s father. Don said `The father would not be at the meeting. ` This appeared to satisfy the husband. Meanwhile Janice discovered more information about the existence of a third daughter

Jessica and Me

called Alice who lived in Watford. This came as huge surprise to Don because his mother had always led him to believe that there was only one sister. Now that there was an extra sister Don wanted to meet her as well before all the sisters came to the end of their lives. This was not going to be easy because of all the animosity that happened in the past. Don had not told his mother about the sisters and began to arrange the party to get them altogether. Don decided to hold the meeting in his garden under a canopy and arranged for food and drink to be supplied by a specialist contractor. First to arrive was Alice along with her family, her grown children were in show business and weren't short of money. When Victoria arrived with her family without her husband it was presumed that he couldn't forget the past. Meanwhile Diana and Julie made their way to bring Jessica to the house but still keeping her in the dark about the reunion. When Jessica came into the garden and was confronted with her sisters she gasped in surprise wondering who these women were and when she was introduced to them as her sisters she broke down in tears and cried with joy at the news. After everyone got over the shock the party got going with the sisters talking about their lives and wondering if they had known each other when they were young if their lives had turned out any different. Victoria and Alice said that their mother kept it a secret on why she had given Jessica away and it was never spoken about from that day. Don asked if any photos of his real Grandmother existed. Alice opened her handbag and gave him a picture of her Mother. Don was surprised to see how the sisters took after their Mother, now he could bring to an end his search for the family.

Don also looked into his father's family and managed to find where his great-grandfather was born. His mother had always said that there was Scottish ancestry in the family but Don found that his grandfather had been born in Clapham and his great grandfather was born in Ware Hertfordshire in 1803.

Diana's family came from Jewish stock in the 1800's. Don did not mind because he wasn't racist and believed that everyone in the world should get on with one another. He often thought how the world

Jessica and Me

would have been if Hitler had embraced the Jews instead of persecuting them. If he had managed to use the Jews business skills to help Germany to get over the problems of the First World War by building up their resources and becoming a peaceful people then there would have probably been no Second World War and everything would have been completely different from there on.

Everything seemed to be working well for Don until he came into contact with the insurance company that were dealing with his private pension. Don decided to list the help of a finance consultant to get the best deal out of the insurance people but it wasn't easy because they were delaying supplying him with the information he needed to be advised what would be the best arrangement. When they eventually came up with the amount of money he could put towards his pension it wasn't anywhere near what he was expecting. It took about six month to finalise the deal and in the meantime Don had to survive on his state pension and all the agro of dealing with the insurance company, Eventually everything worked out for Don but it was hard work getting a result because the company kept misunderstanding what he wanted. It took an email that Don had to cobble together to spell out exactly what the problem was. It showed the difference between what he wanted and what they were prepared to give him. When the company investigated and added up the figures again they realised where the mistakes were being made.

Diana was still working as a receptionist but she was having trouble dealing with the company because they wanted her to go for training to obtain a certificate to enable her to continue working for them. Don thought it wasn't necessary but he asked his wife to get the company to send her a copy of the training manual. When Diana received the manual and read through it, all the contents referred to being a security officer which coincided with the company's main occupation seeing as they were employed to guard property. The only reference made at being a receptionist was a paragraph saying that 'If there were people in the reception area causing trouble and threatening people then the receptionist should call on the services of the guard to sort the problem out and eject the trouble maker.' Don said 'It is a

Jessica and Me

waste of your time.` The company was only insisting on the training because the security firm were probably getting extra money to train their employees even if they hadn`t anything to do with security. Diana said `I do not want to go in for the training. `When the company insisted on the training she decided to hand in her notice. This meant that Don couldn`t rely on his wife's earnings for a while but about three months later the company got in touch with Diana. Saying she could work for them on a part time basis filling in for the receptionist while they were on holiday or off sick. There was no mention of obtaining a certificate so Diana accepted the job and it carried on that way for about three years. The extra income meant that the couple could carry on having holidays and afford little extras including thinking of buy another car.

　Don remembered when he was working the supervisor said to Peter `A new draughtsman is taking over the work that Don is doing. ` Straight away Peter said `Don would be a hard act to follow and everyone would miss him when he retired.` At that point the supervisors jaw dropped open with shock at what Peter had said and he never tried to replace Don knowing that he had made a big mistake in suggesting the replacement.

Jessica and Me

Chapter Fifty-Three

Don noticed his wife wasn't walking to well in fact it was more of a shuffle than how she used to walk. Over the years Diana had slowed down from her normal pace of being a fast walker but Don put that down to her age. The latest problem appeared to be much worse and he eventually persuaded his wife to see the local doctor. The doctor examined Diana's reflexes which appeared to be ok but as a precaution the doctor referred her to a neuron specialist. After a few months the hospital sent a letter giving Diana a date for an appointment and when the specialist did a quick examination similar to what the GP had given her she came to the conclusion that it was psychological saying `It was all in her mind and to come back in six months.`
After four months Diana wasn't improving so Don took her back to the hospital where the same doctor still said `The problem is still the same that is stopping you from walking properly. `Don was not satisfied so he took his wife to see the GP and asked for a councillor and a physiotherapist to see Diana. Meanwhile they decided to go on a cruise holiday thinking it might take her mind off her problems. It was a good break visiting Venice and the Greek Islands. Diana was not to bad taking part in excursions. She managed to dance albeit more of a shuffle but she did get up and try. When they finished the cruise and settled into their home everything seemed ok for the first few days but one morning while Diana was in the bathroom she cried out to Don saying `I am feeling dizzy and I can't walk properly.` Don had to help her back to their bed. When Don asked her what was wrong Diana said `I have read that my symptoms could be vertigo.` Don took his wife to see the doctor that morning and when the doctor asked Diana what was wrong with her she made the mistake of saying she thought it was vertigo. After a quick examination the doctor agreed with her. Diana shouldn't have said anything and let the doctor make her own mind up because now the course was set to go along with treating Dons wife to overcome vertigo when in fact they would find out later that it was more serious than that. The GP

Jessica and Me

gave Diana tablets to ease the dizziness and being sick bringing up bile but the tablets didn't seem to be helping. Diana was feeling worse and after her daughter complained about the lack of action by the doctor she referred her mother to a hospital near Twickenham. The specialist said `You should have a brain scan. ` Don said `It is what I have been asking the doctor to do months ago before my wife got worse. ` He was told it would be too expensive amounting to £700 but when he looked on the internet he found that cost was for a fall body scan. The cost would have only been £250 for a brain scan. Diana agreed to go for the scan but was told it would probably take about two months to get an appointment. This infuriated Don and he complained and asked the doctor to try and make it quicker. After two weeks Don managed to get the appointment brought forward to take place in a week.

When Don and Diana eventually went to the hospital for the scan they found that the scanner was on the back of a lorry outside the hospital. It had a lift to enable the wheelchair to be taken into the unit where the doctor asked Diana to lay down on a bed to be taken through a tunnel for the scan to take place. It took about forty five minutes to complete the scan and when it was over Don asked `How long will it take before my wife would get the results. ` He was told it would take ten days. In actual fact it took fourteen days but Don had to chase up the secretary to get an appointment with the consultant to see Diana.

When the couple went back to the hospital Diana was told `You have a slight swelling in the inner ear, I have referred you to a hospital in London. ` She was informed that it would take about one to two weeks before the consultant could see her but the next day the doctor phoned to say `You should be admitted into the London hospital today because you have a brain tumour. ` She needed an urgent operation to take the pressure off the tumour. Before Diana could get herself ready a bed manager rang to say `The wards are full and I can't arrange a bed for you but I will do my best to get you into the hospital as soon as possible. `

Jessica and Me

The next day a doctor from the previous hospital made a special trip to the London hospital. He managed to arrange for a bed to be made available for Diana and said `I have organised an ambulance to take your wife to the hospital. ` Within the hour an ambulance turned up but it was treating the call as an emergency and could only take Diana to the local hospital. To get Dons wife to the London hospital it took another ambulance to be arranged and when it eventually arrived at the A&E department the sister said there was a bed but it wasn`t ready and the couple had to wait five hours before Diana could get in the bed. By this time it was half past eleven in the evening. When the doctors examined Diana they said `An operation is needed to enable a tube called a shunt to be inserted into the brain. ` The tube would pass through the body to enable excess of fluid to be taken from the brain and distributed into the tummy. This would act as a bypass to relieve the pressure in the brain. The operation was carried out within two days of Diana being admitted into the hospital and it lasted four hours. A butterfly valve acting as a no return arrangement was connected to the tube as well. After four days Diana was allowed home but after a week she wasn`t feeling any better so she went back to the hospital and the doctor said `If you feel worse I will operate in two day's to remove the tumour. ` Diana was surprised that the op. could be achieved in such a short time but after the doctor saw the consultant and discussed the best way of treating her they decided to prescribe tablets to help stop her bringing up bile and stop the head aches being so painful. After further discussions the doctor said `You should come back in a week's to decide when the main operation should take place. ` When Diana went to see the consultant again he informed her that an operation could take place in January 2010 to cut out the tumour. Diana was advised about all the complications that might happen but the consultant stressed that this was only a precaution and the tumour was probably benign and it should be a successful operation.

In January 2009 Barak Obama took the oath to be sworn in as the President of the United States of America. He was the first black man to take his place in the White House and although he had been

Jessica and Me

elected on a large majority the republican party were against his policies especially the health reform bill and his stance in Iraq and his first year in office wouldn't be an easy one but he didn't give up saying he was elected over a four year period and intended to keep his promises on creating change in the way the country was being run.

After Christmas a date was set for the 18th January but when the day came Don phoned the ward to check if everything was ok to go to the hospital. He was told that the ward was full and the operation was cancelled because there were no beds available. Don was furious and complained to the bed manager saying `You have not got any contingency plan. ` To which he agreed and transferred Don to the complaints department. They sympathized with him but they couldn't do anything about the cancellation. Don spent the next few days trying to obtain another date for the operation and after talking to various secretaries and the Neuron admissions dept. set a new date was set for the 18th February. Once again Don had to check if there were any beds available. He rang the ward over the weekend prior to the operation he was told `The ward is still full and we are also blighted with diarrhoea in the ward which is shut down. ` By this time Don was getting very angry and phoned everyone again on the Monday morning. Don eventually talked to a doctor and after some discussion it was decided that Diana should be omitted to the hospital that day. When the ambulance arrived the medics said that the wrong service had been called because they didn't think it was an emergency and after some investigation the paperwork was changed to become an urgent case because the medics obtained permission from the local GP to take Diana to the A&E Dept. Eventually a bed was found in the neuron ward where the surgeons could examine her and decide on the best way forward. The operation was brought forward a day. Don said thank goodness that his wife was being treated as an urgent case. On the day of the operation Dons son said `I think the best way of dealing with the time was to spend the day together. ` To take their minds off the subject they went for a drive. David said `I want to look for a car because in April I will have to hand

Jessica and Me

the existing car back because it was the end of the lease and therefore I need another car.` That day was the longest one that Don and his son had endured for a long time because Diana's operation began at 8 o`clock in the morning and they didn`t see her until 7 o`clock in the evening. Fortunately Diana was awake when Don and his son went into the ward to see her and after spending some time with her the pair came away very pleased with the way Diana had come out of the operation which had taken ten hours.

When the surgeons began to carry out the operation they discovered a lump on Diana's breast and prior to the operation. They rang Don to inform him about the lump but he said `I will carry on and investigate what we have found the next day.` When the doctors saw Don they informed him that the lump could be breast cancer and said `I will carry out a screen test to confirm our suspicions.`

The next day Don visited his wife and as he reached the ward the porter was taking Diana to be screened. He said that Don should go with her. When the doctor saw her she asked Don to approve a procedure that would use a needle to take a sample. The doctor said she had to do this because Diana wasn`t talking very well and she couldn`t understand her. Don said `That would be ok if that what was required. ` This enabled the doctor to carry on. After the examination Don was the only one that could take his wife back to the ward. After his wife arrived and settled in Don realised his car had been parked beyond the time he had paid for and when he managed to get back he found a parking ticket. Don immediately contacted the hospital to ask them to write a letter saying he wasn`t to blame because they had kept him late due to the screening process. They agreed and Don sent a letter telling the parking authority that he wouldn`t pay the charge. After few weeks the car park officials wrote back saying they were investigating his claim and a week later they sent another letter saying they agreed that Don did not need to pay the fine much to his delight. This was the best news he had received for a long time but it didn`t last because the doctors said that the tests confirmed that Diana had cancer and she would have to remain in hospital for further treatment. The doctors prescribed tablets to control the cancer with a

Jessica and Me

view to treating her with chemotherapy but this couldn't be carried out until she became stronger which was proving to be difficult because she wasn't eating too well and didn't have the strength to walk very well either.

Don's daughter was expecting twins and she was having a difficult time because they were two boys but they were not identical so they were positioned in different parts of her tummy with one of them positioned near her rib cage which was affecting her breathing to the extent that she began to suffer from asthma attacks. Julie was 38 years old and Don thought her age might be a problem but Diana and Anna said she should be able to handle having babies at that age. Don was old fashioned thinking that women should have babies in their twenties but the up to date view was that women could be ok having babies in their mid-thirties to their forties.

David and Anna decided to look for a holiday home in Slovakia to rent out during the summer months to bring in extra cash to help prop up their income to enable them to live in the life style they had become accustomed to and they would be able to use the cottage over Christmas holidays.

Diana managed to become strong enough to leave hospital and after spending time convalescing she said to Don `It would be a good idea to look for a property in France to use as a holiday home. ` This was similar to what her son was doing. The couple decided to look in the area near Vienne because this was where they had stayed when they were on holiday in the South of France and they liked the area. It took about six months to find a property but it needed some work to bring it up to the standard required to enable them to carry out renting the property. The following year the work on the cottage was completed and Diana advertised it for rent and she was surprised at the response and although she had her doubt during the renovation she was glad the plan was working and could see a bright future ahead albeit the cancer would always be there and would need constant attention to keep it under control.

Despite the cancer Diana asked her daughter to arrange a surprise party for her mother-in-law by inviting some of her friends and what

Jessica and Me

was left of her family. She managed to get in touch with most of the people that could come to the party but there was one person Diana wanted to invite and that was William who hadn't seen Jessica since Robert died some ten years ago. Diana eventually tracked him down and when she asked him to the party he appeared to be hesitant saying 'I not sure that Jessica wants to see me after all this time.' Diana asked him to think about it as she would look forward to meeting William again. He said 'I will let you know.'

As time drew closer to the day of the 'do' Diana hadn't heard from William and she began to think he wouldn't come and she became more convinced because she still hadn't heard anything when the day arrived for the party to begin. The party was due to start at 5 O'clock and Diana still hadn't heard from William.

Everyone began to arrive while Jessica was kept away from the house until Diana could spring the surprise on her mother-in-law. They were all waiting for Jessica to arrive and when the car drew up outside the house Diana told them to keep quiet and out of sight until she came through the door and when she arrived they all cheered and sang 'For she a jolly good fellow. ' She was surprise and delight that her friends and relations had taken the trouble to turn up for the party.

About half way through the night there was a knock on the front door and Julie rushed quietly to the door and found William standing their wondering if he had done the right thing.

When he appeared through the crowd to stand in front of Jessica, he said 'Hello. ' She looked up at him in surprise and for a moment she was speechless until she managed to say 'Why have you come so late.' William said 'I wondered if you wanted to see me.' He had to tell her something that he had kept secret since he first met her back in the 1940's during the war. Jessica liked things to be out in the open and asked him what he meant by a secret. He said 'When I first saw you in the factory that day it was love at first sight. ' When she told him that she had a husband and a baby boy he was devastated. He vowed to keep seeing her as long as he lived because he couldn't keep away from her. When she asked him to leave after Robert had

Jessica and Me

died he understood. He realised she couldn't respond to his love for her because she was still in love with Robert even after ten years had passed since his death. Jessica said 'I understand the way you feel but I still feel the same about Robert even after all these years, if you want to keep in touch that would be alright but don't expect it to go any further.' Julie said 'I am pleased to see you after all these years, sit next to Jessica and I will get you a drink and something to eat.' William held Jessica by her hand and they recalled the good times they had together including when Robert was around. William said 'I was sad about Robert but I am sure he is looking down on us now and saying we should get together.' To his surprise Jessica agreed with him and said 'Perhaps we could meet each other to see how we get on.' William didn't expect this response and said 'I am pleased you feel this way and this could make up for all the wasted years that have kept us apart.' Jessica smiled and in her mind this was what she had secretly wanted for a long time and maybe this would become a close relationship for the rest of their lives.

THE END